Welcome to Forever

HERO'S WELCOME
BOOK ONE

ANNIE RAINS

NYLA Publishing
121 W 27th St., Suite 1201, New York, NY 10001
http://www.nyliterary.com

Dear Reader

Dear Reader,

Welcome to Forever first released in December of 2015 by a digital-only imprint for Random House. It is my first published book and as such, it holds a very special place in my heart. I poured so much love and heart into Kat and Micah's story and I was so honored when it got picked up for publication. I was surprised and humbled when it then hit the USA Today Bestseller's list within those first few months after its initial release.

Loveswept, the digital only imprint of Random House, has since closed and the rights to this story were reverted to me. I am thrilled to be re-publishing it now and giving Kat and Micah's story a chance to reach new readers.

As always, thank you for reading!

xx,

Annie

Chapter One

K at Chandler stepped inside the darkened building, and her chest filled with the kind of girlish excitement that had always preceded Christmas, birthdays, and the first day of school.

She'd missed this place and the students who'd be coming back today, giving her hugs and making her feel like she belonged. Which was more than she could say for their parents and the school board.

As she flipped the light switch, something crashed at the far end of the building. She heard it once more, a metallic clang echoing down the west hall. Not again.

Kat kicked off her heels and began to run as the sound combined with children's laughter. Over the summer, she'd arrived twice to find that vandals had spray-painted obscene messages on the outside walls—messages she didn't want Seaside's parents to see, especially on the first day of school.

Following the noise, she pushed the side-entrance door open and ran outside just as a blur of color disappeared into the woods. "Nooo!" She grumbled a few choice words under her breath, and stopped. She would never catch the little rascals and the chase would only make her look disheveled for the parents as they arrived for morning drop-off. That would do little to discredit the disapproving opinions that had circulated about her last year, saying she was too young and inexperienced. That a woman her age should be focused on finding a husband and starting a family—not working sixty-hour weeks.

Two cans of spray paint lay at her feet. Red and black. Her breath stilled in her chest. Maybe the kids had drawn a nice flower this time, or a smiley face. Turning, she gasped at the large, dark letters written haphazardly across the side of the school. The F-word proceeded her school's initials.

F--- SES.

SES. Seaside Elementary School. Definitely not the message she wanted to send parents as they arrived today. Glancing at the cans again, she grabbed the red one and did the only thing she could think of to fix the problem on such short notice.

Buck. Duck . . . Luck.

She started spraying. GOOD LUCK, SES. Only it kind of looked more like GOOD FU— "Oh, for heaven's sake." She ran the paint over everything, scribbling it all out. Stepping back, she frowned at the bright red and black paint dripping down the side of the school. At least kids wouldn't be asking their parents what the f-word meant this morning. Although, kids these days knew a lot more than she'd known growing up.

Think, Kat. Think.

She'd just have the wall repainted by afternoon pickup, and hopefully, with the school year opening, the Seaside vandals, as she'd started to call them, would find somewhere else to express themselves.

Right.

She began to walk back to her office, absently twisting the ring on the fourth finger of her left hand. Last year she'd been learning the ropes of being a principal. Yeah, the students had tested her and she'd faced more than her fair share of trials for a new principal. But this year would be different—better.

Seaside, North Carolina, was a small coastal town on the outskirts of one of the country's largest military bases. The community here was a mixture of Marines and retired veterans, which included the town's mayor. With the mayor's daughter enrolled at SES, it was an obvious target for scrutiny. She just needed to show the good things that happened under this metal roof, like the art club and the fundraisers that gave shoes and coats to children who needed them.

Kat retrieved her high heels, a little higher than she was used to after being in sandals all summer, and continued walking toward the front office, giving the ring on her finger another twist. The man who'd given it to her had believed in her ability to do this job. He'd been the one to encourage her to go for it and, even if it meant sixty-hour work weeks and no social life to speak of, she was determined to make this "the best school in the state." The last words tumbled off her lips like her own personal pep talk.

"Talking to yourself?" a deep voice asked from somewhere beside her.

She suppressed a scream as she stumbled backward. No one else was supposed to be here. School didn't start for another hour.

A man jumped forward and grabbed her waist, steadying her on her feet. "Whoa! You okay?" His deep, gravelly voice came with an unspoken promise that as soon as she looked up, he was going to steal more than her breath—her heart or her life, she wasn't sure.

She met his rich brown eyes, shadowed by a ball cap. "Who...? Are you a burglar?" she asked, as the horrible scenes she'd watched on the nightly news flashed across her mind. This was Seaside, though, where nothing worth CNN's time ever happened.

A small smile quirked on his mouth. "Not last time I checked."

Of course not. Burglars didn't rob schools. But he didn't have a kid with him, either, which meant he wasn't an early parent. That only left crazy psychopath. Only, he didn't look crazy. He looked kind of...dreamy...sexy.

"Here." He wrapped an arm around her, which she normally would've resisted, but she was still a little unsteady on her feet. Then he led her to the benches that lined the opposite wall. "I'm sorry I scared you. Are you sure you're okay?" As he removed his hands from her waist, his mouth fell open. "You're bleeding."

She looked down at a large red spot on her blouse. Not blood. "Spray paint," she said, letting out a small laugh. "There are some lovely graffiti artists using Seaside as their canvas lately." She dared to look up at him again. "I'm sorry. Who did you say you were?"

Stepping forward, he offered his hand. "Micah Peterson. I'm the school's new groundskeeper."

She noticed that his skin was rough as she slipped her hand in his. A working man's hands. "I'm Katherine Chandler. School principal." She pulled her hand away. "Please forgive me. I'm usually well acquainted with my employees." And this one she would've remembered. "My assistant principal told me that she'd hired someone over the summer. It's nice to meet you, Mr. Peterson."

"You can call me Micah."

His name alone was enough to make her bones go soft. "Micah, if you don't mind me asking, what are you doing here? It's barely six o'clock."

He shrugged his quarterback-sized shoulders. "Just stopped by to make sure the campus looked nice for the first day of school. There's been a rabbit munching on the chrysanthemums I planted out front. I covered some holes in the sod, too. Looks like we might have a mole."

With a nod, she dropped her guard just a fraction. After all, he was still a man. A tall, dark, and lust-igniting man, who was currently standing alone with her in an empty building.

He scanned the hall, as if not quite sure that they were alone. "I thought I heard yelling. Is everything okay?"

"That was me. And yes, everything's fine. Or it will be once I get that outside wall repainted."

His gaze fell to her hand as she twisted her engagement ring. It was a nervous habit, one that reminded people of her past and usually elicited sympathetic frowns in her direction. Poor Kat Chandler. Her fiancé's dead and she's still clinging to his promise of forever.

Micah Peterson didn't know her history, though. Instead of

sympathy, silent recognition crossed his face. She was off the market. Reflexively, she glanced at his left hand, too—no ring.

Silence swam between them. Heated, awkward silence punctuated by the soft hum of the overhead lighting.

"Well, it was nice to meet you, Principal Chandler," he said in a low voice that made her knees wobble just a little.

Her mouth grew dry as she watched a bead of sweat travel down his temple. In her mind, part-time groundskeepers weren't supposed to look like that. With his T-shirt sticking to the perspiration, she could nearly make out the indentations of well-defined abs. "Please, call me Kat," she insisted in a squeaky voice that made her cheeks burn.

"Kat," he repeated, then gestured behind him. "I better go get my son. Wouldn't want him to be late for his first day of school."

"You have a son?"

"Third grader this year."

She waited for the fact that he was a father to shut down her rampant hormones. It didn't. Her gaze continued to travel down his body as he walked away, her face heating immediately as she realized what she was doing—shamelessly checking out the school's lawn guy. Not that she'd been drooling, but...it seemed that even if her heart wasn't ready to move on, her body definitely was. Her body was practically screaming at her, reminding her of how it felt to be touched—loved.

He turned to wave again and her gaze jumped back to his eyes.

Oh, crap. She hoped he hadn't seen where her eyes were looking —right at where a tight pair of dirt-smudged jeans hugged his backside.

" 'Bye," he said with a slight smile curving his lips.

Yeah, he'd caught her looking.

" 'Bye," she squeaked as she pretended to look for the newspaper that was conveniently lying in front of the double doors. She hurried to pick it up, and then quickly, carefully, walked back to her office, reprimanding herself all the way. She needed to get a grip, and fast. She also needed to change out of her spray-painted shirt. The staff would be arriving any minute and the students would begin filling the hallways in one hour. This job was the reason she woke up in the morning, not sexy groundsmen. She was practically married to the school anyway, and hopefully she and SES would have their own version of happily ever after.

~

AFTER A QUICK SHOWER AND CHANGE OF CLOTHES, Micah drained the coffee from his mug and glanced at the clock on the wall. School started at eight. He still had to get Ben dressed, load the wheelchair in the Jeep, and drive the five miles back to the school, where this morning he'd finally met the principal, looking a little frazzled and more like one of those New York models than a civil servant. Not that he was disappointed.

He clanged his mug in the sink, hoping the noise would rouse the sleepyhead down the hall, and headed in that direction.

Seaside Elementary was the only grade school within a twenty-mile radius, and he wanted to stay close in case there was a medical emergency—or an incident like last year's.

Fresh anger curled his fingers into tight balls at his sides as he remembered the group of kids who'd tormented Ben relentlessly. Maybe because he was disabled, or just because he was different from them—always reading instead of socializing and dispersing random facts without prompting. The bullying had finally crossed the line when the kids had tossed his library books and book bag in the cafeteria trashcan several days in a row, forcing Ben to tearfully ask his teacher for help. Micah still couldn't believe it'd taken them three days to catch on to what was happening. Ben had taken the blame himself, of course, because that's the kind of kid he was. Everyone knew that wasn't the case, though.

Micah flipped the light switch and his muscles softened as he watched his son curl deeper into the covers. The kid could sleep forever. "Come on, trooper. Get up."

Ben moaned.

"First day of school."

More movement stirred under the solar system–themed blanket.

"I made eggs," he said, knowing this would do the trick.

Finally, Ben's head appeared and a groggy smile crossed his face. "Help me up," he pleaded in a sleep-coated voice.

Micah nearly took a step forward, but stopped himself. "You got this, bud," he said, remembering what his son's occupational therapist had told him. If Ben didn't learn how to do things on his own, he'd always rely on others. He'd never be independent.

Ben's thin arm reached for the side rail of his bed and pulled, his tiny muscles bulging as he strained to get his body upright. Then he lined his legs up on the ground to stand. It seemed to take more energy for him to do that simple task than it did for Micah to run five miles every morning at the Marines' physical training center.

After a long moment, Ben's gaze slid toward him with a hopeful gleam in his eyes, as if he'd get some help on this final step. Micah stayed rooted in the doorway. With a sigh, Ben grabbed the arm of his wheelchair and transferred in one jerky movement, a proud smile crossing his sleep-creased face as he looked up.

"Good job, bud." The all-too-familiar pride he got watching Ben succeed tightened his throat. "Go ahead and wheel yourself to the bathroom, and then you can have your eggs at the table." He walked to the kitchen and waited. Ten minutes later, he slid a plate of scrambled eggs in front of his son. "Eat up. It's going to be an exciting day."

Ben hesitated, no longer smiling. That was unusual because Ben always smiled.

"Something wrong?" Micah asked, knowing exactly what the problem was. Ben had loved school until last December's incident.

"What if no one likes me?" he asked in a barely audible voice.

Patting his back, Micah shook his head. "Not possible."

"What if kids laugh at me?"

"They won't."

"But, last year—"

"You've got nothing to worry about. I promise. And so what if they laugh? Ignore them."

Ben stabbed his eggs with his fork. It was crummy advice. Hurtful words were hard to ignore, but the advice Micah's own father had given him growing up wouldn't work in this situation, either. If Ben tried to throw the first punch, the kids would pummel him.

Micah set his plate on the table and started to eat.

"Aren't you going to sit?" Ben asked.

He hesitated. If he sat, he'd probably fall asleep. He'd spent the last three days with his squadron, and then come straight home to relieve Aunt Clara of babysitting duty. In the last four days, he'd barely managed three hours of sleep, which was why he needed to keep moving. Glancing at his son, he hoped Ben didn't see his red-lined eyes, underscored with almost permanent black circles—battle scars of the parent of a child with special needs. "Nope. I have a laundry list of things to do to make your first day at Seaside Elementary perfect."

Ben offered one of his huge, heart-shattering smiles, stabbing at another mound of eggs. "Easy there, buddy. Take too big a bite and you'll spend your day in the ER instead of third grade."

Ben spoke with a full mouth. "No more trips to the ER this year."

Micah nodded, knowing they'd be lucky if that were true.

An hour later, he parked his blue Jeep Cherokee in the front of Seaside Elementary and pulled Ben's wheelchair out of the back. "Ready?"

When he looked at his son, the boy's pale complexion told him the truth. Ben was scared, but he smiled anyway. "Sure, Dad."

His son's bravery gripped his heart and made him, the decorated war hero, feel like a coward. Ben never complained about anything, took everything in stride. But Micah remembered how hard it had been growing up a military brat, drifting from one military town to another. That's why this would be his last assigned duty station before civilian life. No more moving all over the country. When

Micah's commitment was up next May, he wasn't reenlisting. Ben needed a home for once, and a dad to teach him to do things for himself, especially since his mother didn't see fit to call much from whatever assignment she was on these days.

As he walked up beside Ben's chair, he signaled for him to go forward. Insurance had sprung for a top-notch wheelchair this year with one-sided steering. Everyone had concurred that it was time. Ben's muscles were getting tighter as he grew taller, a symptom of his cerebral palsy, and soon, walking would be impossible. "Just don't run over anyone, okay?"

"Okay, Dad." The chair crawled forward at a steady pace.

"See those flowers, bud? I planted those a few days ago," Micah said.

Ben didn't break his concentration. He knew exactly where he was going. Micah had taken him to the school last week to get adjusted to the layout. Each wing of the building was named after sea life. Ben's classroom was down the Sand Fiddler's hall, first door on the left.

Micah stopped just short of the school's front entrance and gave him a quick salute. "I'll see you this afternoon, okay?" Ben was too old for the hugs and kisses he used to give. That'd only fuel the other kids' teasing. But maybe this school would be different, he thought.

"See you later, Dad." Ben returned his salute and continued forward, not looking back. Micah knew if he did, he'd lose control of his body and the wheelchair.

Good boy.

Micah recognized the young principal from this morning greeting the children at the school's entrance.

"Walk," she warned in a sweet voice that did little to slow the excited feet as they stampeded toward her. Her beautiful smile grew larger as she looked at Ben. He usually had that effect on people. Then she waved and—*oh, her heart*—Ben lifted his arm to wave back.

His excitement jerked his body around like a marionette and the lunchbox on his lap toppled to the ground and opened with a loud crash that made Micah flinch. Watching as the scene unfolded in slow motion, he did his best not to run up to his son and grab the falling items as they rolled toward the other students. That's what he wanted to do, but it wouldn't help anything.

His jaw tightened as he watched Principal Chandler kneel down in those ridiculous heels that made her legs, and other assets, look delicious. She began reaching for Ben's sandwich and apple, tossing them quickly in his box and closing it. She didn't hand it back to him, which is exactly what Micah would've done. Instead, she carried Ben's lunchbox, grabbed the books he'd also had in his lap, and walked with him inside.

Seeing that she didn't reappear, Micah guessed she then proceeded to walk with him to class. He ran a quick hand through his hair. How the hell was Ben supposed to make his own way at this school with his principal escorting him around the building? If only she hadn't waved, not that he could blame her for the friendly gesture. Ignoring Ben would have been worse.

Realizing he was still standing at the edge of the parking lot, and probably looking like a crazy person, Micah decided to turn around and head to work. His squadron was waiting. Instead, his feet started to move forward, heading toward the school. As he veered into the front office on his right, the young secretary glanced up.

"May I help you?"

"I'm a new parent here and I want a quick word with the principal," he said, crossing his arms and not budging toward the row of seats behind him. There was no time to wait. He just needed to make sure Kat Chandler knew how to treat his son because there was no way he was going to let Ben have another bad school year.

The woman looked down at an appointment book on her desk. "Um, okay. I'll just see if—"

They both turned as Kat stepped into the office, slightly out of breath. "I just ran into Stanley. The graffiti will be gone by afternoon pickup." She braced her hands on her hips, where his own hands had rested earlier this morning, looking slightly stressed and absolutely beautiful.

Clearing her throat, the secretary jerked her head in his direction. "You have a visitor."

"Oh. Good morning," Kat said, noticing him now. "I'm Kat Chandler, the school's principal." She held out a hand for him to shake as she smiled warmly.

Taking it, he waited for her to recognize him. She didn't. But he'd been wearing a ball cap this morning, and coated in sweat. *Good.* He'd prefer not to lose the first big landscaping job he'd scored in Seaside over this—not that he was going to cause a scene. He just wanted to make sure his son had a great year at SES. Ben was perfectly able to be an independent kid, and part of the reason for that was because he let him carry his own lunchbox.

Micah's jaw clenched at the memory of last year. He wasn't going to tell the pretty principal how to do her job—okay, maybe he was—but for Ben, he'd do anything.

Chapter Two

K at studied the parent standing in her office. He had a deep frown creasing the skin between his dark eyes. There was also something vaguely familiar about him. Maybe they'd met at parent orientation last week. "What can I help you with?" she asked, taking a seat behind her desk, and gesturing for him to sit across from her.

Bracing his hands on his hips, he didn't budge. "You walked my son to his class this morning," he said, his voice edged with slight irritation. "He dropped his lunchbox, and you picked it up and carried it for him."

She nodded, flashing her best principal smile—the one that was supposed to exude confidence and put parents at ease. "Yes. Ben. I did walk with him this morning. He's new here and I wanted to get to know him."

"You should've let him do it alone," he said in such a way that her spine straightened. "He's in a wheelchair, but he's capable. I don't want him to be defined by his disability here. If you treat him that way, everyone else will, too."

Sucking in a breath, she suddenly felt like she was a student visiting the principal's office.

"Mister. . .?"

"Peterson."

Nodding, she spoke slowly, calmly. This was the first upset parent to walk into her office this year, but he wouldn't be the last. Talking parents down from their fear-and-worry-ridden ledges was an unwritten part of her job. "Mr. Peterson. I assure you, I was only getting to know your son."

"And that's nice of you, Principal Chandler, but don't treat Ben different from the other students," he said, his voice as abrasive as the look he was giving her. While he was handsome, she didn't appreciate what he was insinuating. "I don't want my son to suffer because he's in a wheelchair and you feel bad. That's your weakness, not his."

"Weakness?" She took a deep breath, then bit the inside of her cheek, focusing her energy there. This parent was doing more than insinuating; he wanted a fight, and she wasn't going to give it to him. *That* was his weakness, not hers. "Your son didn't seem to mind that I was walking with him this morning."

"Of course not. But walking with the principal doesn't exactly help him make friends, does it?"

Seriously? It was hard for parents to let go. She got that. Harder for some than others, but this dad needed to back off.

"I understand what you're saying, Mr. Peterson," she said, continuing to keep her calm, cool demeanor, "but I assure you that I did not treat your son any differently than I would any other student on this campus."

"You walk every child to class?" he asked, obviously biting back his temper.

"If they ask me to, and I have the time, then yes, I do. Especially the new students. It's easy to get lost if you don't know our school's layout."

"Ask you?" His face was expressionless, but there was a definite emotion firing in those dark eyes of his, and it wasn't anger, despite his stiff posture. "He asked you to walk him to class?" he clarified.

"And carry his books. He said he didn't want to risk dropping them again."

Running a hand through his short, buzz-cut hair, the father surprised her by laughing. It wasn't the kind of laugh that would've put her at ease, though. More of a laugh of someone who was so frustrated, they had no idea what to do. "Figures." He glanced down as his cellphone rang in his pocket, drawing her attention to his fitted blue jeans.

She'd seen those hips before. And the V-shaped torso opening up to a broad pair of drool-worthy shoulders. Her gaze jumped up, and—*uh oh.* She'd also seen those dark brown eyes. *For the love of chocolate.* Why hadn't she recognized him immediately? "Micah Peterson?"

He didn't blink. "Good morning again," he said, true amusement lacing his voice this time.

A gasp caught in her throat. "I'm so sorry I didn't recognize you. You had on a hat earlier and a different shirt." As if the hat and clean shirt were a disguise.

"It seems to me you had on a different shirt, too." He gestured to the fresh blouse she was wearing, free of spray paint unlike this morning's.

"I've learned to always have a spare, just in case. In this profession, it's necessary . . . So, Ben is the son you were talking about this morning?" *Again, duh.* Had her brain overheated from the image of Micah's lower half?

"Listen, I'm not trying to be a hard-ass," he said.

Hard ass? Yep. Very hard. Swallowing, she pulled her mind out of the gutter and straightened. She was a professional, she reminded herself. No drooling over the hot, completely irrational parent.

"First day of school nerves. We all have them," she said. "And you're just looking out for your son. I respect that."

"Right." He nodded as his defensive posture relaxed just a little. "He didn't have many friends at his old school. And it's not easy when the other kids are running around and riding their bikes. Ben will never do any of that. To make matters worse, he sometimes puts up a fight about doing the stuff he is capable of."

Maybe not so irrational. A parent who wanted to do right by their child always squeezed at her heart.

"Don't worry about Ben, Mr. Peterson. Seaside is a great school, and I'm sure he'll fit right in."

His cellphone rang again and this time she averted her gaze to look somewhere less mind-blowing, like at her secretary, Val, who was nosily watching them from her desk. *Great.*

"I have to get to work." He offered what appeared to be a genuine smile.

That's a good smile.

"Of course. We'll see you this afternoon."

As he started to walk away, her gaze traveled down his tall, lean body.

With a sigh, Kat watched the father disappear out of the school's double doors and pointed at her friend. "I knew I shouldn't have given you this job, Val. You're going to be trouble this year." She shook her head and reached for a stack of to-dos on her desk. Thirty minutes later, her phone rang, breaking the steady progress on paperwork that she rarely got to make.

"Trouble in Miss Hadley's classroom," Val said through the speakerphone. "You better get down there quick."

Micah's phone rang for the hundredth time that morning as he sat in the long line of traffic leading to Camp Leon's military base. He had a good mind to turn the whole thing off. Glancing at the caller ID before answering, his chest tightened. *Yeah, I should've turned it off.*

"Hey, Jessica. How are you?" He didn't hide the distaste of her name on his lips, or the fact that he'd rather be doing PT in the desert than talking to his ex.

"I'm good," she said efficiently. "Listen, I don't have time for small talk, Micah."

Of course she didn't. She never had. "What *do* you have time for? Other than the Marine Corps?"

She laughed dryly. Once upon a time, that laugh had been an adrenaline shot to his heart.

Now, it made his teeth grind together. "I volunteered for another deployment."

Stars burst behind his vision. "What the hell, Jess? Ben has been looking forward to us driving to Georgia at Christmas. He'll be devastated."

"He'll understand." There was a dismissive annoyance in her voice.

"I doubt it," he said, his fingers gripping the steering wheel so hard that his arms went numb.

"It's my job, Micah."

"And what do you expect me to do if I get a *mandatory*, not a voluntary, order of deployment? What happens to Ben then?" Uncurling his fingers, he watched as the blood rushed back into his hand.

"Your aunt Clara will take care of him. Just like last time. Or you could get out of it somehow."

"Yeah, how would I do that? Tell my command that I'm pregnant?" he asked.

Silence sizzled between them.

"I never wanted kids. You knew that from the beginning."

"Yeah." He pressed the gas as traffic slowly inched forward. "Will you at least call him later and explain the importance of your career yourself?"

She didn't answer. *Right.* He'd forgotten what a self-centered ex he had. If she hadn't gotten pregnant during their five-month "relationship," they never would've gotten married. He'd thought they could make it work, though. Micah had loved her, or thought he did at least. But the Marine Corps always came first with her, just like with his own dad. And he understood that, hadn't even minded that she'd loved the Corps more than him. But he minded that she loved the Corps more than her own son. Getting married had been a huge mistake. Except for Ben. Ben was the only thing they'd ever done right.

"Fine. I'll tell him tonight," he muttered. Then, after a hurried goodbye, he hung up and entered the military base. A short drive later, he parked and was preparing to get out of his Jeep when his phone rang again. With a low growl, he glanced down at his caller ID—he didn't have the patience for another round with Jessica. He didn't recognize this number, though. "Hello?"

"Mr. Peterson?" a woman asked, her voice tight. "It's Kat Chandler. I'm afraid you're going to have to come back to the school. There's been an accident with Ben."

Chapter Three

This didn't bode well for Seaside Elementary. Ben had barely been here two hours and already he'd been involved in some sort of incident.

Micah walked right in, didn't bother to speak to the office secretary, and headed straight toward Principal Chandler's open office door, pausing at the sight of her—wearing the same fitted skirt that had hugged her body so perfectly this morning.

He glanced over at the wheelchair in the center of the room and back at her. "Where's Ben?"

"He's in class, sitting in one of the nurse's spare wheelchairs," she said.

Which was no doubt oversized for his small frame. "Is he okay?" Micah asked, his voice coming out harder than he intended.

She nodded as she stood and walked around her desk. "Yes, he seems fine. As I said on the phone, I'm very sorry about this, Mr. Peterson."

"You can't monitor every second of the day. I know that." But she could make sure Ben's teacher kept better control over her classroom. Ben had already been nervous about being the new kid. Micah could only imagine how he was rolling with Seaside's punches thus far. But if she said he was fine, he wasn't going to interrupt Ben's first day any more by checking on him while he was in class.

He crouched beside the chair and inspected the tire. Last year's chair had solid rubber tires that never would have gone flat. This one had pneumatic tires that resembled those on a ten- speed bicycle, allowing him to move over more surfaces, including outdoors. "Tell me again what happened."

"A child stabbed it with his pencil," she said, stepping up beside him. "I don't think it was directed at Ben as much as an attention tactic. The school will pay for any replacement parts."

Micah laid a bicycle repair kit down on the floor and started to patch the puncture, doing his best not to notice Kat's long-as-summer legs standing a few feet away. "It needs a patch and some air, just like if you had a bike flat. I keep a kit on me at all times."

"I see." She shifted around, as if looking for something to do. "Would you like some coffee?" she asked.

"Love some." Micah had been up more hours than usual, which may have accounted for his outburst this morning. He'd been an ass, and he knew it. But Ben was his son and, while he was easy to love, it was hard not to worry about him.

Glancing over, he watched her grab two mugs from a cabinet, enjoying the view as her skirt raised two inches along the backs of her thighs.

"He had a flat last month, too," he said, redirecting his attention to the task in front of him. "The mobility guy who sold us this chair said flats could happen, but rarely did." Shaking his head, he reached for the mug of coffee that she handed him. "I guess he didn't realize how active Ben was. Especially for a kid with his level of cerebral palsy."

She pulled up a chair and sipped her coffee as she watched.

Her high-heel shoes were gone, he noticed. There were a lot of things he noticed sitting at this angle. His man parts reacted without consulting with his brain first. His brain knew that checking out Ben's principal was a bad idea. Clearing his throat, he forced his eyes back to the chair and started pumping air into the tire. He refocused his thoughts back on his son. "Ben might've said it didn't bother him, but believe me, it does. He knows you can't control what others do, but today'll hurt. The best I can do is teach him to hold his chin high. It's not as much fun to bully someone who doesn't let it get to them."

"That's pretty good advice." She held on to her mug with both hands, making her look too young to be in charge of a school. When he met her gaze, however, he saw what a quick glance of her appearance didn't tell: It didn't matter how young she looked, she'd already seen too much in life.

Which raised all kinds of questions in his mind that he had no business contemplating.

"Listen, I'm sorry about this morning," he said, lowering his voice and turning back to the wheelchair. "Ben had a rough time last year. I just want to make sure he does okay here."

"No need to apologize. And he'll be fine. We're in this together."

In this together. Those words were foreign to him. Since Jessica had quit her role as mother, he'd been handling everything on his own. Of course, Kat hadn't meant anything by saying that. She was a principal and he was a parent. In that sense, they were a team. But something about those words didn't make him ache. It also made him feel like running out of her office, which he needed to do anyway. His phone was blinking, no doubt signaling a dozen messages from his squadron. "Ben's wheelchair is ready to use," he said, standing.

"That was fast."

"I'm a pro at patching tires," he said, relieved there wasn't damage to the chair. Ben's fragile ego was another story. "I'll pick him up after school." He placed his empty coffee mug on the counter and headed toward the door, feeling her follow behind him.

"Again, I'm s—" she began, stopping when he turned back. "Right. I already said that. Well, hopefully our next meeting will be under better circumstances."

A few lurid fantasies of reasons he'd like to be called back to her office filtered through his mind. Reining in his imagination, he waved. "See you this afternoon, Kat."

As he walked through the front office, he tipped his head at the young secretary, who was smiling like the cat who'd swallowed a canary. *What was that about?* He probably didn't want to know. He had bigger things to worry about. Tonight, he'd have to break his son's heart and tell him that his mother was going back to war—that she'd volunteered to go.

Micah climbed into his Jeep and headed toward the military base. If Jessica was going to be an absentee mother, he'd just have to be a better father. That meant no more dating women like the last one he'd gone out with—Nicole. And certainly no ogling his son's principal. Even if he was interested in dating, Kat Chandler had a ring on her left hand, which made it as clear as the diamond at its center that she was off the market.

DINNER SIZZLED ON THE STOVE IN FRONT OF KAT—A CAN of SpaghettiOs.

"You know, if you keep cooking for me, I might not go back to Doug when he gets home. I might stay with you," Val said, pulling her thick, black hair into a ponytail. "The dad is hot, by the way."

Kat kept her eyes on the food. "Dad?" she asked, trying to sound as nonchalant as possible. She knew exactly who Val was referring to. Her matchmaking best friend always brought up the single, remotely attractive men who graced Seaside. Although, in Micah's case, attractive was an understatement. He was so hot, he practically had steam rising from his muscled body. His social skills, however, were slightly lacking and, as hot as he was, he could be a bit of a jerk. A well-intentioned jerk, but . . .

Kat turned the heat down on the stove and served up two bowls of pasta. "Changing the subject, I spoke to Julie last night. She's coming to town this weekend."

Val emitted a low grunt as she ate. "Alert the presses."

Kat looked over, her mouth quirking to one side. "She says she wants to take me out to the bars and nightclubs in search of my rebound guy."

"Bars and nightclubs? She does remember that this is still Seaside, the place where we were born and raised? Only one bar and zero nightclubs." Val's brows hung low. "Besides, I'm your best friend. I'm the one who's supposed to help you find your rebound guy."

"You know I'm not looking for a relationship right now. It'll just be us sitting around and checking out Seaside's selection. Besides, I was thinking that you could come with us."

Drawing back, Val's eyes widened. "Oh, no. I have never been a huge fan of your sister. Hanging with you two would only spell a weeklong migraine for me."

Kat scooped pasta into her mouth, considering this. "We've been out of high school for nine years. Don't you think it's time to shake hands and make up? Turn the other cheek, or whatever your dad would advise, per the Good Book."

Val's bright blue eyes bore into hers. "She stole my boyfriend right from under my nose. It's unforgivable. And I don't like the way she treats you. When was the last time she even called to ask how you were?"

"Before last night? A year ago maybe. We have busy lives."

Val shook her head, returning her attention to her dinner. "You aren't too busy for anyone. You're the most caring, giving person I know. Julie, on the other hand, is a soul sucker. She's the one who's too busy to grace her own hometown, even after John was killed." Val's expression softened as she realized what she'd said. "Sorry. I didn't mean to—"

"It's fine. I'm done crying into my SpaghettiOs." Unless she'd had too much to drink, which she rarely ever did.

"Did you ever make it to that support group? The one at the Veterans' Center?"

Swallowing thickly, Kat shook her head. "No."

"Why not? I think it'd be good for you. You could connect with other Marine widows."

"Except I'm not a widow. John and I were never married, remember? It just wouldn't feel right. A lot of the people who go to those meetings were married for years. They have kids." Kat reached for her glass of water, her mouth suddenly as dry as paper.

Val watched her for a moment, and then sighed dramatically, setting her fork down. "Fine. I'll *consider* hanging out with you two."

"Really? Yay! It'll be fun, I promise."

Val's gaze lowered to the ring on Kat's left hand. "You might want to put that in your jewelry box while she's here, though."

Staring down at the sparkling, oval-cut diamond, she shook her head. "I can't . . . yet. But I have started packing up his stuff. That's progress."

"Yes, it's . . . *progress.*" There was a playful hint to Val's tone, lightening the mood for both of them.

"It's just hard. I hope you never have to go through it."

Val's body tensed beside her. "Just because I'm dating a Marine, doesn't mean he's going to die."

Crap! She hadn't meant to say what she'd been thinking. She just didn't want her best friend to go through what she had. "I know. I didn't mean anything by that. I'm sure Doug will come home safe and sound. Most Marines come home safe and sound." She heard her voice waver as she spoke, those pesky emotions rising to the surface.

Looking up, she offered her best I'm-completely-together-smile, knowing Val wouldn't buy it the way most did. Kat allowed herself a temporary moment of self-pity—something reserved only for when she was alone or with her best friend—and then she was done. Back to the positive. The future. "He was the one who encouraged me to take this job as principal. He believed I could do it, that I'd make a difference."

"And you are," Val said softly.

"I'm trying, but look at today. It was the first day of school and already there was vandalism and a student popped the tire of another child's wheelchair."

"Two incidents. No big deal. You were perfect."

"Huge deal." Kat set down her spoon, no longer hungry. "Don't you remember how the last school year ended? Seaside Elementary was becoming known for its incidents rather than the fact that we have top-notch teachers and some of the highest academic scores in the state."

Val nodded. "We're a military town. It's kind of natural for the kids to duke it out. Like dogs marking their territory."

This roused a smile from her—one of the reasons she loved Val. "You're comparing my students to dogs?"

"Or wolves. It's the hierarchy of nature, or something like that."

Kat collected her bowl and headed to the sink. "That's it. You're cut off from the Discovery Channel."

"So, what are you going to do?" Val asked, following behind her.

"I don't know yet. But I'm going to do something, in John's honor. I'm going to turn Seaside Elementary into a place where students accept each other, care about each other—"

"And you're cut off from the Hallmark Channel." Val gave Kat's shoulder a playful shove, then jumped as the phone rang in her pocket. "It's Doug," she said, reading her caller ID. "I'll take it outside."

Kat watched her friend disappear out the front door. Glancing down at her engagement ring, she thought about Julie's announcement that she was coming home for a visit. Julie was a lot of things, but Val was wrong about her. Her sister wasn't a soul sucker. She just had a different way of doing things. And if Julie had it her way, by the end of next week, she'd have John's stuff boxed up, the engagement ring on its way to a pawnshop, and a new man in Kat's life, possibly in her bed.

Well, that last part might be nice. She'd just have one ground rule—no Marines.

〜

MICAH GLANCED AT BEN IN THE REARVIEW MIRROR. HE wasn't smiling. It had been a rough first week—not horrible, but it hadn't lived up to Ben's hopes—and now Micah had to stop procrastinating and finally tell him that his mother was deploying again.

"Pizza?" he asked, meeting Ben's gaze in the rearview mirror.

"On a school night?"

"Yeah, why not?" He tried to act like it was a spur-of-the-moment thing. Those rarely happened in the Peterson household, though. His workload and Ben's disability necessitated a schedule, which he did his best to maintain.

Ben scrunched his face.

"All right. Fine. If you don't want pizza—"

"I do," his son protested, slurring his words the way he did when his muscles were tired. And there was that lopsided smile.

Micah turned the Jeep Cherokee into the parking lot for Kirk's Pizza House. It was the only pizza joint in Seaside, and the place was packed. A hostess showed them to the last table in the back and Micah followed, as Ben carefully maneuvered his chair down the narrow aisles.

When they were seated, Ben seemed to shrink in his chair. "You have something to tell me." It wasn't a question. "Otherwise, we'd be having boring chicken and green beans. That's what you laid out this morning," he said.

My kid is smart.

Micah licked his lips, stalling like the old Mustang he'd had when he was sixteen. "Maybe I didn't want boring chicken and beans tonight," he said, silently thanking God when the waitress interrupted, bringing them glasses of water and breadsticks. He wasn't ready to talk about Jessica yet. Couldn't they just enjoy their night for a while before his ex squashed it with her proverbial combat boots? "So, tell me about your day."

Ben blew a breath toward a lock of dark hair falling in his honey-colored eyes. He'd inherited those from his mother. His left arm was too stiff to swipe the hair away, and his right arm—the strong one—was locked on a breadstick, slowly submerging it in pizza sauce. "We had a rally."

Micah grabbed his own breadstick. "A pep rally?"

"Yeah." Talking while he chewed, his son's muddled words were even harder to understand. "Principal Chandler added a new subject to our curriculum. It's called Good Deeds. We'll be emailing the wounded soldiers at Camp Leon and writing letters to people in nursing homes. She's also changing after-school detention to something called the Friendship Club. If you get in trouble, you have to stay after school and work on the campus doing recycling and making new friends."

Micah didn't know what kind of friends were to be made in detention, but before he could think too much on it, the waitress was back to take their orders. He ordered a large pizza, half with just spinach for him and half with ham and sausage for Ben. His little man was a meat lover, and tonight he deserved whatever he wanted. "A club for misbehaving kids, huh?" he asked, recapping the conversation. He reached for a second breadstick, promising himself that he'd stop with this one so as not to ruin his appetite. "That would've been nice last year, huh? A mean kid club."

Ben stopped dipping his bread for a second, and Micah immediately regretted bringing up the bullies.

"Friendship Club," Ben corrected quietly, his voice so low that Micah had to guess at what he'd actually said. "And the kids in the club have to do nice things for everyone."

"Even the girls?" Micah soured his face in a weak attempt to make his son laugh.

Ben glanced up, not even cracking a smile. "Dad, I'm in third grade now. I'm allowed to like girls."

"You are?" This was news to him.

"And I was thinking . . ." The tone of his voice, more confident now with a hint of wanting, made Micah's heart beat in an *uh-oh* rhythm.

"You should start liking girls again, too." His son swiped at his hair, staring at him expectantly across the table. "I won't get in the way anymore. I promise."

"In the way? Anymore?" Micah leaned forward. What was Ben talking about?

"Like with Nicole." Ben's gaze fell on the table.

Micah groaned at just the mention of the name. He'd only dated Nicole a couple weeks. "You know that wasn't you, right? She just wasn't right for me. Wasn't right for us."

"But I think I know who is right for you—I mean us." Ben looked up, eyes wide like they got when he was about to ask for a too-expensive toy or an extra serving of dessert.

Suddenly, Micah was rethinking taking his son out for pizza. The night was quickly turning into a discussion about his love life. Or lack thereof. "Who?"

"Principal Chandler."

Kat's succulent green eyes came to mind. And the sparkling diamond on her left hand. Clearing his throat, he leaned back and scratched the side of his jaw. He was stalling again, looking for the right response to his son's suggestion. "And what makes you think we'd be a good match?"

"Because she also likes spinach on her pizza."

Micah furrowed his brow and followed Ben's gaze to a table across the room, where Kat was eating alone.

As if sensing people watching her, she looked up from a stack of papers on the table and a slow smile formed. Tonight, she wore her corn silk hair down, letting it cascade around her shoulders.

Micah forgot to chew the last bite of his breadstick and started to choke. After plowing a quick fist into his chest to get the food down, he looked back across the room.

She had a concerned tilt to her eyebrows that relaxed as her gaze moved to Ben, who was happily waving her over with his right arm.

"Ben, she looks like she's working," Micah said. And he wasn't prepared to share space with a woman who looked like that.

"People don't work at dinner, Dad," Ben said, a *duh* unfolding in his voice that made Micah all too aware that puberty wasn't far around the corner. Ben waved at her again.

Shifting in her seat, she looked around at the other patrons. Then, she slowly got up and began walking in their direction.

The sight of her made his heart, and other places, rev. No more stalling in this Mustang. Those curves were lethal and that face was one he could look at for a very long time.

He didn't blink.

Good thing for that ring on her finger, because looking at the beautiful woman now, he thought she might be a good match for him, too. She was still Ben's principal, though, and kind of his boss, so getting involved with Kat Chandler was completely out of the question.

Chapter Four

K at smiled warmly at the man approaching her.

"Hey, Kat," he said.

Just the sound of his voice made her breath grow shallow. She'd already stood for a solid second at their table without saying a single word. *Say something,* her brain demanded. "Hey, you two. Looks like we had the same idea for dinner tonight."

Ben nodded, the motion not quite rhythmic. "We never have pizza on a weeknight. It means I'm in trouble."

Micah's dark eyebrows jumped at the claim. "No, it doesn't. Maybe I just want to enjoy my son." He looked at her again, melting all her bones. "Looks like you're alone," he observed.

"My friend canceled. Which is just as well. I have work to do." She glanced back at the papers on her table. Work that would be smeared with pizza sauce before it was all said and done.

"You can join us if you want," Ben said.

She started shaking her head to argue. "No. That's okay. It looks like you're having family time." And her hormones were currently begging her to rip his father's clothing off. What was wrong with her these days? *Get a grip, girl.*

"*Pleeease* join us, Principal Chandler. That'd be so cool." Ben's eyes were large and hopeful as he looked at her.

At his age, the school principal was still a superhero. And she had to admit, she kind of liked being a superhero.

"Dad, tell her we don't mind," Ben said, looking at Micah.

Micah hesitated, and then lifted his eyes to meet her gaze. "We, uh, don't mind."

She read his body language loud and clear, though—he minded. But disappointing such an adorable third grader had to be a sin, she thought, turning back to Ben. "Well, if you're sure." "You can sit right there beside my dad." Ben pointed at the narrow seat.

If she sat there, she'd barely have elbow room. She would be rubbing up against the handsome father that, yes, she was very attracted to despite her earnest wish that she wasn't. Even though he'd been considerably nicer toward her at their last meeting, he was still a parent—one whose trust she was working hard to earn.

"Please. Join us," Micah urged, surprising her and leaving her with very little choice.

"Okay then. I'll just go grab my pizza and put my papers away."

Ben cheered as she walked back to her table.

Why on earth had she just said yes? It was bad enough that she'd practically drooled over Micah's tightly molded muscles as he'd lifted his glass just then. Checking out a student's father crossed some ethical line in the principal handbook, didn't it? She'd just have to spend the dinner focusing on Ben, which wouldn't be too hard. With his adorable glasses and limitless curiosity, he was already leading the pack for her favorite student this year. Not that she had favorites.

She placed her pizza on the table beside theirs and Micah slid over an inch, gesturing for her to sit beside him.

"See?" Ben pointed at the spinach pizza. "That side of the pizza is my dad's. He likes spinach just like you."

She nodded. "Your dad has good taste."

Ben's smile stretched impossibly wider. Then he peppered her with questions as they ate.

What was her favorite color?—green. What was her favorite food?—chips and salsa.

"Which war is your favorite?" he asked.

"War?" Kat glanced at Micah. Until now, he'd been quiet during her interrogation by his son.

"Ben has a special interest in history. Wars specifically," Micah told her. Sitting this close as he spoke to her felt intimate. Meeting his eyes with only a few inches between them felt too close for comfort, but not nearly close enough if she consulted her woman parts.

Kat nodded slowly, directing her gaze and thoughts forward as she searched for an answer. "I guess I prefer peace over war."

Ben awkwardly angled his head to bite from his pizza. When he was done chewing, he smiled at her. "That was a slack answer, Principal Chandler."

"Ben," Micah reprimanded. "That wasn't nice."

"But that's what you always yell at the TV when someone dodges the question on CNN, Dad."

Kat couldn't help laughing. It felt good to laugh. That's why she'd wanted to meet Val here tonight. "It's okay. Ben's right. It was a slack answer. Hmm." She tore off a piece of her pizza and popped it into her mouth. War had stolen her fiancé. She swallowed the thickening lump rising in her throat. She couldn't think about the past, at least not now. "I'll have to get back to you on that, Ben. Is that a better answer?"

With a shrug, he immediately asked her another question, as if he had a Rolodex in his little mind.

"So, let me guess. You're going to be a reporter when you grow up?" she teased, sharing another look with Micah. The momentary meeting of their eyes sent fiery embers through her blood. He reached for the Parmesan cheese on the table and his arm brushed against hers. It should've been awkward, but she found herself mentally willing him to reach for something else just so that she could feel his skin on hers. Squirming, she looked at Ben, whose characteristic smile had faded.

"Reporters don't have wheelchairs, Principal Chandler," he said.

The lump in her throat was back. She set her pizza down and leaned in closer to him, making sure he paid attention. "Reporters come in all shapes and sizes. I'm sure there are some with wheelchairs."

He shook his head, his hair falling in his face. "I've looked. There aren't."

"Well, let me tell you something. At one time, women didn't become principals, either. There's a first for everything. If you have a dream, you follow it."

A little spark lit in Ben's eyes. "That's what Dad says, too. Right, Dad?"

"That's right, buddy."

Kat turned to look at him, surprised at the small smile that quirked on his usually straight lips. If possible, he was even sexier when he smiled.

"His favorite color is green, too. Fatigue green," Ben said.

"Fatigue green?" she asked, looking across the table.

"Like the Marines wear," Ben said.

"Ah." She reached for her glass of water, enjoying Ben's quick, excited speech. It wasn't often she got to sit with one of her students and really get to know them.

"And his favorite food is Mexican, so you guys are pretty close on that one, too."

Raising a brow, she looked at Micah.

He massaged his hands over his face, then glanced at her. "Ben thinks we'd make good, uh, friends."

She straightened, looking between them. "Oh."

"More than friends, Dad." Ben turned to Kat. "His last girlfriend dumped him because of me."

Micah shot Ben another look that seemed to go unnoticed as he rattled on.

"Nicole didn't like my disability," he continued.

Kat frowned. "Well, that's not very nice."

"So my dad's lonely because of me."

"I'm not lonely. I have you, buddy, and that's all I need. Besides,

32

Principal Chandler has a ring." He pointed at her finger. "See that, Ben? It means some lucky guy got to her before you did."

Ben focused on the diamond, his lips puckered in obvious disapproval. Finally, his dark eyes met hers. "That's fake."

"Ben!" Micah leaned across the table and poked his son gently. "Apologize to Principal Chandler right now. That's a very nice, very *real* ring."

She felt like the kid who'd been caught in a lie, standing at the principal's desk with a million and one excuses running through her head. To tell the truth or keep holding on to the lie? Only she hadn't lied. She'd never said she was engaged. Her only guilt was the fact that the man who'd given her the ring could no longer make good on his promise. "What makes you say my ring is fake, Ben?"

He shrugged one shoulder. "'Cause you look lonely like my dad. If the ring was real, you wouldn't look that way."

She rolled her lips together. Her friends telling her so was one thing, but when a kid could see through her, that was a problem.

"Change the subject, buddy," Micah warned. "And quit calling your old man lonely. Your principal is going to get the wrong idea about me and start trying to fix me up with one of her lady friends." He turned to her. "I hate being fixed up, by the way. Especially by my own son. It's embarrassing."

Her shoulders relaxed a notch. "Good intentions," she said quietly, latching onto the escape door in the conversation, and melting into the solid beat that Micah held her gaze. Then she refocused on Ben, who was still frowning at the half-carat antique diamond on her left hand.

Micah was trying not to get turned on every time his skin brushed against Kat's. Trying and failing.

The waitress placed the bill on the table. "Have a good night, guys," she called cheerfully, heading to another table.

He reached for the paper at the same time that Kat did, and their hands brushed against each other lightly. He *really* hoped that Ben hadn't just seen that. For some reason, his son thought it'd be a good idea for him to hook up with his engaged principal. A taken woman was off-limits. He shouldn't have even been looking at her the way he was. Or having the thoughts he'd entertained over the last forty-five minutes.

"No, no, no. You don't have to pay for me," Kat argued.

Micah didn't listen. The bill was in his hand and there was no way a woman was sitting at his table and paying for her own meal. His late mother had taught him better than that. He laid some cash on the table and stood. "We'll walk you to your car and make sure you get in all right."

Ben giggled. "I'll wheel you to your car, Principal Chandler."

She hesitated, still focused on the bill. "Are you sure about picking up the check?"

"Unless you think that fiancé of yours will mind your student treating you to dinner," Micah joked, but something flashed behind her eyes. Sadness?

She stood and they exited the restaurant together, stepping out into the cool night. She headed toward a black Mazda in the parking lot.

"This is me," she said.

"We'll wait until you get inside." Micah looked down at Ben. "Are you taking notes? This is how you treat a lady." *And you don't ever go after an unavailable woman.*

Ben's grin made his gut twist a little. The last thing he wanted to do was hurt his son. Telling him about Jessica's deployment would definitely hurt, but it needed to be done before bed tonight. The sooner, the better.

He looked over at Kat, who was now shaking her purse frantically. She crouched down and began dumping it out on the pavement beside the car. "Something wrong?" he asked, stepping forward and leaving Ben parked on the curb.

She blew out a breath. "I can't find my keys. They've got to be in here somewhere." She shook the bag again. "No jingle. I'll just walk inside and see if I left them in there." She stuffed the strewn contents back in her bag and stood up.

"We'll wait," Micah said, watching as she headed back toward the entrance to Kirk's Pizza House. His gaze ran down her backside as she walked away. He liked this view more than the starry sky that was occupying Ben's attention right now. A few minutes later, she reappeared and shook her head.

"Looks like you'll be riding home with us then."

Her eyes widened. "Home with you?"

"No." He chuckled, shoving his hands in his pockets. "I mean, yes, if you wanted to, but I'm sure you'd rather be with your fiancé." He said it on purpose this time, waiting to see the sadness flicker in her eyes again. What was that? And where was this guy of hers? Why was she eating alone? "I meant that we'd take you to your home, and then we'd go to our own."

"Right." She hugged her purse close to her body, laughing nervously. "I'm so sorry. I'm ruining your father-son night."

"You're not. Trust me." He unlocked his Jeep and opened the door for her. Then he went through the ritual of picking up Ben and placing him in the backseat, folding up his wheelchair and placing it in the trunk. Five minutes later, he was seated in the driver's seat and pulling onto the main road with Kat seated beside him.

"I sometimes ride in the front with Dad, but a man always gives up his seat for a lady," Ben announced proudly.

"That's right, buddy." He turned to Kat. "Where to?"

"Three-eleven Sage Ridge Drive."

Micah stiffened at the address. He and Ben had only lived in Seaside for a few months, but they knew that road well. He glanced in the rearview mirror, surprised that Ben wasn't piping up about the fact that Nicole, the last woman he'd gone out with, lived on that road, too. Ben was too busy staring at Kat, though.

His son's questions started again.

"Do you know what an Osprey is?" Ben asked.

She fidgeted with the ring on her finger as she glanced over her shoulder. "A bird," she said, offering Ben a playful wink. "But it's also a helicopter."

Micah knew his son. Although he'd be impressed she knew that much, the vague helicopter answer wouldn't suffice. And seeing that Micah had been flying an Osprey for the last seven years, Ben knew more about Ospreys than the typical eight-year-old.

"It's a tilt-rotor aircraft actually," Ben said.

"Oh." Kat glanced over at Micah. "Your son is a very smart little guy, isn't he?"

"They can fly vertical and horizontal," Ben continued, "which is different from a regular helicopter."

Kat nodded while he continued to rattle off facts about the military's V-22 Osprey.

Ben had been begging him to take him up in one for over a year now, which was impossible even if Micah's father was the commanding officer of Camp Leon—a CO who'd be very disappointed when he learned that his only son wasn't reenlisting at the end of this contract. Ben needed stability, though. From one parent at least.

Kat pointed to a small one-story house on their left. "That's me."

Micah parked and glanced across the seat at her. She didn't move. Maybe she was waiting for him to get out and open her door, he thought, unbuckling his seatbelt.

"Problem," she said, looking sheepish and sexy as hell in the shadowed Jeep.

He lifted his eyebrows in question.

"I didn't even think about it, but my house key is hooked to my car key somewhere." "You don't have a spare hidden under a mat or something?" he asked.

"I did. But my friend Val took it last week and hasn't been over to put it back. I can call her, though." Kat grabbed her cellphone and began dialing. A few seconds later, she frowned as she stuffed her phone back inside her purse. "She didn't answer."

"I gathered that," he said.

She chewed her bottom lip in a way that made him want to lean over and nibble at her himself. "Anyone else you can call?" *Like your fiancé?*

"I'm really sorry. You can just leave me here and I'll call a locksmith."

With a laugh, Micah shook his head. "I don't think so." He stepped out of his Jeep and began shuffling through the credit cards in his wallet. Finding one that suited him, he walked toward the door. "Be back in a minute, Ben." His son looked half asleep by now, and Micah was willing to bet he'd be drooling before they even left the parking lot. That meant the bad news would have to wait until tomorrow. He hated letting bad news wait. The sooner he told Ben, the sooner he could start healing.

"What are you going to do?" she asked, following him to her front door.

"I'm going to break into your home." He grinned as she pulled back in surprise.

"I don't think that's possible. I have really sturdy—"

Click. The door opened.

She stared at him with her lips slightly parted and her eyes wide with surprise. "It's that easy to get inside my house?"

He nodded, wishing he didn't feel compelled to lean in and kiss her. His gaze flicked back toward his Jeep where, *yep,* Ben was already asleep. Micah smiled, and then cursed under his breath as he noticed a familiar redhead walking down the neighborhood's sidewalk.

He hoped to hell she didn't see them.

"Damn," he muttered, angling his body closer to Kat's, as if that would hide his large six- foot frame.

"What?" Kat followed his gaze.

"I used to date her . . . kind of." They'd only dated a handful of times in what he could probably chalk up to temporary insanity and his buddy Lawson's insistence that he needed to "get back out there." Of course, he'd ended things with her as soon as she'd tossed the C-word at his son. His son had cerebral palsy, but he wasn't crippled.

Kat inspected the woman. "Pretty," she said quietly.

"Pretty is as pretty does. Nicole couldn't deal with Ben's disability. You get me, you get my son. We're a package deal." His entire body tensed just remembering the situation.

Kat's warm hand reached for his, making his tension melt away. *How the hell did she do that?*

"How about I repay your favor in rescuing me tonight, and we have some fun with her?" she asked, as Nicole approached.

He wasn't sure what Kat had in mind, but looking at the beautiful principal now, he'd be willing to plead temporary insanity with her, too. "Deal," he said.

What was she thinking volunteering to pretend she was Micah's new girlfriend?

She wasn't thinking. She'd simply seen that look cross his face when he saw the redhead, and she'd reacted.

Kat looked down at their interlocked fingers, and then met the woman's narrowed catlike eyes. The redhead wore a tight smile.

"Hi, Micah," she purred.

"Nicole." He turned toward Kat. "Kat, this is Nicole. She lives just down the street from you."

Releasing his hand, Kat reached out to shake Nicole's. "So, we're neighbors. Nice to meet you, Nicky." She'd gotten the name wrong on purpose. *What's gotten into me?*

Nicole didn't take her hand. Instead, she stroked the back of the white Persian cat in her arms and gave Kat an assessing stare-down.

Kat tried not to breathe; she was allergic to cats.

"Kitty needed a walk. Helps her sleep," Nicole said, kind of looking like a cat herself with her narrow face and large, green eyes.

Micah stepped in closer to Kat. The woman standing in front of them had hurt him, which spiked Kat's protective nature. Except she usually protected little children. Not muscular groundskeepers, who looked very capable of taking care of themselves.

Leaning into him, she looked up and met his intoxicating eyes. "Honey, you better get Ben home. It's been a long night." All eyes went to Ben, who was fast asleep in the back of the Jeep.

"You're right. Long, but fun." He winked, which did funny

things to her stomach. Then he turned with a tight smile. "Nicole, it was nice to see you again."

The beautiful redhead hesitated.

He wrapped an arm around Kat's shoulders and squeezed. Even though she knew it was only for show, it felt good—*too good*—and she nestled into his hold. She liked her pillows soft, but resting her head against his hard pecs was nice, too. Only they didn't invite fantasies of sleep, but something much more stimulating.

"Okay," Nicole finally said. "Nice to meet you, *Kate*."

Kat would've corrected her, but just as her mouth opened to speak, Micah's other arm reached across her body, brushing against her breasts to open her front door. He hadn't meant to touch her there, she was sure of it, but she shuddered with undeniable attraction. The attraction only intensified as she caught a whiff of his cologne, or maybe that was just him. He smelled like man—hot, sexy man.

Catching her eye, he smiled as his hand still rested on the doorknob. "Is she walking away?" he whispered, the sound of his voice gruff like the unshaven edge of his cheek. Kat suddenly wanted to feel that cheek brushing against hers.

She glanced over her shoulder and nodded. "Um, yes. Slowly . . . Oh, wait. She's looking back—" When she looked at Micah again, she found him closer than she expected. So close their lips brushed unexpectedly. She gave a little gasp, but didn't pull away. Instead, she leaned in, melting into the kiss, forgetting for a moment that they were pretending. That she was only repaying Micah's favor and upsetting the redhead. That this had all been her idea, and the moment was fake.

Warm tingles ran through her body as his hand traveled up her arm and gently caressed her cheek. Her lips parted, inviting the kiss to rocket from sweet to sinful. Micah pulled back and stared long and deep into her eyes.

But holy Godiva. The kiss hadn't felt fake.

"Is she still watching?" he asked in a low whisper.

She looked past him as she attempted to catch the breath he'd just stolen. "No."

"Too bad. I was prepared to kiss you again," he said, releasing her slowly and taking a step back. He held her gaze for a long, heated moment, and then tossed a glance in Ben's direction. Still sleeping. Good. The school didn't need to hear about the principal kissing a student's father.

Did Micah just say he's going to kiss me again?

She ran a tongue over her lips and took a tiny step away also, reminding herself that he was a parent at the school. "Well, thank you for saving me tonight."

"Ditto," he said, watching her. The intensity of his gaze made her dizzy. Or maybe it was the fact that when he looked at her, she forgot to breathe.

Definitely a dad she'd like to . . .The f-word never rolled off her tongue, or her mind, so easily.

"Do you need a ride?" he asked.

Her mouth fell open. "Wh-what?" Had he heard her thoughts? Had she actually said what she was thinking out loud? Oh, geez. Her hormones were way out of control.

"A ride to school tomorrow? You lost your keys. How will you—?"

"Oh." She laughed nervously. And wow, her cheeks were burning.

"What did you think I meant?" A wicked smile crawled over his lips because he knew good and well what she'd thought, and that was mortifying.

"My secretary can pick me up and take me to my car. I have a spare set of keys in the house. It won't be a problem." She stepped over the door's threshold, needing to get inside before the embarrassment killed her. Or before she gave in to her desire and pulled him inside with her. "Good night," she said, her voice breaking a little on the end.

With a wave, he retreated toward his Jeep, glancing back once to offer one of those knee- weakening smiles.

Kat closed the door and leaned against it, sucking in a deep, shuddery breath. What had just happened? She hadn't kissed a man since she'd kissed John goodbye right before his deployment.

But this kiss with Micah had been fake. It didn't count.

Only it had felt real. Too real.

Chapter Five

The next afternoon, Micah parked the Jeep and trailer with his lawn equipment on the side of the school and stepped out. He'd been dreading coming here all day. Half dreading, half looking forward to it. He needed to talk to Kat about the kiss they'd shared last night.

"Dad!" Ben called, waiting for him on the concrete breezeway at the front of the school.

Micah mustered a smile, which wasn't too hard when it came to his son. "Hey, buddy. I thought your teacher said you could help grade papers while I did the lawn this afternoon."

"She did. Just wanted to say hi."

"I can do better than hi." He wrapped Ben in a tight hug, knowing there were no kids around and Ben wouldn't mind this time. "It won't take me long. If your teacher needs me, she knows where I'll be."

"Right." Ben squirmed out of Micah's grasp and started rolling his wheelchair toward the building alone. He'd yet to mention anyone with long-lasting friend potential, but it'd only been a week. School wasn't like the Marine Corps, where life and death situations necessitated that you formed an immediate alliance with the person standing next to you.

Scratching his chin, Micah watched his son disappear back inside the building while debating his choice. He could mow the grass first or go in and talk to Kat. He'd prefer to be clean and smelling somewhat human when he saw her, *so yeah,* talk first, mow later.

He opened the door to the front office and started to say something to the woman sitting behind the desk, but the brunette held up her hand first.

"I know who you are," she said, grinning like they had some inside secret. "And I know who you want." Her brows raised teasingly. "She's somewhere walking around the school with the little hoodlums right now, though."

"Hoodlums?" he asked, not sure that he'd heard her correctly. Weren't all the school's employees supposed to gush over the kids, even the unruly ones?

"This week's troublemakers," the secretary continued. "She's put them in some kind of club, and she's making them do good deeds. You know, wash the blackboards and stuff. A regular Pollyanna."

"Pollyanna?" He was here to see Kat. "I'm sorry. I just wanted to speak to the principal."

"Principal Pollyanna. That's what I call her when she's not listening. And also when she is." The woman offered her hand. "Hi. I'm Valerie Hunt, Kat's oldest friend. Kind of. We weren't really friends growing up, but I knew her when she was knobby-kneed and clumsier than she is now. Therefore, I'm allowed to tease her and still keep my job."

"I see." He glanced around impatiently.

"I'm also privy to all the juicy information that involves her."

This got his attention. He was getting out of the Marine Corps next May, so any gossip he stirred here would stick with him forever. "Juicy information?" he repeated, hoping he'd heard her wrong.

"Usually. But she's been real tight-lipped this week. All I know is she ate dinner with you and your son last night when I bailed on her."

His whole body relaxed. "That's all there is to know."

Val's eyes skimmed over him. "So, where is Ben's mom?"

Maybe he should've chosen to mow the lawn first. He hadn't realized he was walking into an interrogation. "She's active duty," he said.

If Val was surprised, it didn't show. Instead of responding, she continued to stare at him, waiting for him to say more.

"Ben's mom is about to go back to Afghanistan. He doesn't know it yet." So why had he just told the nosiest person he'd ever met?

Her face softened. "Poor kid. That must be hard."

A huge knot formed in the back of his throat. "Maybe I'll just catch Kat . . . uh, Principal Chandler, when I'm done with the lawn." He started to leave, and then walked straight into the leggy blonde who'd invaded his dreams last night. She braced herself against his chest, and looked up at him, surprise making her lips part just slightly the way they had last night after he'd kissed her.

Yeah, he was glad he wasn't sweaty and dirty just yet.

"Micah . . . I mean, um, Mr. Peterson." Her gaze skittered toward her secretary.

"I was hoping to run into you," he said, unable to help the slow smile that spread through his face. Or the way his heart sped up just looking at her. He could get used to the feel of her body against his. "I wanted to talk to you." His gaze flickered behind him, and he lowered his voice. "Privately."

She pulled her hands from his chest with what seemed like the effort it took to pull apart two magnets, and took a tiny step backward. "Sure." She started to lead him into her office, and then stopped. "How about we take a walk outside instead?"

Opening the door for her, he agreed. "Perfect."

They walked at a comfortable distance from each other down the row of flowers he'd planted the week before.

"I wanted to say I'm sorry about last night."

She looked up. "Don't apologize. It was my idea."

"To pretend we were a couple maybe, but I got carried away."

Securing the ball cap on his head, he slid her a glance. "Guess I just got wrapped up in the moment. When I got home, I couldn't sleep. Kissing you was way out of line, and I'm sorry."

Guilt wasn't the only reason he couldn't sleep, though. It'd been a long time since a kiss had made him ache for more. And he'd ached last night in every part of his body.

She stopped walking and faced him. "Really. You don't have to—"

"I knew you weren't available. I apologize for any problems this might cause between you and your fiancé." He cleared his throat and planted his gaze on the mower in the distance. When he looked at her, all he could think about was pulling her to him and kissing her again. And how sweet that kiss had been, or how long it'd been since he'd kissed a woman and felt anything. He certainly hadn't with Nicole.

"It's fine," she said quietly.

He shook his head. "I don't want some guy trying to beat me up."

"Trying?"

His gaze returned to her. "Yeah, well, I haven't seen the guy, but I'm pretty confident in my ability to take care of myself."

She laughed, the sound so sweet that he had the urge to make her laugh again. Time to mow the lawn before his palms started sweating like a high school kid with a tank-sized crush.

"Well, that's all I wanted to say . . . Oh." He reached inside the pocket of his jeans, well aware that her gaze traveled down to watch. "I found this."

"My keys! Where did you find them?"

"I went back to Kirk's this morning. The cashier said someone left them in the bathroom overnight."

Her hand brushed against his knuckles as she grabbed the keys, her skin soft like silk. He wondered if the rest of her felt the same. He had to stop having these thoughts. She was getting married, and not to him. And she was Ben's principal. Two very good reasons to leave her alone.

"Thank you. I had a spare set, but it was giving me the creeps having my keys out there for anyone to use. I was considering leaving early today and getting my locks changed." She laughed lightly.

"You *should* leave early some days. You know what they say about all work and no play," he said.

"It makes a boring Jane. Yes, I know. My mother used to tell me that all the time."

Jessica crossed Micah's mind. His ex was definitely more work than play. "I suspect
you're anything but boring." He watched her throat constrict as she swallowed. It was pull her in for another kiss or walk away, which is what he should've done last night. He tipped his head toward the mower. "I have to get to work."

"All work and no play," she teased, tossing his own words back at him.

"This *is* my play," he said, readjusting his hat. "See you later, Kat." Then, he headed toward his fully-loaded John Deere mower. There was nothing better than taking a ride and letting the vibration shake the stress off his body.

Nothing better.

Except maybe watching a beautiful principal stoop to admire his flowers as her knee-length skirt slid up the backs of her thighs. She had nice, long legs. Standing again, she started to walk away. She also had a nice . . .

He kicked the lawnmower into gear with a loud roar of its engine.

She was a beautiful, engaged principal, who, for all he knew, was just as much all-work-and-no-play as Ben's mother—not what he needed. In fact, Kat Chandler was the *last* thing he needed in his personal life right now.

KAT ENTERED THE SCHOOL AND STOPPED FOR MOMENT, letting the cool air-conditioning hit her heated cheeks. It was hot outside for the beginning of September, and Micah Peterson hadn't helped to cool her down.

"Yeah, he's hot," came a lilting voice across the lobby.

Kat's eyes flung open. "I didn't know you were standing there."

Val laughed with all the delight of a five-year-old. "I think it's great that you have a crush on someone."

Kat looked around to make sure no one had overheard her secretary's big mouth. Micah was a parent. Not only that, he worked for the school. "I don't have a crush on him," she argued in a hushed voice. "He's nice. And handsome. That's all."

"You didn't think he was so nice a few days ago." Val followed her back into the office. "Anyway, I'm heading out. My father has me on dinner duty for another church family in crisis. Are you heading home?"

Kat shook her head. "I'm working late tonight."

"Woo-hoo," Val yipped, sarcasm dripping easily from her words. "That sounds about as much fun as serving up chicken to strangers."

"I'm going to regret hiring you, aren't I?" Kat helped Val stack a pile of random things into her arms, one of which was a romance novel. Kat hoped Val at least pretended to work when there were other people in the office.

"Probably." Val winked and started walking toward the door. "Just don't let him see you watching him."

"What?"

"I know that's really why you're staying late. But don't let him catch you. Men are more interested if they think you're not too into them."

"Thanks for the tip." Rolling her eyes, she opened the door for Val and noticed Ben rolling toward her in his wheelchair.

"See you later, Ben Peterson." Val waved and walked out the double doors of the school.

Thank God. Best friend or not, sometimes she drove Kat batty.

"Your dad is still working outside, Ben," she said, leaning against the wall and waiting for him to look at her. "Did you have a good day at school?"

He shrugged a shoulder, keeping his gaze on the tiled floor.

"Wanna talk about it?" she asked.

He shook his head in a jerky movement characteristic of his cerebral palsy. His muscles resisted everything he did. "Not really."

"Hmm. Want to go for a walk?"

He looked at her as if she had three heads. "In case you haven't noticed, Principal Chandler, I don't walk much." He grinned, obviously proud of his little joke.

"You know what I mean." She gave his dark, shaggy hair a tousle as his crooked smile revealed a small gap between his two front teeth. Then she pushed the square handicap button that automatically opened the double doors of the school, and they headed toward the humming sound of the lawnmower around back.

"Can you push me?" Ben asked, looking up at her with large, hopeful eyes.

Her mouth quirked to the side. "You can wheel yourself."

His shoulders sagged by his side. "But my arm is tired."

Kat remembered what Micah had said about Ben being independent. "I'd rather walk beside you if that's all right."

They continued in silence for another beat.

"I think my mom is deploying again," he said then.

Her mouth fell open. She'd wanted to ask about Ben's mother last night, but hadn't felt right about it. And his file mentioned nothing, which she'd been intending to correct. "Your mother is a Marine?" she asked.

Ben nodded. "My dad is acting funny and I know it has something to do with her. I think she's going back to war, just like last year."

A charley horse–sized cramp squeezed at her heart. "Did you ask your father about it?"

Ben shook his head. "No. He's been trying to tell me. I don't want him to though, even if it's true. Because that'll mean it's real."

"I see." It was the same part of her that hadn't wanted to hear any news about John when she'd found out about the accident involving his squadron. No news meant there was still hope. He could still come home and they would get married.

The mower stopped in the distance, and she spotted Micah walking toward them. His shirt was already soaked through in the front and clung to his deeply defined chest. How did caring for landscapes mold a chest like that one? Was he doing pull-ups in the trees?

"You like my dad," Ben said quietly.

Kat whipped her head to look at the boy, who was smiling broadly at her. "No. I mean, yes. He's nice, but—"

"But you're marrying someone else," he said with a heavy sigh.

They both looked down at her diamond.

"It's complicated," she said softly, aware that Micah was almost in front of them.

"Adults always say that."

"Hey there, buddy." Micah ran the back of his hand over his forehead, clearing the layer of sweat that had collected there. "You two out for a walk?"

Ben nodded. "I finished helping Miss Hadley grade papers."

"Good. You made sure you gave yourself all As then, right?" He winked at Kat, making her belly flutter.

Her feelings about Ben's dad were complicated, too. She wasn't usually one who went dry in the mouth just because a hunky dad stood next to her. Of course, she didn't know many hunky dads, and most of them were married. Or Marines, which were a breed of man she never intended to date again.

"I'll load things up and finish over the weekend, if that's okay?"

"Sure." She nodded, contemplating if she needed to work over the weekend, too. Just the thought of seeing him again made her heart lift in her chest. Val was right. She needed to get more of a social life. Looking forward to the landscape guy mowing the school's lawn was bordering pathetic.

Micah motioned for Ben to move his wheelchair forward, accidentally bumping the

Transformers book bag that hung from its handles. A loose paper fluttered to his feet. "What's this?" He stooped to pick the wrinkled paper up and unfolded it, revealing a drawing inside.

"That's mine!" Ben attempted to snatch it with his right arm. "Give it back. It's mine."

A flicker of something passed across Micah's eyes, and his jaw hardened. "What the hell is this?"

"Dad! *Pleease*," Ben begged. "It's trash."

Kat looked between them, and then took the paper that Micah handed her. It was a penciled sketch of a boy in a wheelchair with various mean words circling the stick-figure boy. *Geek. Nerd. Loser. Dumb.* "Who gave this to you, Ben?" she asked.

Ben looked like he was on the verge of tears. "No one. *I* drew it."

"Ben," Micah warned. "That's not your handiwork. Who gave it to you?" he asked more forcefully.

Ben looked away, his mouth tightly shut. He wasn't going to talk.

Kat crouched down, resting her hands on the arms of Ben's wheelchair, and lowered her voice. "Whoever drew it, they're wrong." She waited for him to meet her eyes. "None of those things are true. You know that, right?"

Sniffling, he nodded. "I'm definitely not dumb. I'm much smarter than your average third grader."

This made her smile. "And you're not a nerd, or a geek, or a loser. If you don't want to tell us who drew that picture, you don't have to."

"Now wait one minute," Micah said behind her, his voice hard-edged like it'd been earlier in the week.

Kat didn't turn back. Instead, she continued talking to Ben. "But if you change your mind, I'd really like to talk to the person who drew that picture. A kid has to feel really bad about themselves to want to tear someone else down."

Ben blinked. "I didn't think about that."

She lifted a shoulder and stood, ironing her hands over her skirt. "My office door is always open. I'm a good listener, and I happen to know that you're a good talker."

Ben's contagious smile was back. "Okay." His gaze moved to his father.

Kat hesitated before looking at Micah, too, already suspecting what she'd see in his expression—something similar to what she'd seen after she'd walked Ben to class on the first day of school— unmasked disapproval.

Not looking at her, Micah reached for the drawing in her hand and gave it another quick glance, growling under his breath. "We'll talk at home," he said to Ben.

It was obvious he didn't like the way she'd handled the situation. Would he rather that she bully the answer out of his son, though?

"Have a nice weekend," he said tightly, walking with Ben toward his Jeep Cherokee in the parking lot.

" 'Bye, Principal Chandler," Ben called, not looking back.

"'Bye. See you Monday!"

And with that, the first week of school was over. Kat blew out a breath. Not too bad. Everyone had survived, and next week would be even better—as long as she kept her hard and fast attraction toward a certain parent in check, and proved to him that she had his son's best interests at heart. Because she did. Ben was a great kid, and she was going to make sure that he, and every other student at SES, was successful this year.

~

MICAH STARED AT BEN ACROSS THE DINNER TABLE THAT night. He'd made salads on purpose. Ben hated salads and, for the life of him, he didn't know how to punish the kid. Ben needed to tell on his bully, so that the brat could be tossed in that Friendship Club the school was constructing for mean kids.

51

"You don't protect the people who hurt you," he said, studying Ben's forlorn features.

"You protect Mom," Ben countered.

Micah started to argue, stopping short when the doorbell rang. He pointed a finger. "Not the same, but hold that thought."

He walked toward the front door and opened it, already knowing who would be there. "Hey, Lawson. Maybe you can talk some sense into my boy."

Lawson pulled off his cowboy hat and hung it on a hook in the hallway as he followed Micah toward the table. It was Friday night. Lawson had been showing up on Friday nights since their first deployment together. Micah had saved his life in the desert and somehow that translated into having weekly meals together.

Ben's eyes lit up when he saw him. "Uncle Lawson!"

Yeah, and somehow weekly meals translated into family. That was fine by Micah, too. Ben needed family. Other than Micah, all Ben had was a mother who had chosen the military over him and a grandfather who, as the CO of Camp Leon, *was* the military.

Then there was Aunt Clara and Uncle Rick who lived next door. They were a big part of the reason that Micah had decided to stay in Seaside once he got out of the military. Clara and Rick had always been home to him, no matter where he'd gone growing up, moving across the country, wherever his father's job sent them. Every time he'd visited Seaside, he'd felt that ring of familiarity in his heart—the one he guessed people got when they came home.

This was his home.

Lawson, all six foot three of him, stood in front of the table and frowned at the salad like a disappointed child.

Micah tried not to look at him for fear of laughing. This was a serious meal. Ben needed to tell him who was bullying him at school.

"A salad?" Lawson muttered. "Really? I don't know if I mentioned it on the phone or not, but I ran six miles this morning. And spent all day in the field. I probably sweat off at least two gallons out there, man."

Nice visual. "You mentioned it." Micah sat and picked up his fork, stabbing at a leaf of lettuce. "Ben, tell Uncle Lawson why we're having salads for dinner."

Ben squirmed in his chair. "Because salads are good for you."

"Wrong answer," Micah said sharply. "Some kid at school is picking on Ben. Drawing pictures of him and calling him names."

"What kid?" Lawson asked, his eyes darkening. He was a good friend, and loved Ben as much as he would a real nephew.

"He's not saying," Micah said through tight lips. He wanted to shake the answer out of his son right now and then barge down to the bully's house and lay into the kid until he cried uncontrollably. And after that, lay into the kid's parents for raising such a brat. Not that he'd actually do that, of course.

But Ben wasn't saying. No matter how much the kid had hurt his feelings, he didn't want to see his bully get in trouble with his overprotective father. Micah got that. It's the same thing he would've done, but it didn't keep his blood from singing through his veins.

"Fine. You can add doing the dishes every night to your list of chores," Micah said.

"Dad!"

Lawson raised a finger quietly, seated now with a fork in hand. "How's he supposed to wash dishes?"

Micah and Ben both looked at him like he had vines growing out of his ears.

"I can wash dishes, Uncle Lawson. I hold the dish in my left arm and wash with my right. Just takes *forever*." He emphasized the word "forever," rolling his eyes.

"Keep complaining and I'll add folding the laundry." Micah noticed the slight tremble in Ben's chin. *Oh, geez.* He hoped his son wouldn't start crying. Lawson hated it when Ben cried. The man got all shifty and looked like he was being held hostage or something.

"If you're so big and tough, why don't you just tell me this news you've been trying to break to me all week," Ben said then.

Micah steeled himself, holding his fork suspended in the air. "What news?"

"You know. The news about Mom." Tears shone in Ben's eyes. His cheeks were already a ruddy red from the emotion swirling through him. Cerebral palsy didn't just affect his son's muscle tone, it also made him an extra emotional kid. It was something Micah understood, but it still socked him in the gut every time he saw Ben's tears.

Lawson shoved more lettuce in his mouth, keeping his head low. Micah guessed he was regretting not going home for a boring night of TV or finding a date for tonight instead.

"How did you know your mom was deploying again?" Micah asked.

Ben pushed aside his plate as a tear glided down his freckled cheek. He sniffed, looking like he was doing his best not to fall apart, and Micah knew he was. "I didn't. Until now."

Chapter Six

K at watched her younger sister park and step out of her little
Honda Civic. Julie was an inch taller than she was, which
had always grated on Kat's nerves growing up, and a little tanner,
thanks to her morning yoga routine, which she did outside. Even so,
people had always mistaken them for twins. They were nearly iden-
tical, on the outside at least. Personality wise, they were worlds
different.

Julie's gaze flicked toward the window.

Spotted. Straightening, Kat guessed she had to help with her
sister's bags now. There couldn't be more than a couple. Julie was
only staying for a weekend because she had to get back to her job as
a yoga instructor at her boyfriend's health club in Charlotte.

"Julie!" Kat was surprised by the genuine enthusiasm that rolled
off her as she bounded down the steps and toward the car in her
driveway.

Setting her bags down, Julie opened her arms, looking genuinely
happy to see her, too. Of course, Julie was always happy to see everyone. Other than Val, she didn't have any enemies. Growing up, Kat
would've said that her younger sister was perfect, or as close to
perfection as it came.

"Hey, sis!" Julie stepped back and gave Kat an assessing look. "How are you?"

With a close-up look, Kat could ask the same. "I'm good. You?"

Julie brushed her hair from her face, seeming to breathe in the air around her. "The drive was a long one, but it feels good to be home."

That was a statement that Kat never thought she'd hear her sister say. Julie had gone away to college right after high school and, while she was religious about making the obligatory holiday visits, she rarely came back to Seaside otherwise. Which raised all kinds of questions about what she was doing here now. Before Kat could ask, though, Julie popped the trunk of her car and Kat stared with her mouth agape at the one, two, three, four . . . six bags in the trunk. A car this small shouldn't even hold six bags.

"Let's just get these to my room and then we can catch up," Julie said, heaving a duffel bag over her shoulder.

Her room?

Kat had envisioned Julie taking the couch. There was no spare room here. Unless Julie stayed in the master bedroom, where John's things still resided. Kat hadn't slept there in over two years—since she'd been notified that he was killed in action. That room had been theirs together. How could she sleep there knowing John was never coming home?

Julie's gaze lowered as Kat twisted the engagement ring on her finger, the concern etching itself deeper into the fine lines of her face. Then she lugged another bag on her shoulder and started walking toward the front door.

Kat followed her inside. "Just how long will you be staying exactly?"

As if she didn't hear her, her sister continued walking down the hall, poking her head into both rooms, and then heading inside the master. "I assume you're using the one that looks lived in, so I'll camp out here if that's okay." A smile brightened her face as she plopped down on the king-sized bed and looked at Kat.

"You can't stay in this room. And please get off the bed," she said, her tone becoming the one she used when disciplining her students—polite but pointed. She refused to put Julie's luggage down in this room. It was off-limits.

"This was your room with John," Julie said, not budging. Her eyes tilted sympathetically.

Kat hated when people's eyes slanted in pity. "Stop that."

"Stop what?" Julie asked, the slant diving deeper.

"Looking at me like I'm not okay. I am okay. Just because I don't use this room, or that bed anymore, doesn't mean anything."

"I know." Julie nodded. "Have you even touched this bed since he's been gone?"

Not since she'd gotten the call from John's sobbing mother, informing her that they'd identified his body. "Please, just get up," Kat snapped, trying her best not to sound rude. "You can sleep somewhere else. I'll give you my room and I'll take the couch."

Julie stood, shaking her head. "I'm not kicking you out of your own room. If anyone is taking the couch, it's me. The couch will be perfect, actually." She lifted her bags and started back down the hall. "Are you at least going to therapy?" she asked.

Kat didn't answer. Work was her therapy. And Val.

"You never were good at taking care of yourself. Too busy taking care of everyone else around you," Julie continued.

Kat huffed, doing her best to keep up as Julie strode directly toward the kitchen. "I'm taking care of myself. You don't even live here. You have no idea if I'm taking care of myself or not. Which I am." Kat rested her hands on her hips, her brows lowering as she watched Julie open the refrigerator and peer inside. "What are you doing?"

"Seeing just how well you take care of yourself." Julie glanced over her shoulder. "You're living off cold pizza and mustard?"

Point taken.

"Kirk's pizza is the best," Kat said weakly, as if that were a viable defense.

"Well, we're going out to dinner tonight anyway, right?" Julie shut the fridge and leaned against the counter. "We'll work on finding you that rebound guy tonight and get groceries tomorrow. It's a wonder you're still breathing." Her sister winked playfully.

"I'm the older sister. I'm the one who is supposed to be making sure you're okay."

Julie's smile wilted only slightly. "All good." Her catchphrase for as long as Kat could remember. Everything was always "all good." And Kat usually believed her. But Julie was suddenly home, and the dark circles under her eyes made Kat wonder at the reason.

"How soon do the bars open in Seaside anyway?" Julie asked, flashing a wicked grin.

"Only one bar in Seaside, remember? Heroes. And I believe it's open right now."

"Good." Julie headed toward her suitcase. "I'll freshen up, we'll grab a bite, and then we'll work on getting you laid."

Kat spewed the drink of water she'd just sipped onto the floor in front of her. "Who said anything about having sex?"

Julie chuckled, looking her over. "Sis, you are wound tighter than a forty-year-old virgin. But okay, fine." She held up her hands in surrender. "You can start by getting wasted drunk tonight. How's that?"

Kat's shoulders relaxed a notch. Drunk sounded nice. "Perfect."

MICAH RELUCTANTLY WALKED THROUGH THE DOOR OF Heroes, Seaside's only bar. It was a popular hole- in-the-wall that catered to the local military. How had Lawson talked him into coming here after the dinner from hell, when Ben had stared at his lettuce like eating it was some new form of torture? He just wanted his kid to be happy. Was that too much to ask?

"Ben'll be fine with your aunt. Aunt Clara is awesome." Lawson bumped his shoulder, seeming to read his mind. "You need some time off to unwind."

Drinking wasn't Micah's idea of unwinding. Unwinding was

tilling dirt. Riding his mower. Fishing. "Aunt Clara?" Micah teased. "She's my aunt, you know? Not yours."

Lawson shrugged. "What happened to what's mine is yours?"

"I never said that." Micah frowned. "And keep your voice down. You're making us sound like an old married couple."

Lawson's gaze skimmed over him. "Nah. You're not my type, bro. Bar or table?"

"Table." Micah hated the bar. The bar was for people who wanted to talk about their problems. And while Jeff, the regular bartender here, was a good listener, Micah wasn't in the mood. He'd rather drink and listen to Lawson talk.

Truth be told, he'd really rather go home.

They headed toward a round table in the back corner, as Lawson scanned the room for women. Micah guessed he'd be ditched within the hour. Then he could nab Ben and maybe catch the tail end of a game on TV.

Settling into his seat, Lawson whistled under his breath. "Don't look now, but a smokin' hot brunette just walked through the door."

Micah turned to look.

"I said *don't* look." Lawson shook his head, and then flashed a charming smile at the waitress standing next to him. "I'll just have a Coke to start with, sweetheart."

The young woman flushed as she nodded. "And for you?" she asked, smiling at Micah.

"A beer, please." Turning, he looked at the woman who'd just walked in again. "That brunette you have your eye on looks familiar. I think she works at Ben's school." He watched the woman join a table with two other women and his mouth went dry. "Kat." And another woman who looked a lot like Kat. He hadn't started drinking yet, and he was already seeing double.

"I spotted her first, buddy. But because you saved my life in the desert—"

Micah faced Lawson. "Her name is Val, and I'm not interested in her. I know her friend. Don't look—" His words came out as Lawson craned his neck to stare at the table of women.

His head bobbed approvingly. "Which one is yours? She-Ra or Cinderella?"

"She-Ra?" Micah asked, lifting a brow.

"Yeah. You know. Princess of Power." Lawson waved a hand. "I'm guessing you're into Cinderella. She's more your type, all sweet and innocent looking."

"Cinderella? Your man card is in jeopardy right now, man. Her name is Kat Chandler. She's Ben's principal."

Lawson's smile grew as he rubbed his hands together. "Ben told me about her the other night. Said you like his principal a lot. Emphasis on a lot."

The waitress set a beer in front of him. "Ben wants me to like her a lot. He feels guilty about Nicole. Thinks I'm lonely."

Lawson drank from his Coke. "You are lonely. Why don't we buy a round for the pretty ladies over there? I can't decide between Val and She-Ra. She-Ra looks pretty hot. I'll leave Cinderella for you, though." His brows bounced playfully.

Micah started to peel the label on his bottle. "I'm not buying Ben's principal a drink."

"This isn't school, it's a bar. And she's not a principal right now, she's a woman. A fairest- of-them-all specimen," Lawson said, mixing up his fairy tales—not that Micah would admit to knowing the difference, much less point that fact out.

Micah leaned back in his chair and nursed the beer in his hand. "What are we? Twelve?"

Lawson waved the waitress back over. "Three refills of whatever the ladies over there are having."

"Got it." Scribbling on her notepad, she flushed again as she met Lawson's eyes. It was enough to make Micah gag. Women fell over themselves around the guy, acted like he walked on water.

"It's the cowboy hat," Micah said, when she walked away.

Lawson grinned. "Whatever works. You can borrow it sometime

if you want. If you're feeling like you need a little help in the romantic field."

Screw tiny sips. He took a huge gulp from his beer. "I don't need help. Thanks."

"Uh-oh. She's bringing the drinks over." Lawson grabbed a menu and pretended to read, lifting his gaze, none too casually. "They're looking at us," he said through the corner of his mouth.

Micah turned in his chair and met Kat's eyes. *Wow.* Lawson was right. She wasn't a principal tonight. She looked . . . like a goddess. Or, yes, Cinderella with her pale skin and flowing blond hair that hung past her shoulders.

And there was no man in sight. This was the second time that he'd run into her outside of school and she'd been without a guy. She obviously had one. Women didn't just wear diamonds on their left ring finger for no reason. Whoever the hell her fiancé was, he was lucky to get to take her home. Maybe her fiancé was in the military and deployed, he considered, which made him feel even worse for checking her out.

She-Ra, as Lawson had deemed her, stood up and headed in their direction. When she got to their table, she leaned forward, bracing her hands on the table in front of her. "Thanks for the drinks, guys."

She was thin, but light muscles twisted up her arms. It wasn't a look that Micah normally found attractive, but, considering she was a clone of Kat Chandler, it worked.

She stuck out her hand and shook both of theirs. "I'm Julie Chandler. That's my sister, Kat, and her friend Val."

Lawson was in full charm mode. "I'm Lawson and this is my buddy Micah. Are you ladies all alone tonight?" he asked.

With a smile, her gaze landed on his cowboy hat. "Hopefully not for long. Want to join us?" Micah started to say no, but was stopped short by Lawson's "Hell, yeah."

A moment later, the five of them sat comfortably around the other table.

"We keep running into each other," Kat said, leaning over to him as Lawson captured Val's and Julie's attention.

"Great minds think alike." It had come out smooth, hopefully charming, but then Micah shook his head. "Actually, this wasn't my idea. To be honest, I'd rather be at home with Ben." He looked at Kat. "No offense. You're beautiful company."

Her hair swept across her face as she glanced down to look at her hands. "Thank you. And this wasn't my idea, either. Val and Julie decided I needed a night out."

"Why is that?" he asked.

A shadow of emotion crossed her expression as she looked at him. "Oh, you know. I work too much, I guess."

"We've talked about that, Kat," he said, taking another sip from his beer, and motioning toward her ring. "When you get married, you won't want to spend all your time away from your husband."

Her smile faded.

"Sorry, just saying. I know this from experience. Ben's mom loved her work more than she loved us. The relationship was doomed from the beginning."

Crap. By the look on her face, he'd really stuck his foot in his mouth. He tried to backpedal.

"I'm sure your marriage will be different, though. And he's a lucky guy."

Maybe he did need to wear a damn cowboy hat, because his charm was nowhere to be found right now.

Lifting her beer for the first time since he'd sat down next to her, she took a sip. And another. Then she took such a long pull on her bottle that Micah wondered if she'd pass out from the lack of oxygen. After several more swigs, Val and Julie stopped to watch her, glancing at Micah in question.

"What did you say to her?" Val asked, accusations etched all over her face.

"He didn't say anything," Kat said, raising her voice. "I need another drink."

As if on cue, the waitress came with bottles for everyone except Lawson, who took another soda.

"If I said something—" Micah leaned in close to her, catching the scent of her perfume.

Damn. She smelled amazing.

"You didn't." Rolling her lips into one another, she kept her eyes on the drink. "It's just, well, I'm not engaged any longer."

"Oh." His gaze lowered to her ring.

With a shrug, she looked around the table. "That relationship is in the past, and I'm moving on."

Crap, crap, crap. He'd really screwed up this relaxing night out for her. He wasn't sure what the story was, but he was starting to suspect it was the reason behind the haunted look he sometimes saw in her eyes. His hand found hers under the table and he offered a gentle squeeze.

"I'm sorry," he whispered.

"You didn't know." She forced a smile at him and looked at Val and Julie again. "But tonight isn't about that. It's about catching up with my two favorite women, and enjoying a few drinks."

"That's not *exactly* what I had in mind," Julie said, lifting her brows.

Kat wobbled a little on her seat, and Micah instinctively placed a steadying hand on her back. The touch zinged through him, and, *yeah,* he could think of some things he'd rather do than drink, too.

Grabbing the fresh bottle that the waitress had placed in front of her a moment earlier, Kat held it up to the group. "Well, drinking myself into oblivion is *exactly* what I have in mind."

The room was spinning as Kat tried to focus on Micah's mouth. He was saying something, but his hand on her thigh was very distracting.

And why had she just told him she wasn't engaged? That opened all kinds of doors. Now there'd be questions, and answering questions when you were drunk was never a good idea.

She looked across the table at her sister and friend, who were laughing hysterically at something the other guy had said. What was his name again? All she could remember at the moment was the kiss that she'd shared with Micah the other night. It'd been a nice kiss. Better than nice. That kiss had set off fireworks inside her, lighting up places that had been dormant far too long. "Kat?"

"Hmm." She blinked heavily at Micah and felt that dorky smile crawl through her cheeks. *Great, just great.* She'd never be able to face him again, which was too bad. She kind of liked this sexy lawn keeper.

"I think you've had too much to drink." His brows hung heavily over his chocolate fudge eyes.

"Yum."

"Yep." He nodded definitively. "I'm taking you home right now." All conversation stopped and everyone at the table turned to him.

"I'm taking her to her home, and I'll be going back to mine." Micah cleared his throat.

"Ladies, you don't have to finish your night quite yet. I can vouch for my friend here. He'll get you home just fine," he said, leveling his gaze at Lawson.

"And who'll vouch for you?" Julie asked, looking at Micah. "How do we know you're not going to take advantage of my sister while she's falling all over herself?"

"Hey!" Kat objected. "I'm not falling over." She swayed on her chair as she waggled a finger. "And I can vouch for Micah. He's a perfect gentleman."

Val's gaze narrowed on Kat, her lips lifting lightly at the corners. "I'll vouch for him. Micah should definitely drive Kat home tonight."

And either Kat's vision was jumping from all the alcohol, which was possible, or Val's eyebrows waggled over her mischief-filled eyes.

Kat shook her head. Val thought they were leaving to rip each other's clothes off—or at least that's what she was hoping. But she was wrong. Raging hormones or not, Kat couldn't sleep with Micah. She barely knew him, and he was a parent who also happened to work for her.

She'd have to be a lot drunker than this to cross those lines.

"Are you ready?" Micah asked, turning to her and smiling.

"I can't just leave. I'm the reason we're all here." Her words slurred on top of each other, as she looked across the table at Val again. "I can't just leave you."

"It's fine. Really. I'll call you tomorrow and you can complain about how awful your headache is. Because it's going to be painful." Val smiled as if the thought were a pleasant one. Kat shifted in her chair, and then relented. "Fine." Going home sounded good actually. She tried to stand before both feet were flat on the ground. *Rookie-drunk mistake.* The heel of her shoe got caught on the leg of the chair, and her body flung to what would've been the floor, if Micah hadn't been standing there. Instead, her head hit the hard rock wall of his chest.

He pulled her up gently and steadied her on her feet. "I'll help you to my Jeep."

She nodded, feeling sick as her head started to spin faster. "Okay. I guess. See you at home, Julie." Her words sounded slurred even to her own drunken ears. How much had she had to drink? She couldn't remember, which was a bad sign. She remembered the first three drinks, and those were buried under several more.

Micah's arm hugged her waist tightly as he helped her exit the bar and walk through the parking lot.

"You're strong," she said, giggling. Yep, she'd be mortified in the morning. This thought started her laughing hysterically.

Leaning her against his Jeep, he held a hand to her stomach to keep her from tipping over while he unlocked the door. His hand resting just south of her waist lit a fire low in her belly. She was hysterical and turned on, and every other contradicting emotion. Definitely in no condition to be interacting with co-workers and parents of her students.

"What's so funny?" he asked.

"Nothing. It's just, I'm wasted." She laughed even harder. "I never get wasted."

"Good to know." He started to guide her to the passenger seat.

When she tried to step up, she wobbled out of control and his strong arms wrapped around her again. "Okay," he said. Then with one quick motion, he lifted her off the ground and placed her into the seat of his vehicle.

"Have you thought about that kiss?" she asked, as he leaned in close to fasten her seatbelt. She couldn't control what was coming out of her mouth. "Because I have. A little." She started laughing again. Val had warned her that she was a horrible drunk, and evidently, it was true.

"What have you thought about it?" he asked, his voice low and bristly. Her buckle snapped into place with a loud *click*. He could step back now, but he didn't.

And she didn't want him to. What was the point of being drunk if you couldn't say and do what you wanted, and then apologize for it in the morning? No one blamed a drunk, they blamed the drink. "I thought that I liked it. The kiss. It was amazing." She held her breath as he lingered in front of her, his hand still resting on the seat's buckle.

"I thought the same thing."

"You did?" She swallowed thickly, as her heart rode up her throat.

His brow lifted. "You sound surprised."

"I'm out of practice." She nibbled on her lower lip, drawing his gaze there. Then his gaze flicked back to her ring. Just the thought squashed the flutterings in her chest, leaving a deep ache that vibrated with the alcohol. "He's been gone for two years," she said.

Micah's brows pinched together softly.

Explaining about John in her state wasn't a good idea, though. She might start crying, which she didn't do in front of others anymore, and right now all she wanted to do was forget everything but their kiss. *That* she wanted to remember. "You could kiss me again," she said softly.

His smile deepened and, *damn*, he smelled good.

Leaning in closer to her ear, his hot breath melted her as he whispered, "Kat, you've had too much to drink. I'm taking you home now."

Before she could process what he'd said, he stepped back and shut the Jeep's door, the sound as offensive as if someone had crashed cymbals in her ears. A moment later, he reappeared on the driver's side and cranked the engine, another sound that made her wince.

She closed her eyes, unsure of what to do with her drunken emotions.

"If I kiss you again, I want to be one hundred percent sure it's what you want. Not because my almost ex is walking up and you want to help me out. Not because you've had too much to drink and want to escape."

She suddenly felt very tired, as the Jeep Cherokee headed out of the parking lot. "So, you are going to kiss me again?" she asked. Before she could hear his answer, though, her eyes closed and the sounds of the road and his voice, and the blood thundering in her head, blurred together. She remembered their kiss, the feel of his stubble roughly brushing against her cheek, and the way he had smelled like pine and fudge brownies.

No, wait. His eyes reminded her of fudge brownies. He didn't smell like them.

Her eyes fluttered open. Yeah, she was definitely going to regret tonight in the morning.

Especially the part where she'd offered to kiss him and he'd rejected her. She'd *really* regret that part.

Chapter Seven

M icah ran toward the parking lot on Monday afternoon. *Crap.* He was going to be late picking up Ben. And it was against regulations to wear his uniform in public. He guessed having his dad as the commanding officer of Camp Leon helped with some things.

Tires squealed as he pressed the gas pedal. This was the sucky part about being a single dad—having no one else to depend on, but himself. Although, he had Aunt Clara and Uncle Rick now, too. That was the great thing about living in Seaside—it came with extended family. Aunt Clara was the equivalent of Mayberry's Aunt Bea. Uncle Rick was mostly quiet, a good listener, and Micah had fond memories of him tossing a baseball a time or two in the backyard as a kid. There were no memories of his own father doing that with him.

As soon as he was off the military base, Micah lifted his cellphone to his ear and dialed Aunt Clara's number. She'd have no problem picking Ben up from school. She was always asking to do more for them, wanting to cook and do their laundry. She was a godsend some days—most days.

He waited, anxiety building with each unanswered ring.

Great.

After dialing Clara again with no answer, he reluctantly dialed the school.

Kat's voice came on the other line after just a few rings. She'd avoided him this morning as he'd dropped Ben off, no doubt embarrassed about Friday night when she'd slurred and stumbled and, in the sweetest possible way, had almost thrown herself at him. Or she was mad about what could be perceived as his rejection. "Hello."

"Kat, it's Micah Peterson. I'm really sorry, but I'm running late. I'll be there in ten," he promised, speeding up to make that promise even close to true.

Her voice was soft, reassuring. "Ben's fine. Slow down and don't kill yourself getting over here. I was planning on working late anyway."

His foot reflexively lifted on the gas pedal. "Of course you were. Thanks," he said, breathing a heavy sigh of relief.

"I guess I owe you after the other night. Thanks for getting me home safely. And I still haven't repaid you for taking me home when I lost my keys. Or for finding my keys, for that matter."

He tried to bite back his words. He'd been tossing around the idea of inviting her to the Marine Corps ball in a few weeks—ever since she'd admitted that she wasn't engaged. Going alone this year wasn't an option. Single people got stuck at the bar, and he hated the bar. Thanks to his father, he'd learned not to drink at these functions. The old man was adamant that he always keep a professional appearance at work and during off-hours. But there were no off-hours when you were the son of the commanding officer of the military base. Someone was always watching and, according to his father, Micah needed to be an example of exemplary behavior at all times.

The problem was that if you didn't drink at such a function, you got stuck being designated driver for all the other guys without dates. *All* the guys being as many as could legally fit in his Jeep Cherokee last year.

Micah flinched at the memory, and then flinched again as the memory concluded with one of the guys losing the entire contents of his stomach in the backseat of Micah's Jeep.

Not this year.

So he had two options. Invite Nicole, who'd shattered Ben's heart when she'd called him a cripple a few months back. *No way, no how.* Or invite someone else. Kat was the only single woman he knew in Seaside at the moment. She was also attractive.

"We could call it even if you'd agree to be my date to something," he said, only a few short minutes from Seaside Elementary now. He waited a long moment for her answer, each beat of silence punctuated loudly by his pounding heart. "'Date' is the wrong word. If you'd attend a function with me and save me from a night of prolonged, boring conservations. It's next month. All you would have to do is wear a dress and you'd get a free meal out of it." He'd wait to tell her it was the Marine Corps ball until after she agreed, he decided. In his experience, women either loved getting dressed up and being paraded around, or they despised it. He suspected Kat, with her workaholic ways, was in the latter group.

The silence continued on the line. At this rate, he'd be waiting for her answer while standing face-to-face with her at the school.

"Actually, if you said yes, I'd owe *you*," he said, unable to stop talking.

"Really?" she finally asked.

He smiled to himself. What was he doing? He needed to ask someone who didn't make his heart sputter all over the place every time he caught a glimpse of her. He liked Kat, which was all the more reason *not* to take her to the Marine Corps ball.

Except taking her almost made going sound fun. The thought of dancing with her, holding her close—*yeah, I could get excited about that.*

"Okay," she finally said.

Her answer was so soft that he had to wonder if he'd imagined it.

"My sister and Val have actually been getting on me about going out more. Maybe this will shut them up."

"So we'll be helping each other out. Win-win." He parked and climbed out of his vehicle, breaking into a slight jog as he approached the school's entrance. "I'm here, by the way."

"I'll go get Ben. See you in a minute." A dial tone replaced her voice.

His chest was already swelling in anticipation of locking eyes with hers. Yep, something about her had his heart pouncing in his chest like a dog after a treat. And as much as he wanted to avoid her, he also needed to see her. It'd been better when he'd thought she was engaged. At least then his attraction had promised to never amount to anything.

With her being single, attraction could only escalate to more. He wasn't ready for more, and might never be—at least not until Ben was grown. That's what his brief "thing" with Nicole had shown him. His son needed his parents right now, but with Jessica out in the desert, he would have to make up for her absence by being that much more involved.

He pulled open the front door of the school and came face-to-face with Kat as she walked beside Ben's wheelchair. They were smiling and something inside him ached seeing them together. Ben needed a strong woman figure in his life, who accepted him for who he was—a boy, not a problem.

Her smile dissolved as she looked at him and her gaze traveled down his body. He remembered that he was still in his uniform, which was against regulations, but there'd been no time to change.

"You're a Marine?" she asked, taking a small step backward, her face growing pale and accentuating those large green eyes of hers.

That's when it hit him. She hadn't known he was a Marine. Had she thought he just took care of people's lawns for a living? That was the plan eventually, yeah, but not yet.

"Hi, Dad." Ben wheeled forward, oblivious to the disapproval radiating from his principal.

"Hey there, buddy." Micah forced a smile, keeping his eyes locked on Kat. "I guess I've never formally introduced myself. I'm Sergeant Micah Daniel Peterson."

Her eyes glistened in the dark hallway. Most people were impressed by his title. Not her. She looked like she'd seen a ghost as she took another step backward.

"Dad?"

Micah reluctantly looked down at his son. "Yeah, buddy?"

"Why are you still in uniform?" Ben asked. "Isn't that against the rules?"

Scratching his chin, Micah wished he wasn't. "I was in a hurry to get to see you, buddy." His gaze shifted back to Kat.

"I, um, have to go," she said quietly.

It was an excuse. She didn't have anywhere to go. He'd mowed the lawn here enough to know that she stayed late and was always the last person to leave. He also now knew that she had no fiancé to go home to, either.

"Kat?" He started to go after her, but she didn't turn back.

"'Bye, Ben. See you tomorrow," she called over her shoulder, her voice as shaky as the long legs walking away from him.

Turning back to his son, he hooked his head. "Come on, Ben. Time to get home." He'd talk to Kat about her reaction later, when he didn't have his son as an audience.

Just before they reached the double doors of the school, he turned to look at Kat once more, but she'd already slipped back into her office, hiding from him and the uniform he wore with honor. But he had no idea why.

Kat watched the father and son leave through the front doors of the school. *Oh, boy.* What had she gotten herself into? She couldn't go anywhere with him. A Marine?

Plopping into the chair behind her desk, she cradled her head in her hands. Why'd he have to be a Marine? He was just supposed to be the sexy guy who kept the school's campus looking pristine. Only, how in the hell had she not known he was a Marine? His hair was a buzz cut and the friend he'd been out with the other night was obviously in the Corps. She'd seen the SEMPER FI tattoo on his arm.

She hunched over her knees, feeling like she was going to be sick.

How had she let herself have feelings for this man without even knowing this aspect of his life? Well, the feelings would subside, and she'd just back out of the "function" he'd mentioned on the phone earlier. Maybe one of the teachers who worked here wanted to be his date. There was a laundry list of single women at the school who'd probably claw at the chance.

A sliver of jealousy ran through Kat with the thought. Then she jerked her head upright, gasping at the sound of a loud crash on the other side of the school. There it was again, coming from just beyond the west wing. She recognized the noise. The Seaside vandals.

The heels of her shoes clicked loudly as she walked down the long, shadowed hallway. If the kids could hear her, they'd better run because she was in no mood to be understanding tonight.

The *click, click, sheeesh* of the spray can grew louder as she neared the school's side entrance. She was going to march down there and collect those kids by their scruffs. Then she was going to call their parents and tell them what a bunch of spoiled, misbehaving brats they'd raised. At least that's what she wanted to do.

Pushing through the double doors, she was temporarily blinded by the light of the sinking sun. As she crossed the door's threshold, her heel caught on the doorframe, flinging her body forward onto the rough pavement. *Omph!* The wind was knocked out of her in one quick *whoosh*.

She didn't move for a long second. The kids were gone, she was sure of that. She could hear their laughter trailing through the woods in front of her. She was also sure that she was going to feel like someone had beaten her with an umbrella tomorrow morning when she woke up.

"Kat?" a deep voice asked.

She lifted her head to see Micah standing there, watching her. She groaned.

"Are you all right?" He moved quickly toward her and crouched down to inspect her leg, which had bright red blood from a large gash spilling onto the sidewalk. She shook her head.

"Did you see them?"

"Who?"

"The kids. The Seaside vandals?"

Micah glanced around. "No one. Just you."

"I heard noises. I know they were here. I heard—" She followed his gaze and cursed under her breath at the large dark letters still wet and dripping down the side of the school.

CHANDLER SUCKS.

Nice.

"Here. Let me." Micah offered her a hand and helped pull her up, waiting to let go until she was steady on her feet, his gaze still heavy on the gash.

"What are you doing out here?" she asked numbly.

"Ben said he left his sketchbook at the picnic table." He held up a wired notebook. When he did, a folded piece of paper slipped out. He bent to pick it up, his lips pressing into a hard line as he opened the paper and looked at the drawing inside. "Not one of Ben's." He handed it over.

Kat studied the poorly drawn stick person sitting inside a wheelchair. The words "dumb" and "ugly" were scrawled across the top. "Who would do this?" she asked, looking up into Micah's dark eyes.

"I don't know. But I'm going to go find out," he said, turning and walking with a mission.

"Wait, I have a better idea." She stopped following him as pain seared through her leg. "Ow."

"You sure you're okay?" he asked, looking back at her. His brows hung low over his eyes, no longer angry, but tilting with concern.

She nodded. "Yeah."

He walked back toward her and took her arm. "There's a first aid kit in my Jeep. Let's get that scrape cleaned up."

Her body jolted with his touch, and something about his concern made her heartbeat quicken.

But he was a Marine. And Sergeant Micah Peterson's fate could end up being the same as John's. He could die, and leave her more alone than before she'd met him.

When they reached the Jeep, Micah pointed at Ben. "You and I are having a talk tonight." Ben's face paled as he handed him the notebook with the drawing on top. Then he turned back to Kat. "First things first. Sit and give me your leg," he commanded.

Her blood drained to her toes as his hands closed around her calf and he reached for a first aid kit in the glove compartment. Betraying her, her body grew warm and tingly, though it could have been from loss of blood—she hoped. She didn't want to like his touch, even if he was only smearing an alcohol wipe on her gashed knee. She didn't want to find his callused hands intoxicatingly sexy or let her mind wonder how his skin would feel rubbing against other places.

"How're you doing?" His eyes met hers.

She swallowed the thick knot of pain and bone-melting lust in her throat. "I can't go to that function with you," she said, her voice quiet.

He watched her for several long seconds, his grasp still tight on her leg. "You've already said yes, Kat." He reached for a Band-Aid. "You don't strike me as one of those people who goes back on their word."

"I'm usually not, but—" She shook her head.

"I normally wouldn't press, but I really do need a date to this thing." He placed the Band-Aid neatly on her wound, continuing to watch her. "You sent out an email this morning asking for parent volunteers for this friendship gang you've started."

"Friendship Club," she corrected. "And, yes, one or two additional adults would help."

He raised a brow as he released her leg. "I can be your backup."

This made her smile. He made it sound like the kids were a bunch of criminals instead of misguided students. "Actually, there was something I wanted to talk to you about," she said.

"Ben helped me with the after-school group today." She glanced over at the third grader in the backseat of Micah's Jeep. "He was a great helper. I could really use him in the afternoons, and you wouldn't have to rush to get over here every day. Plus, when you're doing the lawn, he's here anyway. Why not have him do something worthwhile?"

"By hanging out with a bunch of delinquents?" Micah gave his head a hard shake. "I'm not sure that's such a great idea."

Kat lifted her chin. "I think it'd be good for him."

Micah studied her. She'd expected that he'd be furious when she suggested the idea, but he actually seemed to be considering it, which surprised her. Ben had enjoyed helping her today, and she'd made sure not to treat him differently than any other kid in the group. She even thought that Ben looked happy out there working with the kids, showing them that he was just like them in more ways than not.

"You would still need another adult. And if I agree to let Ben help, I'll have a vested interest." He was staring at her with the intenseness of a soldier watching his target. "I'm off duty in time to be here most days."

She smiled softly. Had he really just agreed to her request? So easily? Maybe one date wouldn't kill her, as long as she kept her feelings in check and did her best to pretend that he wasn't an incredibly hot, and nice, guy. Hotter and nicer every time she saw him.

"So, is it a deal, then?" he asked. "Ben and I help you with the after-school gang and you attend the Marine Corps ball with me?"

Her head pushed forward. "The Marine Corps ball? That's your function?"

"Yeah." He smiled, uncertainty playing in his eyes and at the corners of his mouth.

Kat started shaking her head. She couldn't surround herself with hundreds of men in uniforms. One man in uniform was too many. "I'm sorry." Her throat was tight and she suddenly needed air, and lots of it. "I'm sorry. I can't be your date, Micah. The answer is no."

Holding her gaze, he didn't look mad, but he wasn't smiling any longer, either. "All right," he said easily, the tone of his voice not quite matching his rigid posture. "My loss, I guess."

Her gaze traveled back to Ben, who looked devastated. Then, for the second time that afternoon, she lied and told Micah that she had to go, gesturing back toward the empty school. "See you tomorrow, Ben." She waved, and did her best to walk, not limp, away as quickly as she could.

An hour later, Julie met Kat at the door when she got home. "Do you always work this late?" her sister asked with a slight huff.

Kat set her briefcase down and breathed in the aroma of a home-cooked meal. "You cooked?"

"Of course I did. And worked like hell to keep it warm because I expected you home over an hour ago."

Kat inspected her sister, dressed in a tank top and yoga pants. Her hair was pulled back neatly in a ponytail. "Sorry. You didn't have to—"

Her sister held up a hand. "No time for chitchat." She pointed to a chair at the table. "Sit." Kat didn't argue. A meal cooked on the stove beat a microwave dinner any day. If her sister kept this up, she might not mind her staying indefinitely. Which wasn't true. They'd shared a bedroom growing up and their constant bickering had tended to escalate until they fought every night instead of having a bedtime story from their mother. "Thanks, by the way. This is nice." And exactly what she needed after the afternoon she'd had.

Julie shrugged her thin shoulders. "Someone has to take care of you. And what else was I supposed to do while I waited for you?"

"You don't have to stay here. You can go home, you know?" Kat's stomach rumbled in response to the smells that swirled together in front of her. "As you can see, I'm fine."

Her sister sat quietly and picked up her fork.

"I'm sure your job and that boyfriend of yours need you more than I do," Kat continued, her hand nearly shaking with anticipation as she sawed the knife through the tender meat on her plate. She'd been too busy to eat lunch. And after her near run-in with the vandals, and then Micah, her insides had been too twisted to notice how hungry she was. Until now.

Julie cut her steak with all the focus and precision of a surgeon. Watching her, warning bells began to ring in Kat's head. "Julie?"

"We can discuss this later. I don't want the food to get cold."

The bells grew louder. "Discuss what?" Kat asked.

Her sister shook her head. "I might be staying a little longer than I expected, that's all."

"How long?" Kat steeled herself as the bells shrieked in her ear. A week? A month? Longer? How on earth would they survive living in the same house for an extended amount of time?

"I lost my job," Julie said flatly. "And my boyfriend. Which means I also lost my apartment. *His* apartment," she corrected. "So, you see, I have nowhere else to go." She looked up and extended a wobbly smile.

"I see." Kat's appetite took a step off a very high building and plummeted to its demise. She loved her sister, but she didn't want to live with her. She'd just gotten used to living alone, and it suited her. But she wasn't about to kick her sister out on the streets, either.

Reaching across the table, she laid her hand over Julie's. "You can stay here as long as you need to."

Chapter Eight

K at stared at the group of sullen-faced kids. For once, she was
glad she couldn't read a child's mind. If she had to guess,
they were all contemplating how to make her assistant principal,
Dora Burroughs, pay miserably for holding them after school.

Dora had the students writing sentences, which did nothing to
help the kids see the error of their ways. It didn't change the way
they felt about themselves or allow them to give back to their
community, either. Dora was an old-school administrator. She
hadn't liked Kat's ideas of turning after-school detention into a
club, but she wasn't the head of SES. Kat was—at least for another
year.

"I've got it from here, Mrs. Burroughs," Kat said.

The older woman frowned at her, sending wrinkles diving from
the corners of her mouth. She had white hair that still had a golden
tint from the days when she'd been blond. Kat tried to imagine that
Dora had gone into this job because she loved children, but Kat
never saw any evidence of that. All she saw was the stern, unfor-
giving manner in which her assistant principal treated the kids who
walked into her office. And unfortunately, Dora was the same way
with the school's employees.

Thank God, the school board hadn't made Dora Burroughs principal at Seaside.

Dora scanned the group of six students, seated at their child-sized desks. "Have a good afternoon, children." Then, without a word to Kat, she walked briskly out of the room.

Sucking in a breath, Kat forced a smile at the students. She'd taken them outside the other day to pick up litter on campus. Holding up six plastic trash bags now, she watched as the smiles in the room faded. "Oh, come on. It's better than writing sentences, and a little sunshine is good for you. You can think about why you're here as you make our school the best it can be."

Val is right. I do sound like Pollyanna.

The students followed Kat down the hall and out onto the side of the campus, where the Seaside vandals had graced her with a new message yesterday. Stanley had taken care of that for her this morning, and hopefully the wall would stay clean this time.

Each child took a bag from her and veered in a different direction.

"Don't stray too far!" she called, wishing Val had been able to stay later and help her. Micah was right. She did need backup, and asking Mrs. Burroughs was out of the question. So was asking Micah, who'd offered his services in exchange for something she couldn't give him. She liked to think she was a strong woman, but when it came to her past, she felt like her heart was exposed, vulnerable to everything around her, which so often seemed to reflect the military life. Sure, she could've moved to a town that wasn't so close to Camp Leon, but this was her hometown. She belonged here.

Kat jumped as one of the children screamed behind her. Turning, she saw several of them swatting at the air wildly. Then she heard a buzz speed by her ear.

Oh, no. Bees!

"It's okay, children. Stay calm," she said shakily, as a bee buzzed by her own head. It buzzed by again. She *hated* bees. "Keep calm," she repeated, but her own heart rate was skyrocketing. When she was a kid, she'd once disturbed a hive and had to run for her life as they'd swarmed after her. Where had these bees come from?

All the students were screaming frantically now, even though there couldn't have been more than a couple of bees. "Get away!" she heard several of them cry.

"It's going to be okay," she said again over their high-pitched terror, but she doubted they heard her. Or if they did, that they believed her. There was no doubt in her mind that they heard the next voice, though.

"Stay still and they'll leave you alone," a deep baritone commanded.

Kat froze. So did all the children. She was pretty sure she knew exactly who was standing behind her, and he'd just seen her doing the "bumblebee in your pants dance," as her sister used to call it. Taking a breath, she willed her heart to slow down. Then, after a moment, she turned to see a big, strong man with ink black hair and chocolate fudge eyes standing with his arms crossed at his chest.

"You okay?" he asked.

It seemed like he was always asking her that question.

She nodded, turning to assess the children, who all stood frozen like little statues. Clearing her throat, she said "All right, guys. Looks like Mr. Peterson was right. The bees are gone."

She watched as the students slowly relaxed, and then turned to Micah. "Thank you." Her gaze moved to Ben who was parked beside him. "You probably would've known to ignore them, too, huh?" she said, her voice softening.

Ben nodded. "But if a bee was buzzing around me, I probably would've screamed like a girl, too, Principal Chandler."

"She is a girl, buddy. She's allowed to scream like that." Micah's smile widened as he looked back at her.

"I didn't . . . we didn't . . ." Her shoulders relaxed. "You're teasing me, right? Does that mean you're not mad at me?"

"Mad?" His dark brows lowered. "For what?"

"For going back on our agreement." She turned to check on the students who were talking among themselves, and then faced him again.

He stood, big and tall, watching her. "I'm not mad. In fact Ben and I were just walking over to see if you were still open to letting us help. To show that there's no hard feelings."

Guilt curled through her stomach as she remembered their original deal.

Seeming to read her mind, he added, "No expectations. You don't have to be my date. I understand."

"I'll do it," she said quickly. "I'll go with you."

"You don't have to—"

"That was the deal, right?" she said shakily. "And I always keep my end of a deal. I'll go. I could use the help, and I think it'd be great if you showed the kids how to work outside. Kids need that stuff, right?"

"I think so." Micah shoved his hands in his pockets.

"The school will provide whatever tools you need to work with the group. I want you to work with us. Both of you," she said, looking at Ben. "And I want to go to the ball with you." She met Micah's eyes again.

Okay, the last line was a boldfaced lie. There was no part of her that actually wanted to go to the Marine Corps ball, but a deal was a deal and she'd do anything for these kids, including going out with a Marine.

Slowly, he reached out his hand for her to shake. "Then it's a deal."

Electricity shot through her as she slipped her hand inside his. That was another reason this was probably a very bad idea. The chemistry between them was undeniable. Explosive even.

Pulling her hand away, she released a shuddery breath. "Yep. A deal."

THE NEXT AFTERNOON, MICAH LOOKED AT THE SIX children making up the Friendship Club. None of them matched any of the America's Most Wanted descriptions hanging up at the entrance to Dail's Grocery Store. If he hadn't seen the rascals laughing at the assistant principal behind her back yesterday, he might be tempted to say the kids looked sweet.

The first one lined up in front of him was Shaun, a redheaded boy, who was a little overweight. There was a splash of freckles on the bridge of his nose. He'd allegedly stolen another kid's lunch for three days running and threatened to beat the kid to a pulp if he told.

The next two kids, Kyle and Bogie, were lanky blonds with eyes that actually sparkled with mischief. They'd tripped a younger kid in the hallway and made him drop all his stuff. Then they'd laughed along with everyone else in the hallway as the kid had cried.

Marcus was a small African-American kid with shiny new sneakers and a smile that ate up half his face. Micah wasn't sure what he'd done to get tossed into the group.

Shelby Cooke was the only girl. She had long brown hair and wore a blank expression. From what Kat had told him, she'd been to hell and back in the last year. Her father was in jail these days and Shelby and her sister were living with their aunt, recovering from years of unspeakable abuse. Now, Shelby was striking out at the world and everyone around her.

Then there was Ben, who hadn't done anything wrong.

Micah clapped his hands in front of him as he stared at the kids outside the Sand Fiddler's wing. It was a section of the school that he hadn't landscaped yet. Before the bell had rung, he and Kat had exchanged ideas for the group. The kids needed to stop treating others with disrespect and start doing worthwhile things that didn't tear anyone down in the process.

Micah pointed to a couple pairs of gardening gloves and a few hoes on the ground. "See those?" He didn't wait for the children to respond before handing out the three hoes and two sets of gloves. "There's a job for each of you. Follow me," he said, leading the kids, minus Ben, to the land that bordered the fence. While he instructed three of the children on how to use a hoe, Kat showed two students what a weed looked like. Since there were no plants behind the school yet, pretty much everything was a weed.

"This is stupid," Shaun said, his brows merging into one bushy, rust-colored line above his eyes.

"So is stealing other kids' lunches." Micah pointed at the weeds and headed back toward his son, who was sitting quietly, hands in his lap and a tired look on his face. No doubt he wanted to work with the others, but couldn't. The story of his life.

"I have a job for you, too, soldier." Micah motioned for Ben to follow him to a wooden picnic table on the side of the school. On the table, he laid three pots, a bag of soil, a small shovel, and a packet of seeds. "You're a smart guy, right? Get to it."

A small smile cracked on Ben's freckled face. "This is the best job anyway." His voice lifted on the end of his words; swinging easily from disappointment to the happy child he tended to be.

Always looking at the positive. Another of the many things that Micah loved about his son. He patted Ben's back and headed to where Kat was standing.

"You have a job for me, too?" she asked, shading her eyes with her hand as he walked toward her.

"Why? Have you been bad?" he asked, not meaning for it to sound suggestive, but her cheeks flushed anyway.

"Only according to the school's assistant principal." She sighed, and then sat on one of the benches lining the walkway.

Micah sat beside her. When he did, he could smell the scent of her perfume. It was one of those flowery smells that usually gave him a headache. This one made him want to lean in and take a deeper whiff. "What's she got against you?"

Kat shook her head. "I don't even know. Maybe that I got the job she wanted. Or she thinks I'm screwing it all up."

Micah glanced over. Sitting this close to her, he couldn't help remembering the kiss they'd shared last week. It'd be so easy to do it again, and see if she still made that little whimper when their lips met. He'd thought about that whimper a lot. It was as sexy as the woman sitting next to him.

"If Mrs. Burroughs wasn't a woman, I'd offer to kick her butt for you." He grinned, watching Kat laugh beside him.

"Then we'd be just like these kids, solving our problems the wrong way." She focused on the group with the hoes in hand. "Do you think it'll work?"

She met his gaze and he had to force himself not to lift his hand and swipe a lock of hair out of her face.

"The gardening thing, I mean," she said.

"If it doesn't, you'll have a bunch of unruly kids with green thumbs."

She laughed lightly, still holding his gaze. "Better than a bunch of unruly kids with pages of handwritten sentences, I guess."

"True." He swallowed, rubbing his hands over the thighs of his jeans as he refused to blink. He also refused to lean closer, touch her, do all the things that he'd been increasingly fantasizing about. "Kat," he said, unsure of what he'd say next. A Marine always had a plan of action, but interacting with Kat was uncharted territory.

They both looked up as Ben's cry broke through the heat radiating between them. Bogie had his hands braced on the arms of Ben's chair and was leaned in close to Micah's son's face. Micah got up and started stalking toward them. As he got closer, he heard Bogie's words.

Stupid.

Cripple.

Loser.

"Back away," Micah commanded.

Bogie straightened. "Just checking your son's theory, sir." A sarcastic smile molded to his thin, dimpled face.

"Theory?" Micah crossed his arms at his chest.

Bogie grinned, talking loud enough for the others to hear. "Ben thinks talking to his seeds will make them grow faster. Tell them, freak."

"Hey!" Micah snapped. "You will not talk to anyone here in that manner."

"It's science," Ben said, keeping his gaze low. "If you speak positive things over a plant, it grows faster. And it's greener, too."

Bogie snickered. "So, I'm testing to see if Ben shrivels up and dies if I call him bad words."

Micah didn't want to, but he instinctively glanced in Ben's direction and saw the tears shining in his eyes. His son would always have difficulty fitting in with his peers. He'd always struggle. As he turned back to Bogie, he heard the other kids whispering behind him. The Marine in him definitely wanted to win this fight for his son, but he couldn't very well take on a bunch of elementary-school kids—no matter how much he wanted to. And this wasn't his fight. It was Ben's.

"Go back to your work, Bogie." His jaw was tight as he spoke; his words coming out like machine gun bullets, quick and powerful. Once Bogie had walked away, he squeezed Ben's shoulder. "Take care of your plants, son." Micah headed back to the bench with an anchor of guilt and worry weighing him down. He'd hoped this school would be different from the others, but Ben was the same child wherever he went. He was different, which wasn't a bad thing. It just meant that the other kids noticed, and some would be mean.

That was something that Micah couldn't control or change, and he hated that. He was Ben's father. He was supposed to protect him, and he couldn't. All he could do was stand by helplessly and watch his son learn yet another hard lesson of life.

Kat rested her hand on his shoulder as he returned to the bench with a heavy sigh and sat beside her. "If you think helping with the club will be too much for Ben, I understand. I'm sorry. I didn't know—"

Micah shook his head. "No. I think this is exactly what he needs. It'll be good for him to be here." It just might break Micah watching. "He's staying." Looking at Kat, he added, "We both are. And those kids will learn some respect."

The next morning Micah was yawning before the day had even

gotten started. He took a sip from his coffee as he watched the men in his squadron arrive for a little basic training. They'd jumped out of a V-22 Osprey a thousand times, but he still liked to do refresher trainings every now and then, especially when there was talk of another deployment coming up next year.

He'd be a civilian by that time. As much as he hated to leave his men, it was what was right for Ben. And he was excited about the prospect of staying on the ground, working in the green, and just enjoying his role of being a dad.

"Working two jobs is starting to take its toll, I see," Lawson said, coming up beside him. "You make plenty of money, man. I don't know why you're helping out at the school."

Because I am preparing to leave the Corps. Lawson didn't need to know that just yet, though. Micah shrugged and took another sip from his coffee. "Maybe I like to stay busy."

"Sergeant in the Marines. Single father to a son with special needs. Sounds pretty busy to me. Want to know what I think?"

Micah slid a glance in Lawson's direction. He usually didn't want to know what Lawson thought, but he cocked a brow anyway. "That it's time for you to get your hair cut again? And buy a new razor?" he asked, observing the shadow of growth along Lawson's jaw.

His friend frowned. "This afternoon, all right?" He crossed his arms at his chest. "I think you're high on Kat. And as a buddy, I have to tell you, it's a hard crash coming down."

"I don't have time for romance, or whatever it is you're insinuating." He took another heavy sip of his java. "And, if you remember, Nicole was your brilliant idea." Micah's gaze sharpened on his friend. "And by brilliant, I mean bad."

Lawson nodded. "Agreed. Sometimes that happens. Rare as it is. Besides, I never told you to date her. I told you to *date* her." His voice dropped as he made air quotations around the word "date."

Micah shook his head, unable to suppress a smile. "One of these days I'll learn to stop listening to you. Like today, maybe." He straightened, the coffee's effects not yet meeting his tired voice.

"Now go get your gear ready. We're doing dry runs on the floor this morning. We'll practice getting our gear on and then we'll review the flight manual."

Lawson shook his head. "We all know how to get our gear on properly. We're not idiots."

Yeah, but mistakes happened, and in their line of work, mistakes often cost people their lives. They'd both learned that the hard way. "Is that the way you talk to your superior?" Micah asked, keeping his eyes focused on the others. It was a low blow, pulling the rank card, but Lawson was under his command right now. Technically, Micah wasn't even supposed to be hanging out with him or having him over for dinner every week—not that he'd ever let a rule like that stop him.

"No, sir," Lawson said, staring at him for a solid second. "What crawled up your butt and died?"

Micah's jaw locked. A little respect at work would be nice, though.

Lawson offered a sarcastic-as-hell salute and started moving toward the adjoining room, where the other Marines were gathered. "I'll go get my gear, *sir*."

"You do that, Phillips."

Chapter Nine

A week later, Kat could already feel her heart pounding as she drove to the Veterans' Center with a box of John's things in the trunk to donate. One box. Baby steps.

Julie leaned forward in the passenger seat beside her and changed the music. "I hate that song."

"Pretty strong word," Kat mused, glancing over.

"What's a strong word?" Julie popped her gum and stared at her.

"Hate. You don't really hate the song. You just don't like it." The silence that followed prompted her to look over at her sister again.

"Right. Okay. I really dislike that song." Her sister rolled her eyes playfully, the corners of her mouth turning up. "But I really *love* this one, which is another strong word. I really just mean I like it a lot. Does that word work for you?"

"Perfectly." Kat smiled to herself.

"This word stuff is really getting annoying, you know that? And the array of plants you've placed by the kitchen sink, the ones you talk to all the time, that's pretty creepy, sis."

This made Kat laugh, and laughter was good. It eased the panic that'd been swirling through her all morning. Moving on in her actions and thoughts were one thing, but folding up John's favorite shirt to give to someone who was alive and could actually wear it, that was hard. There were memories tied to every single thing she had of John's—memories she worried she'd lose without them.

"One of the kids in my after-school group has been teaching us about talking to plants," Kat said, trying not to think about the box. "It really works. You should see this kid's specimens."

"Specimens?" Julie popped another bubble. "You're teaching kids to talk to plants? You know the parents will sue you when their brats all end up in padded cells."

Kat tsked. "There's actually a science behind this stuff. There have been research studies proving that when you talk to plants, it affects their growth. And I think the kids are learning about choosing their words and actions wisely."

The kids that weren't teasing Ben mercilessly over his theories, at least.

"The kid is the son of the school's groundskeeper," Kat continued. "He's also the guy helping out with the group."

Julie cracked her window and tossed her gum, making Kat nearly swerve into the next lane. "Julie! The gum will hit other people's cars. You can't just toss it on the highway."

Her sister stared at her for an exaggerated beat and continued. "You know what I think? I think you're going gaga over this kid's science stuff because you've got a thing for his dad." Julie waggled her eyebrows. "Perhaps, Mr. Rebound Guy?"

"You know I'm not ready for that kind of thing."

"What kind of thing? Lust? Dating? Sex?" Julie asked, drawing out the last word in a teasing manner.

"All of it," Kat said as Julie snickered.

"Come on, sis. Sex is the greatest physical activity God ever invented. Yoga and sex."

"God didn't create sex for exercise. It's a bonding thing," Kat argued. "An act of love."

Geez, I really am Pollyanna.

"All I'm saying is, if you don't use it, you lose it."

Kat's brain stuttered on her sister's claim. "If I don't have sex, I'll lose my female parts?"

This made Julie burst into laughter.

Kat's gaze slid over. "Let's talk about something else, okay? What about you? Why did you and your ex break up?"

Julie redirected her attention out the window, suddenly quiet. "We just grew apart."

"After three years? Did something happen?"

Julie shook her head, but Kat caught the subtle darkening of her eyes as she glanced over.

Something had hurt her sister badly enough that she had left a job and man she loved.

And badly enough for Julie to pack her bags and return to Seaside, which Kat never thought would happen.

They didn't need to talk about it now, though. They also didn't need to talk about her sex life, or lack thereof.

"Okay, another subject change." Kat started on the first topic that popped into her mind. "So, there's a little girl in the Friendship Club, Shelby Cooke. She's had a rough life so far. Her father's in jail for abusing her and her sister, among other things."

Julie was looking at her again, her shoulders relaxed. "That's terrible."

Kat rolled her lips together, hating this topic as much as the last. But at least this one had a happy ending. "Shelby is safe now, but she's dealing with a lot emotionally. She's lashed out at her teachers and some of the other students. I don't like it, but I've had to ask her to stay after school several times already this year."

Julie nodded, urging Kat to continue.

"Anyway, I overhead Shelby talking to one of the plants this week, just like Ben. The children are only supposed to say positive things, and she was, but I don't think Shelby has had a lot of experience with being spoken to nicely."

"What was she saying?" Julie asked.

"Actually, she wasn't talking. She was singing a song her mother used to sing to her when she was alive."

Julie shuddered as she rubbed her hands along her arms. "I just got chills. That's amazing."

"What we're doing for these kids is going to make a difference."

"Yeah. Sounds like it." Julie pulled another stick of gum from her purse and popped it into her mouth. "And you're probably right."

Furrowing her brow, Kat glanced across the seat. Her sister never admitted that she was right about anything. "Right about what?"

"You shouldn't have sex with this guy, whoever he is. Definitely not. The way your eyes light up when you talk about him, you'd lose your heart fast. He can't be your rebound guy."

"John died two years ago. I'm way past a rebound guy."

"But you're still wearing his ring." Julie gestured at Kat's finger. "So you're actually not past rebounding. And this guy sounds like he's perfect for you. He's into teaching kids and saving the world. Right up your alley. So I suggest you stay as far away from him as you possibly can."

Chewing her lower lip, Kat pulled into the Veterans' Center parking lot, noticing Val's car parked on the side. Val often baked goodies for the local veterans and dropped them off. It was the closest she got to representing the preacher's daughter that everyone expected her to be.

Kat parked and turned to her sister. "Micah, the school's groundskeeper, is the one taking me to the Marine Corps ball." Her voice was flat, hammered down by the truth of Julie's words. Micah *was* the perfect guy for her.

"The lawn guy is also the Marine? The hot guy from the bar?" Julie clarified, pushing her neck forward in disbelief.

Panic rose in Kat's chest. "Yep."

Julie snickered. "Sister, you are in deep trouble."

Micah stared at the woman standing across the store for a long second.

"Earth to Mikie." Lawson snapped a finger in front of him. "Who are you staring at anyway?" Lawson's gaze followed his and stopped. "Oh. Kat and that other girl from Heroes." A wide grin spread across his unshaven face. "The one you're intent on telling me you're not interested in. Even though you were more than happy to take her home that night."

Something protective rumbled through Micah and his jaw tightened. "I just dropped her off at her house. She'd had too much to drink." *And she'd been an adorable drunk.* He jabbed a finger in Lawson's shoulder. "And didn't you end up taking Kat's sister home that night?"

Lawson nodded, a fond smile forming on his face. "I think she liked me. It's hard to say because she was too busy fussing at the brunette that I also took home." He frowned as his gaze slid toward Micah. "I'd like to tell you they were fighting over me, but"—he shook his head— "the cowboy hat has lost its mojo, man. And unless they're actually clawing at each other and pulling each other's clothes off, it's not pleasant to watch two women fight."

Micah chuckled, returning his attention to Kat, who was still browsing through the dresses, no doubt looking for one to wear to the ball in a few weeks. His heart sped up just thinking about holding her close against him. He imagined whispering how beautiful she was in her ear and watching her skin flush with each compliment. He liked that about her. She had no idea how heart-stopping she was, and no idea what a turn-on her dedication to her job was.

"I'm tired of looking. What do you think of this one?" Lawson held up a tiny white child's dress with lace edges. "Think Sabrina will wear this one?"

An image of Lawson's three-year-old niece came to mind. "She'd look adorable in anything," Micah said, grinning at the boyish nature his friend took on when he talked about the little girl.

"And if she takes after her mother, she'll continue with that trend, and you and I will be kicking some teenaged behind in a few years."

Micah raised a brow and returned his attention to Kat, who was now holding up a long, black dress with rhinestones accenting the collar. She'd look gorgeous in it. His gaze caught on the low-cut front. If she wore that, he'd be too busy drooling to speak that night.

"You want to go over there and say something, or should we continue being the creepy stalkers across the store?"

"I'm not stalking her." Micah pretended to look through the dresses some more. "What's this dress for again?"

"Sabrina's christening. My sister elected me to stand beside her for the event."

"Probably because of the hat," Micah joked, knocking his hand down on the cowboy hat's rim.

Lawson readjusted it, and then his eyebrows rose. "Hats aren't allowed in church, man. It's because I am the favorite uncle." A large grin spread across his face.

"Aren't you the only uncle?" Micah laughed as his friend's smile faltered.

Lawson's gaze lifted back to the women. "Don't look now, but you've been spotted."

Micah whipped around and looked at Kat, who was still in the women's dress section, oblivious to his presence. A low growl of frustration emerged as he glanced back. "Very funny. I better go over and say hello before I end up strangling you."

"Right. And I better say hello to Jewels," Lawson said.

"Julie," Micah corrected. "Her name is Julie."

"Right." Lawson walked ahead of him, taking the lead.

Micah prepared himself for when Kat turned around, knowing that her beauty and those expressive eyes of hers would make him feel like a hormonal teenager again. He'd never enjoyed being a teenager. He preferred to operate according to his head, not what was inside his boxer shorts. He shoved his hands into his pockets, and then she turned around, taking him by surprise. She really did get prettier every time he saw her, in contrast to his ex-wife, who'd only lost attractiveness with time because of her bad attitude.

Kat smiled as he approached, and that's when he knew the whole, indisputable truth. It wasn't his head or what was inside his boxers that he needed to worry about. *His heart was in deep trouble.*

~

"Don't look now," Julie said, standing in Seaside's finest dress shop, "but your boyfriend is here. And he's walking straight toward us."

"Boyfriend?" Kat turned and her heart skidded to a stop. "Micah." She hurriedly placed the dress back on the rack and forced a smile, willing her breath to slow down. He was just a guy— an incredibly gorgeous guy, who just so happened to be another Marine. Some luck falling for two uniformed men in one lifetime.

Falling? Had she really just thought that she was falling for him? Because that wasn't allowed. They may be going to the USMC ball together, but she absolutely was not going to give her heart to him. *Nuh-uh.* They weren't even really dating.

"Hi," he said in that deep voice that gave her immediate hot flashes.

He'd gotten to her faster than she'd expected. Opening her mouth to speak, she prayed comprehensible words would come out. He was just a man. "What are you doing here?" she asked, her voice shrill. Just a man, she reminded herself—a heart-stoppingly gorgeous man with dark chocolate eyes that did funny things to her knees. Not only that, he was good with kids and a devoted father.

Micah grinned. "Dress shopping. You?"

"Me, too. But, um, why are *you* dress shopping?" she asked.

He gestured to his friend standing beside him. She recognized him from the bar the other night, and offered a friendly smile.

"It's for my niece, actually," Lawson said, holding up a child-sized white dress. "She's getting christened on Sunday." Then he gestured toward the dress that Kat had been looking at.

"Looks like you're buying a dress, too." He drove an elbow into Micah's side. "What do you think? Think it'll look good on your date?"

Micah cleared his throat and, if Kat wasn't mistaken, he looked a little embarrassed. "Of course."

Kat looked back at the rack, taking a moment to regain her composure. Every time she saw him, he was way better looking than she'd remembered. How was that even fair? "Yeah? I'm not sure." She ran her hand over the silky fabric.

"I am. I'm sure you'd look great in a heap of rags," he said.

Nervous laughter tumbled off her lips, as clumsy as the rest of her body seemed to be when he was around. "I'll take that into consideration," she said.

"Great pickup line, man," Lawson teased. "I'm sure you'd look great in rags, as well, miss," he told Julie, who responded with a cool look of disinterest.

Kat took the black dress back off the rack. "I guess this'll do. I'm tired of looking."

"Not a shopper?" Micah asked.

She dared to look at him again. "Not usually." Usually she had too much work to do to be out shopping on a Saturday afternoon.

"So do you ladies have plans tonight?" Lawson asked them.

Kat watched the two men exchange a look. "Yes," she said at the same time that Julie answered, "No." They looked at each other.

"Your plans were canceled, *remember*?" Julie said, one brow arching slightly—the little matchmaker. She was just as bad as Val.

"Right." Kat nodded slowly, laughing nervously under her breath. "I guess I forgot about that." She looked back at Micah. "Looks like I don't have plans tonight, after all."

"The thing is, there's a garden exhibit later." Micah shoved his hands in the pockets of his perfectly fitted jeans. "I helped create the designs for it. There'll be miles of a garden that I'd bet gives Eden a run for its money . . . I'd be honored if you came with us. Both of you."

Kat wanted to say yes so badly that the only acceptable answer was no. It was on the tip of her lips, ready to leap off, when her sister's answer came first.

"I wish I could, but I have a, um, thing, I just remembered." Julie shrugged, her gaze skittering toward Lawson. "But Kat would love to go. Wouldn't you, sis?" Her thin elbow plowed into Kat's side, the same way that Lawson's had done to Micah a few minutes earlier.

After rubbing the spot and slicing her gaze at her matchmaker sister, Kat nodded slowly. She didn't have one viable excuse not to go. "Yes. Of course."

Chapter Ten

After spending the rest of the day shopping with Julie, Kat made her way to the garden exhibit that Micah had invited her to—alone. Her loving sister had successfully forced her to come here tonight, which was probably a bad idea, and then gone home to attend to her "other plans." Knowing Julie, those plans included lying on the couch and watching sappy black-and-white movies on the TV.

Parking, Kat looked out into the gravel parking lot and spotted Micah walking toward her. Also alone. He reached her door before she could move and pulled it open.

"You came," he said in that deep baritone voice that she thought literally made the ground beneath her shake as she stepped out of her car.

"Of course I did. I have to see what kind of competition is trying to sweep you away from caring for the school's lawn, right?" As if that were even part of the reason she was here. "Where's Ben?" she asked, reminding them both that she was also his son's principal. Being his boss and his son's principal were two very good reasons not to be having hot flashes right now.

"I may have designed the gardens, but the layout wasn't my

doing. It's not exactly wheelchair-friendly here, so Ben is with my aunt and uncle tonight. They live next door to us."

"Oh. I didn't realize you had family nearby," she said, wishing he wasn't standing so close. At his current distance, the temptation to reach out and touch his muscled chest, which was currently pushing against the limits of his T-shirt, was nearly unbearable. He wore a leather jacket over his T-shirt, but it was unzipped, like an open door inviting her in.

"My dad, too. He's the commanding officer of Camp Leon."

"Commanding officer? Wow." She wondered if John had known him. What if Micah's father had been the one to send him to war? The thought sent a shiver over her body. She was supposed to be moving on—focusing on the present and not the past. And she was. Presently, she was falling in lust, hard and quick, with a hot guy that she'd kissed once. It had been a couple weeks, but she still remembered the way his lips had felt against hers. He'd had new growth of hair along his face that could only be felt and not seen.

She shivered again as the memory of their kiss replayed in her mind. "You're cold," he said.

"No, I'm fine."

"Here." He removed his leather jacket and held it up against her. "The wind off the ocean makes for chilly nights."

Slipping her arms into the cozy confines of his jacket, she took a deep breath, catching the faint smell of cologne. She closed her eyes, loving the deep rustic scent, then snapped them back open, hoping Micah hadn't noticed.

The corners of his mouth lifted as he watched her.

"Salt air," she said, hoping that explained the giddy grin on her face.

He nodded and started walking. "Wait till you get in the gardens." His eyes gleamed as he looked at her.

"Can't wait." She followed him through a gate, where suddenly she was overwhelmed by an explosion of color, too vibrant for the end of September. "It's incredible," she said, as they continued walking through intense shades of green. And she was in awe of the fact that Micah had helped to create it. "I've never seen most of these plants before. Are they exotic?"

He laughed, seeming to enjoy her complete naïveté when it came to all things green. "Not really. Most of the plants you're seeing are native to North Carolina."

She looked around, gaining a new appreciation for the plants and flowers around her. Most days she was so busy, she didn't stop to take in what was happening right outside her window.

"These are roses, by the way," he said, gesturing toward the rust-colored flower blooming beside him. A playful glint lit his soft brown eyes as he watched her.

She dug her elbow into his side. "I know that, Mr. Wise Guy."

Leaning into her, he said, "I just wanted to hear you laugh again. I like the sound."

Her face straightened. "No one's ever complimented my laugh before."

"Then maybe you don't laugh often enough."

When he looked at her, her knees went weak. "Um, gardening is a rare interest for a kid. What got you curious?" She cleared her throat and redirected her attention. After all, this was Seaside. Anyone could spot her here with Micah and get the wrong idea. Or the right idea because, as much as she wanted to persuade herself otherwise, she was here as a woman, not a boss or a principal.

"I was kind of a bully back in the day. I could never live up to my dad's image of what I should be, so I acted out. The kids in the Friendship Club have nothing on the trouble I caused."

A wicked grin spread, carving out deep dimples in his chiseled cheeks. "Dad dropped me off at my aunt Clara's one afternoon, and she found me cursing the world and every plant in her backyard."

Kat laughed softly, leaning in closer to him as a soft breeze rustled through the bushes.

"That's when she taught me how to make things grow. It'd felt like magic back then."

"Not anymore?" she asked.

"With plants, yeah. Anything green. I just wish I had the same touch with Ben. Sometimes I see him struggling and I feel so helpless." He motioned toward one of the benches that lined the paths and they sat.

She felt immediately warmer with his body shielding the wind. "I don't think growing up is supposed to be easy. That's why kids have parents to help them through it, and I know you do that for Ben."

"Yeah, well I try, but Ben only has one parent at the moment." His lips compressed into a hard line.

"Where's Ben's mom?" she asked, hoping she wasn't prying too much.

Looking down at his hands in his lap, he blew out a long breath. "In Afghanistan right about now. She volunteered for another deployment. Sometimes I think she loves those soldiers more than she does her own son."

"I doubt that's true."

He looked at her. "Would you leave that boy on purpose? I wouldn't. Jessica grew up in foster care. She never had that sense of family. I guess that's part of the reason why." He sighed heavily. "It's hard on Ben. It doesn't help, either, that he's different from the other kids."

"Sounds tough." Unable to help herself, she reached over and squeezed his hand gently, urging him on.

"I'm not trying to be a downer. Never discuss your ex on a date. Isn't that the number-one rule in the book of dating?"

Kat sucked in a breath at the mention of the d-word, pulling her hand back to her own lap. "Not that this is a date," he corrected.

"Right. It's not." She hadn't woken this morning expecting that she'd be spending her night walking around with Micah through the most magical gardens she'd ever seen. Dates were planned. This wasn't.

He held her gaze for a long, pulse-igniting beat. "It just feels like one," he said, his voice low, meant only for her.

She couldn't argue his point. It did feel like a date. She was wearing his jacket, and he was sitting so close to her right now that their legs were brushing up against each other. She swallowed. If she didn't look away at this very moment, he'd probably kiss her. And secluded on their bench with no one else around, no one would have to know.

She kept her eyes locked on his. They were magic eyes, with a myriad of browns mixing together, light and dark.

Then his body leaned in slowly as if to tell her a secret. And yeah, she really, really wanted to hear that secret. Her heart pounded in her chest as he moved even closer. So close she could barely think, barely breathe. Then her eyes started to close. She'd worry about the consequences of kissing Micah tomorrow. Tonight, she didn't want to worry. She just wanted to kiss this man until her entire body melted into one big, feel-good puddle.

When nothing happened, her eyes fluttered back open. He was watching her with a large grin stretching along his face. It was a good face, she decided. One she could stare at for a very long time.

"What?" she asked, her chest rising and falling as if she'd just sprinted across the parking lot.

Why the heck wasn't he kissing her right about now?

"Just checking," he said. Then he leaned in and kissed her.

She sighed softly as his tongue touched her outer lip, and then reached inside her mouth. His hands moved up her shoulders, pulling her gently to him. Bracing both hands on his chest to keep from falling into him, she kissed him back, and it felt good—too good.

After a long moment, the kiss slowed like a ride at an amusement park. She half-expected her hair to be up in the air, a huge mess from their rollercoaster kiss.

"What were you checking?" she asked when she had words to speak again.

"If you were ready for me." He smiled. "If *I* was ready for you."

"And?"

He kissed her lips again, more softly this time. "And I'm still not sure."

∾

IT WAS ALMOST MIDNIGHT BEFORE MICAH LEFT THE gardens. After walking Kat to her car at the close of the exhibit, he'd returned to help with cleanup. Now, he blinked through heavy lids as he drove home, unable to keep his mind on anything other than the woman who'd been on his arm all night.

What was he getting himself into? He was supposed to be focusing on Ben. That's what he'd decided after his brief thing with Nicole. Ben needed one hundred percent of his attention, and that left no room for a relationship.

So why had he kissed Kat tonight?

Because she was beautiful. That's why. Not just that, but funny, too. And smart. And she was incredible with Ben and the other kids. She was great—which left him with a choice. He could either pretend like nothing had happened tonight, or he could entertain letting someone else into his and Ben's life.

His pulse quickened at just the thought of taking that leap again. And it wouldn't just be his leap. Anytime he leapt, he took Ben with him. That made dating anyone a risk—a risk often best not taken.

As if on cue, his phone buzzed at his side. He glanced at the caller ID, thinking he'd call whoever it was back tomorrow. When he saw his aunt's name on the phone's screen, however, he immediately pulled it to his ear. "What's wrong?" he asked.

"Now calm down," she said. "Ben's okay."

"Then why are you calling me this late?"

"Ben had a nightmare. That's all."

Micah could hear the shakiness in his aunt's voice, which did nothing to calm his growing nerves. "A nightmare?" Ben never had nightmares. Not since "Uncle" Lawson had let him watch that crazy horror flick with the talking doll. "What was it about? Aunt Clara?"

She sighed heavily. "His mother in the war. I know I said I'd watch him tonight, but he's asking for you, Micah."

Massaging his right temple, pressed down harder on the gas pedal. "I'm ten minutes away. I'll get him on the way home."

"Good. And I'm sorry," she said, still shaky.

Micah couldn't help but smile. "For what?" he asked. "For being a saint of an aunt and watching my kid tonight?" *So that I could kiss Ben's principal.* "I'll see you soon." He hung up the phone and hurried home as fast as his Jeep would allow. He'd left Ben with Clara so that he could see the gardens that he'd helped design. For the last few months, he'd worked on the layouts at night when Ben was sleeping. Getting this opportunity was a big step in starting up his own landscaping business after he was out of the Corps. And in providing Ben with some form of stability.

Kissing Kat, however, wasn't a step in the right direction. If they got involved, there'd be dates. Ben would be left with Aunt Clara a lot more, and he was fragile right now with Jessica deployed. The timing was piss-poor for starting a relationship, and he knew it.

So there it was. His choice was made. He'd just have to pretend nothing had happened tonight. He and Kat would run the Friendship Club, he'd take her to the Marine Corps ball and stay just long enough to please his father and keep him from being DD to a bunch of drunks the rest of the night. Then his deal with Kat would be over. If he could keep his eyes, and hands, off her in that silky black dress, he'd be fine.

And most important, so would Ben.

～

"STOP STARING AT ME." KAT FROWNED AT VAL ON Monday morning.

"Can't help it," Val said, sitting behind her secretary's desk. "Something is definitely up with you. It's written all over your face." She circled a finger in the air, growing giddier by the second. "This has something to do with Micah Peterson."

"Micah?" Just hearing his name made Kat cross her legs under her desk and made her lips tingle at the memory of their fireworks kiss.

"Uh-huh. Something happened with him over the weekend," Val accused.

How did her best friend do that? Val always knew when she was holding something back.

But she wasn't ready to talk about what had happened with Micah over the weekend just yet. And, really, she shouldn't have been kissing a parent at all—not that she had any regrets. She didn't. He'd put a smile on her face that hadn't budged since Saturday night.

"Fine. Don't tell me now. You can spill the juicy details over chips and salsa on Tuesday at dinner."

Kat gathered a stack of papers from her office mailbox and continued walking. "We'll see."

"Ah-ha!" Val pointed another accusatory finger. "You just admitted it. Something *did* happen."

Kat didn't look back. Her kiss with Micah was the last thing she needed to get out on the gossip network at Seaside Elementary. "We'll talk Tuesday." Slipping into her office, she closed the door and breathed a sigh of relief at the brief moment of privacy

After several minutes of sitting behind her desk, she slammed a folder on her desk and groaned. She couldn't concentrate on what she was supposed to be doing. Her brain was consumed by the kiss, just like a hormone-ravaged teenager. Like when she'd first met John.

Her right hand absently went to the diamond on her left ring finger. She hadn't been able to envision dating someone else before, but with Micah, she could. Even if he was a Marine— which was crazy.

A ragged breath shuddered through her. Maybe his being a Marine was one of the things that attracted her to him. Even though the career choice had stolen John's life, she'd always admired his courage and strength. She admired his sacrifice for his country, too.

But it hadn't just been his sacrifice. She'd also sacrificed something —her future.

Now, maybe she could begin again. With Micah.

Crazy thoughts. Ridiculous thoughts.

Her phone rang on her desk and she snapped upright before picking up the receiver. "Yes?"

"Problem in the Seagull hall," Val said.

"What kind of problem?"

"Kimberly Flowers."

Kat groaned. "Okay. Thanks." She'd needed a distraction, but she wasn't in the mood to deal with the mayor's daughter today. Or any day for that matter. She stood and walked past Val's desk, going down the hall toward the culprit.

From the classroom's doorway, she saw immediately what had happened. Curling a finger at the tall girl with long, ash blond hair, she signaled her to step into the hallway. Kimberly had caused trouble before. So had Kimberly's parents.

"You smeared red lipstick on the substitute teacher's chair?" Anger scalded Kat's neck. If there was one thing she wouldn't tolerate, it was disrespect against a teacher. Not in her school. And the poor sub was wearing white linen pants of all things. Didn't she know you weren't supposed to wear white after Labor Day?

The ends of Kimberly Flowers's mouth quirked. "It was just a joke. Everyone thought it was funny, Principal Chandler."

"Funny? Did Mrs. Pilar think it was funny?" Kat shook her head. "Well, guess what, Kim? You'll be staying an hour after school for the next two weeks."

The girl's expression twisted. "But I have soccer." Her mean-girl voice suddenly sounded like a whiny three-year-old's.

"Not for the next couple weeks, you don't." Kat crossed her arms under her chest.

Mirroring her, Kimberly crossed her arms, too. "We'll see. My dad won't let you keep me from soccer."

The twinkle in Kim's eyes just about made Kat want to raise the penance to a month. "I'd love to talk to your father. In fact, while you return to your seat, I think I'll go call him and share the good news."

Kim's twinkle dulled just a touch. *Good.*

Kat waved at the substitute teacher, Mrs. Pilar, whose left eye appeared to be twitching. Yeah, the Flowers family had that effect on her, too. Starting back down the long hallway, she had to admit, she was impressed with herself. Most teachers in this school backed down to the third-grade girl just because of who her parents were. Backing down had only made Kimberly Flowers a bigger bully, though. And if Kat backed down . . . well, the girl would probably turn out to be just like her bully parents, who, unfortunately, Kat would now be dealing with this afternoon.

Val's brow lifted as Kat stormed back through the office. "So what are you going to do about Kimberly Flowers?"

"What do you mean what am I going to do? The only thing I can do," Kat said. "She has to be treated like everyone else around here."

A snicker escaped her friend's lips. "You've been a great boss. I'll put in a good word for you if you need me to."

"For what?" Kat asked, unamused.

"Your next job. Mayor Flowers is going to have your head if you make his only daughter spend her afternoons talking to plants."

"He won't. I'll make him understand. A child has to be taught her boundaries. At this rate, that girl will be in the state penitentiary by the time she's drinking age. He certainly doesn't want that, right?" Kat slipped a hard candy out of the bowl by Val's computer. "I'll be at my desk if you need me."

"One more thing," Val said. "You have a visitor. I told him he could wait in your office."

"Him?" Kat looked through the frosted glass window of her office door where the tall, dark outline of a male body waited on the other side. Her belly fluttered. "Thank you, Val. Please make sure we aren't disturbed."

"Sure will . . . and we'll discuss what happens behind that closed door when we have our chips and salsa tomorrow night."

Chapter Eleven

H is plan was to go into Kat's office and avoid discussing the kiss. Pretend like it never happened because that's the way it needed to be.

Micah's mind knew that, but his heart shredded the idea to pieces as soon as she walked into the room, looking all flustered and flushed. A rush of testosterone shot through him and all he could think of suddenly was locking that door, pushing her up against the wall, and pressing his mouth against hers.

"Hi." Her voice was soft and sweet. He wanted to turn it to a raspy pant. *Damn.* He'd been celibate for too long. Maybe Lawson was right and all he needed was a good lay, but definitely not with Kat. Sleeping with her could only mean falling deeper under her spell.

"Did you need me for something?" she asked, stepping closer. She was wearing a floral dress that flirted with her legs, brushing up against them with every step she took.

Yep. He definitely needed her for something. Clearing his throat, he ran a quick hand through his hair. "Yes." He nodded, but for the life of him, he couldn't remember what he'd come here to ask her. Something about the after-school program maybe? Or Ben?

He focused on her rose-colored lips that tasted like honey. He loved honey, and he could think of a lot of places he'd like to taste it at the moment.

A smile crossed her mouth as if she knew exactly what he was thinking. "We can't talk about that here. This is where I work," she said, lowering her voice.

He shook his head. "No. No, I didn't come here to talk about that." A nervous laugh escaped his lips. That's what he'd come here *not* to talk about. "I, uh . . . I came here to talk about the Friendship Club."

"Oh. Okay." Taking a seat behind her desk, she motioned for him to sit at the chair in front of her. The idea of doing so made him feel like that bully being called to the principal's office all those years ago. Except he'd never wanted to clear his principal's desk and have his way with her. For one, his principals had all been about a hundred years old when he was growing up. So that ruled that out.

She stared at him expectantly. "What's on your mind, Micah?"

He swallowed and took a step toward her desk. "You," he said, doing his best not to tell her exactly what he was thinking.

Her eyes widened.

"I want to go out with you again," he said, surprising himself, too. He'd made a conscious decision *not* to date Kat. Only, he'd been fantasizing about another date since they'd hugged goodbye at the gardens this weekend. He'd been fantasizing about a hell of a lot more than that.

A beautiful smile crossed those delicious honey lips.

"Except this time I want it to be real. I want to pick you up at your house, bring you flowers, and get you home by a reasonable hour." *Then follow you inside.* He leaned forward, bracing his hands on her desk. "Will you go on a date with me, Kat? This Friday night?"

Suddenly, her smile dropped. "I, um. I can't." She held up her hands. "Not that I don't want to. I do. But I kind of have this obligation."

"Obligation?" he repeated, stunned that he was being turned down. He didn't ask women out often, but when he did, he didn't get turned down. He never should've asked her out in the first place. "What kind of obligation?" he asked.

Color rose through her neck and trickled into her cheeks. "I volunteer at the Veterans' Center once a month, in honor of the men and women who've fallen. This Friday is the one I'm scheduled for. I help serve dinner. Then we play bingo. On Saturdays, there's a dance and I sometimes help out with that, too. Only bingo this month, though. No dancing."

He straightened, keeping his gaze on her. "Good. You can save your dancing feet for me next weekend." He winked at her, feeling a little less rejected by the thought of her spending her night with a bunch of older men. At least that's who he always imagined hung out at a place like that. Younger vets usually occupied the local bar or could be found playing a game of pool or taking up water sports at the nearby beach.

"You can help me serve on Friday night if you want," she said then. "The Veterans' Center is always looking volunteers."

He shook his head ruefully. There was enough on his to-do plate already. Adding another volunteer job to his long list was definitely pushing his limits, and he hadn't meant to ask her out anyway. It'd been a moment of insanity. "I should probably hang out with Ben," he said, even though he'd spent nearly every night for the last two weeks with his son. Aunt Clara had been urging him to take time for himself lately. "He's having a tough time these days with his mother's deployment." *And the fact that Jessica hasn't called even once.*

"Well, you can bring him, too. I'll put him to work calling out bingo numbers."

Micah scratched his chin, considering this. "Ben would probably like that. He's really happy to be helping out after school."

"Good." She smiled, meeting his eyes head-on, and holding his gaze for a long, sizzling beat.

If he brought Ben, he definitely wouldn't be following Kat inside her home at the end of the night, which both relieved and disappointed him.

"Will you still bring me flowers and get me home at a reasonable hour?" she asked, leaning forward on her desk, making her blouse lower just enough for the disappointment to outweigh the relief. He wanted this woman in every way he'd never wanted anyone else before. He wanted to hold her, kiss her. Take that little whimper she did when he kissed her and turn it into a moan.

"I have this thing about flowers. I never cut the stem, and I talk to them when no one's looking," he said. "My son taught me that. I would only bring flowers to a woman that I trusted to continue spoiling them as much as I do."

"Oh, I can be trusted." Her green eyes danced as she looked at him. "I've never liked the idea of cutting the flower stems, either, actually. It seems kind of sad and barbaric, but . . . they are pretty."

Micah gave his head a quick shake. "I've never had a woman say that to me. Kat Chandler, you might just be the perfect woman," he teased, cutting himself off before he finished his thought. *For me. You might just be the perfect woman for me.*

And that thought scared the hell out of him.

"Then it's a date." She tucked a loose strand of her blond hair behind her ear.

He nodded. A date. Dating was not what he'd come here to talk about, but whatever that was had long been forgotten, buried under a thick blanket of smoldering desire.

"Was there something else you wanted to discuss?" she asked.

"Nope. Just us." The last word caught him by surprise. *Us.* He needed to get out of this office fast before he said, or did, something else he'd probably regret later.

∽

"I am not putting my hands in the dirt," Kimberly Flowers protested that afternoon. "When my father finds out—"

Kat held up a hand to quiet the girl. When Kim's father finally got around to checking in with the assistant she'd talked to earlier, he'd be outraged. She was well aware of that. "You don't have to touch the dirt today. You can sit at the picnic table and watch Ben do his work, and think about why you're here."

Kimberly cast a glance at Ben, who was sitting at one of the picnic tables. "Why does he get to work at the table? Because he's in a wheelchair?"

"That's right," Kat said, taking her time as she responded, choosing her words wisely. "And if you say one negative thing to him, you'll add another week to your punishment."

Kimberly shrugged and, without another word, started walking toward Ben. She sat down at the very end of the bench. Ben looked at her, said something that Kat couldn't make out, and continued working.

For a moment, Kat watched the after-school group, up to nine kids today. Their rows of dirt bloomed from the ground across the back lot of the school and green sprouts were beginning to peek through, lifting toward the sun. While most of these kids had put up a fight at first, they all sat on the earth now, watering their seedlings, patting the dirt, and some, thanks to Ben, were even talking excitedly to something that would never speak back. The kids were pouring their very souls into this project. Being here wasn't a punishment, it was an opportunity, and she was proud of that.

The faint sound of a mower started in the background. *Micah.* Kat shielded her eyes from the sun and searched for him. Then her heart sank to her knees as she spotted a man dressed in an expensive suit heading across the lawn in her direction.

She swallowed as his frown creased deeper into his otherwise smooth skin. His gaze flicked toward Kimberly at the table and back to her. Something told her this was Mayor Flowers's lackey, and he had a message from his boss.

"Miss Chandler?" the man asked when he was standing in front of her.

She nodded. "Principal Chandler. And you are?"

"Jack Markus, Mayor Flowers's assistant." He glanced at

Kimberly again. "I have to say, the mayor was disappointed when he heard about what happened at the school today."

So disappointed that he'd sent his assistant to do the talking for him, Kat thought, forcing a smile. "As was I. Anytime a student disrespects a teacher, it's a very serious matter."

Mr. Markus nodded with a practiced smile. "I understand. Certainly you can appreciate that the mayor doesn't want his daughter staying after school with students who have more severe behavior issues, though."

"Actually, Kim's actions today were right on par with the behaviors that the other children here have exhibited."

Irritation traced itself around Mr. Markus's dark features: his eyes, his chin, and his compressed lips. "But Kimberly has extracurricular activities that demand her attendance. Why don't you send home some punitive assignment, and I'll see to it that it gets done."

Kat crossed her arms. "If the mayor wants his daughter to attend a public school and be treated like every other child here, then she'll also have to abide by the same rules and punishments. It is one hour after school. Yes, she's missing soccer practice, but I spoke to Coach Donaldson and she's in favor of Kimberly being here."

"But Mayor Flowers is not," Mr. Markus said pointedly, his smile unbudging.

Kat swallowed back her nerves and raised her voice, hoping she exuded confidence instead of the anxiety currently swirling through her. She was well aware of this family's position in the community, but she had a position to uphold at this school. "Kimberly cannot participate in school sports or any extracurricular activity until she serves her time here. If you want to take her home, you're free to do so, but until she's served her two weeks, she's banned from soccer and anything else that takes place on this campus."

Mr. Markus's gaze crossed the lot toward Kimberly once more, his smile finally fading to something that looked a lot like . . . disdain?

"You're making them talk to plants?" he asked.

Kat nearly flinched at the disbelief in his voice. Yeah, she was walking a narrow line, straight toward unemployment. "It's more than that. These kids are learning about responsibility. They're working together as a team, which is a skill they're going to need in the future." She met Mr. Markus's wary gaze. "I don't expect you to understand."

After a long pause, he nodded. "I do understand. I've always thought Kimberly could use . . . some direction. Being the only child of two very important people has got to be hard on a kid." He smiled at Kat, his first sign of being a real person. "I'm not saying the mayor won't protest, but I'll talk to him."

Kat sucked in a breath. "Thank you. That's nice of you."

"She's got to learn, right? Isn't that the purpose of school? More than just reading and math."

Kat nodded. "Right."

"I'll pick Kimberly up in half an hour," Mr. Markus said, taking a step back. "I'll just go wait in the car."

Kat turned back to the Friendship Club and watched the kids with their different chores, a giddy smile stretching her face uncomfortably. She'd stood up for what she believed in and hadn't backed down. And it'd worked.

The mower came to a stop thirty feet away and she locked eyes with Micah, sweaty from the heat. He removed his ball cap and waved at her. Waving back, a flutter of heat tore through her, rivaling the pride she'd just felt in her administrative capabilities. He was an employee. A parent.

But she didn't care because he was also the first man to make her feel this way in a very long time.

～

MICAH LEFT THE SCHOOL THAT AFTERNOON AND DROVE straight to his aunt Clara's. "Listen to your aunt, you hear me?" He pointed a finger at Ben, seated in his wheelchair beside the Jeep.

"Great-aunt," Ben corrected, glancing over his shoulder at the older woman standing behind him in the driveway.

"We'll be fine. Go on," Aunt Clara urged, waving him away with her hand. "I've got him."

Micah had grown to feel less guilty about leaving Ben here in the last month. He guessed that was progress. And Ben was starting to ask to come over, even when Micah had nowhere to go.

He wasn't sure how he felt about that. A single man should want his freedom, not feel overwhelmed by it.

Tonight, though, he had no desire to leave Ben. Meeting his father at Camp Leon sounded more like a punishment than a good time, although for the life of him, he had no idea why the senior Peterson would want to punish him. Micah hadn't told anyone about his plans not to reenlist next year. Not yet.

After hopping back in his Jeep, he drove all the way to the military base with the windows down. His father had said he wanted a tour of the "birds" which is what he called the V-22 Osprey. There was always a spark of pride in the old man's eyes these days when he spoke about Micah being an Osprey pilot. Funny, he'd discouraged the decision when Micah had first announced he'd be applying for flight school. He'd been a twenty-two-year-old officer at the time and the options were endless. The obvious choice, though, according to his father, was to follow in his footsteps.

Instead, Micah had done six months in pre-flight classes before he was even allowed to set foot in the large aircraft. As soon as he had, he'd felt that unparalleled surge of adrenaline. The Marine Corps had never been his dream, but a new dream took hold of him when he sat in the pilot's seat that first day. He did another three years after pre-flight before he was actually considered a pilot, and he'd suffered more than a little ridicule from his good ol' dad during that time.

Colonel Peterson was waiting for him when he pulled up. Parking, Micah took a deep breath. He loved his dad, but sometimes, most times, he didn't like him very much.

"Hey, Dad." Micah waved and headed in his direction.

"It's Colonel Peterson when you're on the job. You know that. And where's your uniform?" his father asked in the brisk manner that he'd always used to communicate with his only child.

Micah slid his sunglasses over his eyes and avoided the question. "What do you want?"

His father's lips tightened. "Walk with me," he commanded.

"I already did my PT today. So if it's exercise you're after . . ." Micah contained a grin as his old man's gaze slid over. A lot of grunts would go limp-kneed at the look, but Micah had learned a long time ago that his father was all smoke and mirrors. And while Micah was usually anything but a smart-ass—that was much more Lawson's style—he enjoyed joking around with his father.

They didn't walk far. Just to the edge of the fence, where there were several straight-backed and uncomfortable-as-hell metal benches. They sat in silence for a long moment. Micah recognized this maneuver, too. He'd gotten the silent treatment a lot as a child, expected to squirm as he wondered what was going on. Not now. Micah was a grown man, and he really didn't care what his father's opinions were anymore. All he cared about was the fact that he was missing dinner with his son right now in order to be here at his father's beck and call.

Slapping his hands on his thighs, he glanced over. "Well, this was great, Colonel. If that's all you needed—" He started to stand.

"It's time you moved up in rank," his father finally spoke. "I hear you didn't take the classes required to qualify you for a rank change last month."

Micah shrugged. Yeah, he'd been a little busy last month designing gardens that had made grown men weep. "That's right," he said, not feeling the need to justify himself. He slid his sunglasses back over his eyes instead, and crossed a foot over one knee.

"You'll take the required trainings and apply for rank next month."

His father didn't say as much, but Micah recognized an order when he got one. He'd been taking orders his entire life. Tightening and relaxing the muscles in his jaw, he nodded. The alternative to agreeing with his good ol' dad's order was telling him where he could stick it. And then admitting that he wouldn't be reenlisting next year, so upping rank wasn't exactly a priority. Micah wasn't ready for that battle of wills just yet, though. Not while he was still in the planning stages—building his client list for landscaping and pulling off exhibits like he'd done last week. His father was a man who was . . . effective at getting his way, and Micah didn't want to leave him any room to crash his plans.

"Well, if that's all, sir." Standing, Micah offered a sarcastic salute, which could've just as easily been his middle finger going up. Then he headed back to his Jeep, hating that he hadn't told his father where he could go with his orders. Micah had made a calculated move, though, just like the military had trained him so well to do. His father had won this little battle, but the war was definitely going to be his.

Chapter Twelve

K at's stomach turned at the mention of Mayor Flowers being on the other line.

"Thanks, Val. Put him through." She plopped down in her black leather office chair and sucked in a deep breath. The mayor was just a person, a parent like any other. She'd simply explain that Seaside Elementary was cracking down on misbehavior this year, and no student was exempt.

"Principal Chandler." The mayor's voice was deep and smooth. She imagined him wearing the plastered smile that politicians wore as he sat behind his cherry desk, paid for by the good citizens of Seaside. "I hear we have a problem."

She grabbed the stress ball from her desk drawer and squeezed. "We do, sir. But as I told Mr. Markus, two weeks and your daughter is free to go back to her normal after-school routine."

"You see, Ms. Chandler . . ." the mayor began.

Kat noted that the "principal" title had been dropped.

"That's the problem," he said. "Kimberly has sports she has to attend to. She can't be held behind with a bunch of, shall we say, less-than-honor-student children, to pick up litter and do gardening. I'm sure you can see why a man in my position couldn't have that."

Kat closed her eyes, squeezing the ball in her hand until pain seared through the divots in her knuckles. "When you enrolled Kimberly here, sir, you told me that you wanted her to be treated like everyone else."

"And I do, Katherine."

Now her last name had been dropped, too. Next, he'd be calling her Kat.

"How about I make a generous donation to support your little effort? The Friendship Club, is it? I'm sure you could use some monies to help the kids out. Does five hundred dollars sound sufficient?"

Kat's mouth fell open and she dropped the ball on her desk, then she looked up as someone knocked on her door. The person behind it didn't wait for her to reply. He just slipped in.

Micah.

She held up a finger, silently asking him to hold on. "That's very generous of you, Mr. Mayor." And part of her was doing the math. Five hundred dollars could buy new equipment.

They could even build a greenhouse. And she'd always been interested in doing a recycling program at the school. She could start by having the after-school kids organize it.

The mayor chuckled. "Good. I'll have my assistant—"

"But the answer is no. Sir, this club is making a difference in these kids' lives, on school property and off. I know it is. And your daughter means too much to me as a principal to let her get away with treating others with disrespect. This is the period in her life when her moral code is being developed. The lessons she learns here, as a student at Seaside Elementary, will influence who she becomes as an adult. If she doesn't serve her time in the club, she can't play sports. That's my decision."

Kat locked eyes with Micah. The world was spinning and he was her focal point.

"I see." The mayor cleared his throat, his tone of voice sharpening dramatically. She could no longer hear the plastic smile behind the receiver. "That's a shame, Kat," he said. "I was hoping we could work this out civilly."

"I hope you understand." A sick feeling crawled through her stomach as she listened.

"I do. I understand that you're the youngest principal to ever work at one of the Seaside schools. There was a lot of talk about whether or not you were up for the job when you came on. Personally, I think it was the sympathy vote that got you into office. Everyone knows the story about you and your fiancé."

Her throat tightened so much that her hand actually went to her neck to pull the loose fabric of her shirt away. "Maybe that's true, Mayor Flowers. But hopefully it'll be my professional achievements that keep me in this position."

Micah took a step closer, his brows lowering with weighing concern.

"We'll see," the mayor said. "Have a good day, Katherine." And with that, the line went dead.

With a shaky hand, she set the phone back in its cradle. For a long moment, she was afraid to move, afraid to talk, to look up and meet Micah's dark eyes.

"Everything all right?" he asked, moving around to her chair. He reached out a finger and gently tipped her chin upward, forcing her to look at him.

With eyes burning, mostly out of anger, she shook her head. "I think . . . the mayor just threatened my job if I don't let Kimberly off the hook." Now her entire body was shaking. *Damn it.*

Micah pulled her into his chest, wrapping his strong arms around her. "You did the right thing," he whispered.

And she knew he was right. She *had* done the right thing. "But what if—"

"Doesn't matter," he said, as if he knew what she was going to ask. "Honor, courage, commitment. That's what a Marine stands for. I'd say you just showed all three of those qualities."

She pulled her head back to look at him. Then she watched

numbly as he dipped his head closer to hers, hovering at her lips and waiting for a signal that she wanted him to.

And hell yeah, she wanted him to.

She clutched his T-shirt and pulled him the rest of the way, moaning slightly as his tongue slipped into her mouth. His hands caressed her mid-back, then traveled up past the hem of her shirt. Good thing he'd closed her office door behind him.

The phone buzzed on her desk. Kat's eyes snapped open, locking on Micah's. The machine buzzed again. Reaching over, she pressed the call-receive button. "Yes?"

"Kat?" Val's voice blared into her office. "What happened with the mayor?"

Kat cleared her throat. She'd have to kill Val later.

"And is Mr. Peterson still in there with you?" Val asked.

Micah removed his hands from Kat's body and straightened as Kat pulled her clothing back into position.

"Yes, he is," she said, unnerved by the shaky quality to her voice. Val would know exactly what was going on in here. Val always knew. Her brain was wired toward romance and sex.

"What are you guys doing in there anyway?" Laughter played in her friend's voice.

"We'll talk about it tomorrow night, okay? Over chips and salsa." Kat pressed the hang-up button and looked at the dark hunk of muscle in front of her. She had no intention of confessing anything to Val. Not yet. Whatever was developing between her and Micah was private, and she didn't need anyone else's opinion about what should happen next.

"I, uh . . . I'm sorry." Concern etched itself on his forehead.

"Sorry?" Her smile evolved to a small laugh. "I was just about to thank you."

❦

"If you want my opinion," Val began a little while later.

"I don't." Kat dipped a tortilla chip in a small bowl of salsa at the center of the table. "But tell me anyway."

Val smiled. "Take the money from the mayor and move on. Kimberly Flowers will always be a spoiled brat as long as she's under those people's roof."

Those people, meaning the mayor and his wife.

A waiter stood at the end of their table and cleared his throat. "Are you ladies ready to order yet?"

Val's gaze traveled over him, making no attempt to hide her inspection of his young, athletic frame. Then she looked down at the vinyl menu and pointed. "I'll have the chicken enchilada special." She closed the menu and handed it back.

"And you?" The waiter turned to look at Kat.

"I'll have the same." She handed her menu to the man and waited for him to leave before continuing. "I considered taking the money. More to save my job than to appease anyone. But I can't. John was the one who convinced me I could do this job. I wasn't going to apply for principal, but he said that I was a natural born leader. He had faith in me." She took a shuddery breath. "Just before he went on deployment, one of the last things he told me was that he believed I could lead this school and make a difference in those children's lives. If I backed down with Kimberly . . ." Kat circled her finger around the rim of her glass. "I don't know, I feel like he'd be disappointed in me somehow."

Val's eyes held that sympathetic slant.

"I know he's dead. You don't have to remind me," Kat said. "But I still feel him, like he's watching over me." Now, instead of sympathy, Kat saw worry in her friend's eyes. "And I'm not crazy, either. I just want to make him proud, even if it means losing my job."

Val reached across the table and grasped her hand. "You know I love you, but I will *never* understand you." She smiled, her usually teasing eyes only full of kindness now.

"I love you, too." Kat stared at their interlocked hands and then at the solitaire diamond on her finger. "Did I tell you that I have a date this weekend?" she asked, changing the subject.

Val pulled back and bounced on her seat. "No, you didn't! I knew this was coming. Details. I need details. I haven't gotten juicy details about your sex life in over two years."

"And you're not getting any now, either. I said date, not sex."

"Same thing." Val waved a hand. "Where is he taking you?"

"The Veterans' Center."

The look of sheer disappointment nearly made Kat spew her soda across the table in laughter.

"It's my night to volunteer. He said he'd love to go. He's bringing Ben, too."

Now Val looked like she might start crying. "You're going on a date to play bingo with a bunch of old men and a child? I had much greater hopes for Micah Peterson than that."

Kat laughed at her friend, and then took a sip from her soda. "He might've pressed me against the desk in my office yesterday and kissed me, too."

Val was bouncing again. "Now we're talking."

Kat spared some of the details. Like the fact that she hadn't been able to think of anything other than Micah in the last twenty-four hours. "You have to promise to keep this just between you and me. I don't want it getting out that I'm seeing a student's parent. Or someone that works for me, for that matter."

Val held up two fingers. "Scout's honor."

Kat lowered her brows. "You're not a Boy Scout."

"You know what I mean. Of course I promise. The last thing I need is for you to get fired and old Dora Burroughs to take your place."

Kat reached for another chip. "You'd be in the unemployment line standing right next to me. Our current assistant principal would never keep you on."

Val feigned insult. "I'd never give her a chance. I'd pack my stuff right along with you. We're best friends, right?"

Kat nodded. "I'm so lucky to have you in my life. You've been with me through a lot of hard times these last few years."

"Maybe I should come this Friday and be with you for some more good times. I could spy on you and your date." Val used her fingers to place imaginary quotes around the word date, making Kat laugh.

It probably did sound lame, but the truth was, she'd be happy to go anywhere with Micah right about now. And keeping to a non-date kind of situation was less likely to gain unwanted attention from people who were looking to tear down her reputation. Like the mayor. Volunteering wasn't date material. It was innocent.

No one had to know about the less than innocent thoughts tramping through her mind.

When dinner was over, they walked together to the parking lot.

"Thanks for buying dinner," Val said, veering toward her car. "I'll get yours next time. You might be unemployed by then, so . . ." She winked as she ducked inside her little coupe.

Kat waved. "See you tomorrow, bright and early." She climbed into her own car, her body feeling like lead, and headed home to find Julie asleep on the couch with an old black-and-white classic playing on the television. Kat sat down beside her and turned off the TV.

Julie stirred as she did. "Hey, I was watching that."

"Yeah. I can see that." Kat smiled.

Julie's eyes cracked and then her face scrunched as if the light was eating her alive. She flipped her body restlessly to face the back of the couch and pulled her blanket over her head. Guilt gnawed at Kat's stomach as she flipped the light switch. If Julie were going to be staying for an indefinite amount of time, she'd need a real bed. Maybe this weekend, Kat would finish cleaning out the master bedroom, change the sheets, and open it to Julie. Just the thought made her entire body tense, which pissed her off a little. It was just a room, no big deal. Or it shouldn't have been.

Standing, Kat glanced back at her sister one more time and then headed down the hall. "Good night."

But Julie was already breathing hard, sleeping like a log, the way she always had. It was nice to have someone else in the house—not quite so lonely. Not that she'd ever considered herself lonely. She had Val. And other friends. Her co-workers. And now a sister, who deserved better than a couch.

Kat nodded to herself as she passed the master bedroom, promising herself that this weekend she'd do better. It was time to make space for new things in her life, new people. Micah crossed her mind and her heart kicked hard. New beginnings.

Chapter Thirteen

"I have a sprout, Mr. Peterson." Tony, one of the young boys in the Friendship Club pointed at the green stalk emerging from the ground.

Micah squatted beside him. "Yes, you do. Good job, son."

Tony's proud smile dropped and his eyes went back to the plant. "Thanks," he said quietly. Micah tried to remember Tony's story. He thought maybe Tony's father was in jail. *Crap.*

He'd just called the kid "son." Patting Tony's back, he asked, "Want to help me till another row of dirt? Kimberly over there doesn't have one yet."

Tony was smiling again. "She ain't gonna put her hands in dirt, Mr. Peterson. Are you crazy?"

Micah laughed. "Must be. Come on."

Two other boys joined him and Micah watched proudly as they tilled several more rows and pulled weeds together as a team. He caught Ben watching, too. There was a familiar look of disappointment on his face. Then Kimberly leaned in beside him at the picnic table and he smiled widely.

His son had a crush on the mayor's daughter. And Kimberly appeared to be listening contentedly to Ben's endless chatter, no doubt an explanation of how something worked. She liked him, too. A friend.

Micah's throat tightened as he leaned against the fence. He didn't see Kat walk up beside him until she touched his arm.

"You okay?" she asked.

He gave a quick nod. "Yep. Just amazed at what the kids have done out here."

Her gaze swept over the corner lot of the school. "It is amazing. Silly question, but what do we have growing anyway?"

"The better question would be what don't we have." He pointed at the rows of flowers popcorning out of the ground along the back fence. "Those are marigolds, mixed in with some chrysanthemums." Next, he pointed to the large rectangle of land in the fence's back corner. "The vegetable garden has squash, tomatoes, zucchini, and onions. In a week or two, we could make a pretty nice salad with what the kids have grown."

"We should." Kat leaned up beside him, too close and still not close enough. "We could make a salad pizza."

"A salad pizza?" He frowned, soliciting one of her singsong laughs he'd come to love.

"You're going to dishonor these veggies by putting them on a pizza?" Micah angled his body toward hers and lowered his voice. "So, are you ready for our date tonight?" he asked.

She didn't look at him. Instead, her hand absently went to the ring on her left hand. "I know what you're thinking." She looked at him and his heart did funny things as he stared into her eyes.

She was breathtaking. He had a sudden urge to take her in his arms and kiss her until her knees went weak. "I doubt it," he said, flashing her a wicked grin.

"You work with Marines all day. Why would you want to volunteer your Friday night to be with a bunch of veterans?"

"I wasn't thinking that. Trust me. I said yes because I want to be with *you*. Anywhere. And I'll be a veteran one day. Besides, I happen to like bingo."

"You do?" Her verdant green eyes tilted skeptically.

"Doesn't everyone?" He leaned in closer, changing the subject. "What do you make of Kimberly's attention to Ben?"

Kat's gaze slid toward the picnic table. "She's smiling. Flicking her hair. I think I see a little crush forming there."

"That's what I saw, too. I don't have the heart to make that girl get up and plant her row of seeds right now. Ben needs a friend. Sitting at a picnic table allows him to garden like the others, but it also ostracizes him even more than a wheelchair out here. I just want him to fit in."

Micah crossed his arms, continuing to watch Ben with Kim. "He's just so smart. Sometimes I wish he didn't understand how different he is. This . . ." Micah gestured toward Ben and Kim together. "This is something I rarely see, another student sitting and laughing with him." His jaw tightened. "Anyway. I know what *you're* thinking." He cast a teasing glance in her direction. "You're asking yourself what you got yourself into when you agreed to go out with me tonight, and now you wish I'd come down with some awful sickness so I'd have to stay home."

Her mouth fell open. "I would never wish that. And I know exactly what I'm getting myself into."

"Yeah?" He caught her gaze and held it, nearly wishing he'd arranged for Ben to stay with Aunt Clara tonight. If it weren't for all these kids right now, he'd be pressing the good principal against the fence and making her moan like he had the other day in her office. Short little moans, startled and urging him on at the same time.

"Looks like our hour is up, and the kids don't seem to be counting down the seconds anymore." Kat beamed at him.

"Dirt is good for the soul." He nodded at the man headed in their direction. "Looks like the mayor sent his assistant again. Everything okay with that?" he asked.

Kat shrugged and stepped forward to shake Jack Markus's hand. "Mr. Markus. I'm glad the mayor reconsidered letting Kimberly stay after with us today."

Jack wore a deep frown. "He didn't really have a choice. Sports are Kimberly's life." He looked at Kimberly sitting at the table. "If I were you I'd tread lightly, though, Principal Chandler. Maybe let Kim off on a shorter sentence. The mayor doesn't take kindly to losing battles."

Micah remembered that the race with the mayor's last competitor hadn't been pretty. "It's two weeks," he said without thinking. He stepped closer to Kat and she looked up at him with surprise.

She turned back to Mr. Markus. "He's right. And look at her. She's already made a friend out here."

"A disabled boy?" Jack shook his head. "Be glad the mayor sent me instead of coming out here himself."

"What's that supposed to mean? That disabled boy happens to be my son." Micah crossed his arms and stared the suited man down like a misbehaving grunt.

"No offense, Mr. . . . ?" Mr. Markus waited for Micah to introduce himself.

"Sergeant Micah Peterson," Micah said tightly. "And Principal Chandler is the one who makes the rules at this school. Not you and not Mayor Flowers."

Mr. Markus shifted uncomfortably with Micah's tone of voice. "I understand that. It's just"—he lowered his voice— "Kimberly will raise havoc in that house until her father has no choice but to stir up trouble. That's how she is. And I have to say, I'm not sure I could stand up to Kimberly that well, either."

Everyone's eyes turned to the little girl seated at the table with Ben. "She looks harmless," Kat said, knowing better.

"Trust me." Mr. Markus straightened and waved as Kimberly noticed him. She immediately grabbed up her book bag and said a quick goodbye to Ben. Ben's gaze lingered after her as she walked briskly to the mayor's assistant. The brief joy Micah had sworn he'd seen on Kim's face was now gone, replaced by a grown-up look of annoyance.

"This place sucks," Kim declared, loud enough for everyone to hear her. "I need to talk to my father right now."

Micah and Kat watched the two walk away.

"I don't know about you, but I won't be voting for Mayor Flowers next year. If he can't control things at home, he certainly shouldn't be in charge of the town of Seaside," Micah said.

Kat laughed. "He was a respected member of the military. He's a veteran. I'd say he's handled quite a lot."

Micah shrugged. "Speaking of veterans . . ."

She turned her body toward his. "Speaking of veterans . . ."

He smiled. "I've never looked forward to hanging out with a bunch of retired military more in my life."

Her lips curved slightly. "Me, neither."

Kat frowned at herself in the mirror that night.

"Stop obsessing. You look gorgeous." Julie laid back on the bed and watched her. "You must really like this guy."

"He's a friend."

"Uh-huh." A wicked smile spread through Julie's cheeks. "No sex for two-plus years, Kat. It's time." Her voice carried a teasing quality that reminded Kat of their younger days, sharing a bedroom and every detail of each other's lives.

"You're immature. You know that?" Kat said, just as she would've back then.

Kissy sounds followed her as she walked toward the bathroom and closed her sister out. "Let me know if the doorbell rings." Behind the door, Kat leaned against the wall and closed her eyes, forcing herself to take a slow, relaxing breath. She had to admit, the no sex thing for two years was starting to get to her, which was why she was thankful Ben would be with them tonight. That would ensure that her hormones stayed in their cage.

After the threat of retaliation from the mayor, another make-out session would be a great release. But not with Micah. She already had feelings developing for him and she wasn't ready. Physically, yes. But emotionally, not yet. She twisted her engagement ring.

She went to the mirror to comb her hand through her hair one more time, then turned as the doorbell rang across the house. Here went nothing.

Or everything.

Kat opened the bathroom door and headed down the hall toward the sound of Micah's deep voice greeting Julie.

"Look who's here," Julie announced as Kat came into view. Then with pronounced enjoyment, Julie added, "And look who's *not* here."

Kat searched the room as if Ben might be hiding under a couch cushion.

"He's home with my aunt Clara tonight." Micah took a step forward and offered a small potted plant with a pretty pink flower budding at its center.

She smiled at the gesture as she accepted the plant. "It's lovely. Thank you. I hope everything's all right with Ben."

Micah waved a hand. "Apparently, it's not cool to escort your parent on a date with your principal."

Despite her nervousness, Kat laughed.

Julie reached for the plant in her sister's hand with a peculiar look. "I'll take that. *Nice* flowers," she said, obviously not understanding the gesture.

Kat understood it, though, and she loved it. Taking his hand, she allowed him to lead her to the door.

"Hey, Micah." Julie took a few retreating steps and then leaned in toward him, lowering her voice to what was supposed to be a whisper. "Show my sister a good time, will you? It's been a long time coming."

Mortified heat rose up in Kat's cheeks. *For the love of chocolate.* She hoped he had no idea what her sister was talking about. When she looked up at Micah, though, it was obvious by the large grin on his face that he did.

He squeezed her hand tighter. "Don't wait up," he called to Julie behind them, and then he led Kat to his Jeep.

～

BRING FLOWERS—CHECK. OPEN HER CAR DOOR—CHECK.

Micah mentally reviewed the checklist his aunt had rattled off before going out on his date with Kat tonight. He didn't need a checklist, though. It'd been a long time, but he remembered how to treat a woman on a date. "You look beautiful tonight, by the way," he said.

Kat brushed a strand of hair from her face and smiled at him. "Thank you. I hope Ben isn't scarred for life because his father and principal are out together."

"He's fine. Just didn't want to hang out with a bunch of old people this evening," he said. "And he wasn't referring to the folks at the Veterans' Center."

Kat laughed. "Isn't your aunt older than us?"

Micah nodded. "Yes, but she's apparently a lot more fun."

The real truth was, Ben was matchmaking. Even though the last woman Micah had dated had shred his heart to pieces, Ben still believed his father could find the missing link in their family. He'd stopped believing his real mother was that link a long time ago.

"Do you think eyebrows will raise when you walk in with someone new on your arm tonight?" Micah asked.

Kat shrugged, drawing his attention to the smooth, bare skin on her shoulders. "Probably, but it won't stop the regulars from flirting with me." She pulled the cardigan that had slipped down to her elbows back up, and then cinched it tight across her chest.

"You cold?" he asked, instinctively turning on the heater.

"No, I'm fine. Just nervous, I guess."

"Because of me? Don't be."

"I haven't been on a date in a long time. Not since . . ." Her sentence fell off and Micah watched her hand absently fidget with the ring on her finger.

"Not since your fiancé died?" he asked.

She nodded. "I'm sorry. I shouldn't bring that subject up. It's in my past, not my future."

"It's okay. It's part of who you are. What happened?" he asked, uncertain if he really wanted to know.

She hesitated. "Are you sure?"

"No. But tell me anyway." He listened as she sucked in a long breath.

"Well, he proposed the night before he was set to deploy. He was going to be gone for nine months and then we were planning to get married when he returned."

He heard the pattern of her breathing change, nearly felt the aching of her heart as she continued.

"I did all the wedding planning while he was away. Bought the dress. Made the arrangements. We were going to marry down at the docks. I'd already gotten permission from Mr. Blokey . . . I was going to hang lights at the archway and we were going to recite our vows there. I wrote my own. And Val was going to be my maid of honor, of course. Julie, too. I wanted to have both of them standing beside me on what I knew would be the happiest day of my life." She paused, turning to look out the passenger side window. "He never came home, though."

He'd heard this story before. Not Kat's specifically, but others like it. It was a tough handout from life.

"So, that's my story." She laughed nervously, turning to look at him again. Micah suspected it was a laugh or cry moment, and Kat was a strong woman. He'd realized that over the last few months. Even so, he wanted to stop the vehicle and wrap his arms around her. "Why do you still wear the ring? If you don't mind me asking."

She pulled her hand closer to her face to inspect the diamond. "I know it's time to take it off. It's just comforting to keep it on. It's all I have left, really. I guess I'm not ready to remove it just yet."

"You will be. One day."

She nodded. "Right. I'm on a date for the first time in years. That's progress. Even if it is at the Veterans' Center. I'm sorry. I know this isn't ideal."

"It's fine. And besides, I have different arrangements for when we leave here." Micah parked in front of the large metal building and got out before she could reply. Then he ran around and opened her door.

Help her out of the vehicle—check.

Her hand slipped easily into his as she stepped out of the Jeep. "What kind of arrangements do you have planned?" she asked.

He ran a thumb over the back of her hand. "I guess you'll have to stick with me to find out," he said, leading her inside with only one thing left on Aunt Clara's checklist to do at the end of the night: kiss her.

Chapter Fourteen

"Good night, sunshine." A balding older man patted Kat's back and cast a wary eye at Micah. "I know how you Marines think, but don't even try to sleep with the lady on the first date."

Kat nearly choked on the Coke she was drinking. "Mr. Vincent!"

He laughed heartily. "That's old-fashioned of me, isn't it? Just make sure you call her in the morning if you do. See you next month, Miss Katherine," he said with a wink.

Kat grimaced. "Sorry about that," she said when Mr. Vincent was gone. Bringing Micah here was as bad as she imagined it would be to bring him home to meet a clan of extended family. These people felt more like family to her than the few blood relatives she had left. She had her mom, widowed now, who lived close by. She rarely saw her, though. Then there was Julie, who had suddenly decided it was time to start acting like sisters again.

"Don't apologize." Micah sat on a metal folding chair as she finished collecting the bingo cards. "I grew up in a house full of men. I work with a bunch of men. Sex jokes are the norm," he said.

"Well, I work in an elementary school. My life revolves around kids and cranky people who sit behind a desk. It's not the norm for me." Thus the reason for her burning cheeks, only made worse because she'd been fantasizing about Micah's hands running over her body all night. She turned to him and realized he was still watching her, as if she was the most fascinating thing he'd seen all day. "All done. Ready to go?" she asked.

He held her gaze for a long beat with those bone-melting eyes that made her stomach turn nervously. Then he stood and took her hand. "Thank you for letting me come with you tonight."

She lowered her gaze. If she didn't, she might be compelled to step closer, to press her body against his, surrounded by a room full of people who would never let her forget her actions. "The vets here mean a lot to me."

"Me, too. There's one thing we have in common." A slight smile formed on his lips.

He had a nice mouth, she decided, liking the way it was surrounded by a dark five o'clock shadow at this late hour.

"Care to go investigate more commonalities with me?" he asked.

A breath shuddered through her. The Veterans' Center was more like working together at the

Friendship Club. Sure, they'd been flirting, even kissing. Whatever happened after they left this building, though, would be different. This was a date, where the possibilities ranged from mediocre conversation to wild, unbridled sex to something more. Something real. She took a step toward him that felt like a leap off a very high cliff, then stopped to catch her breath.

"You okay?" he asked, still watching her.

She took the hand he offered, wanting to feel his skin against hers as much as needing something to keep her grounded. "Yes. I'm fine. Let's do this."

He cocked a brow that made her squirm.

"I mean let's go," she said.

A light sprinkle of rain fell as they walked toward his Jeep at the far end of the parking lot. "Should've brought an umbrella," he mused, hurrying to open the door for her. His hand brushed against hers as they both reached for the handle.

"Not for me. I love the rain." She stepped inside and smiled back at him, wiping a damp strand of hair from her eyes.

"Two things we have in common." He shut the door and entered on the driver's side.

"So where are you taking me?" she asked as the headlights flooded the quickly emptying parking lot. They might have walked slowly, but the older gentlemen and women who frequented the Veterans' Center drove like maniacs.

Micah's mouth quirked on one side. "My place."

∾

HER BLOOD RAN HOT AGAIN. *HIS PLACE?* "WH . . . WHY are we . . . ?" Maybe she'd been out of the dating game too long. Maybe sex on the first date was the norm now.

"Ben is at my aunt Clara's tonight. I thought I'd take you to my house and show you my garden."

"Your garden?" she repeated, unsure she was understanding him. *His garden?*

He laughed, seeming to read her expression. "Don't sound so excited."

"No, I am. I'm beginning to love gardens. The one you showed me the other night was amazing. It was like nothing I've ever seen." She just hadn't expected he'd take her to see another garden tonight.

He looked over. "It's kind of my baby, so . . ."

She nodded, willing to go almost anywhere with him tonight. "I'd love to see your garden, Micah."

She would just leave this part out when she was recapping the night for Val and Julie later. A date to the Veterans' Center to play bingo with veterans and then a tour of Micah's garden. She was going to sound pathetic. But the date did happen to be with the hot groundskeeper at the school, and that definitely wasn't pathetic.

Five minutes later, Micah pulled into the driveway of a one-story house that was covered with cedar-shake siding. Kat leaned forward to watch the rain bounce off the house's metal roof. Even with her rain-blurred view, it was breathtaking. "Wow." She sighed, taking in the rugged, yet fanciful home. It was one she might've bought for herself if she'd been in the market.

Micah watched her. "Ben and I haven't lived here long. I have big plans for this house, though. And my garden."

"Sounds like you two will be staying awhile?" She regretted the hopeful tone in her voice.

The rain fell harder now, pelting against the windshield. She leaned back into the passenger seat. She'd always loved the rain, but without an umbrella, there was no way she was stepping foot outside. Not after taking so long to do her hair and makeup. And not while wearing a white linen dress that would show everything underneath if she got drenched.

"I hope to make this my forever home," Micah said. "Ben needs stability. Heck, I was raised in the military. I've never stayed anywhere longer than five years. My contract is up next May, and I'm not planning on reenlisting." He blew out a breath. "You're the first person I've told that to."

Kat's lips parted as she looked at him. She'd just assumed he'd leave. All Marines left. *Or they never came home,* she thought, pulling her thoughts back to the present immediately. Now wasn't the time or place to be thinking of the past. "I had no idea. I think that's wonderful. For Ben," she added.

Micah shrugged. "I have a nice little side business started with my landscaping. I want to expand to designing gardens like the ones you saw last week. That's where my passion is."

"That's a great dream."

"Think so?" He turned to her, his eyes darkening. They stared at each other for a long beat. "Looks like we're stuck in here awhile," he finally said. "Unless you want to get completely soaked."

No. She didn't. She tried to remember what she had on underneath the dress. She hadn't obsessed over that part. Because the dress wasn't coming off. It was staying on, and staying dry.

"I don't mind waiting out the storm."

"Me, either." He leaned in closer to her and reached out to

brush a lock of damp hair from her face, his finger passing over her cheek slowly.

She swallowed thickly as her heart began to race. "You're the first person I've dated since. . ." She didn't complete her sentence. He already knew the rest. "I might not be good at this anymore," she whispered. At what exactly, she wasn't sure, because the dress was staying on, she reminded herself.

He leaned in even closer. "Good at what?" he asked in a deep voice that radiated up her legs, through her body, and resided in her chest.

"Whatever we're doing here."

"Talking?" His voice was barely a whisper against the beating of the rain. "You're good at talking, Kat." He guided her chin toward him and his lips brushed lightly against hers.

"Kissing? You're great at that, too." His tongue slid into her mouth, exploring for just a moment as his hands did the same, running along her skin, awakening her body with the power that no cup of java ever had.

She arched to his touch, wanting the man in front of her. Screw the ramifications. Her body needed more of his touch. Right here, right now.

Micah pulled back and looked at her, his eyes molten with desire. "A Jeep isn't the place to make love to a woman. I want you, Kat, but I don't want it to be here," he said, his voice deep.

They couldn't stop. Not now. Please not now.

He pulled his body off hers and returned to his driver's seat, breathing heavy himself. Running a quick hand over his short hair, he looked over at her with a teasing glance. "Will you melt?" he asked.

She shook her head quickly, her body still quivering from his touch. She was having withdrawal from the absence of his weight blanketing her already. Screw hair and makeup. She *needed* to feel his touch.

"Good," he said, leaning in and kissing her lips tenderly. "Then let's make a run for it."

She nodded, suddenly willing if that meant that they could keep going.

Rain pelted her hot skin as she opened the door to his Jeep Cherokee and ran, squealing softly as cold puddles splashed her ankles. She didn't care. All she cared about right now was Micah.

He unlocked the front door and pulled her inside, immediately covering her mouth with his in a long, bone-melting kiss that told her he still wanted her. "You're wet," he said, running his hands over her rain-soaked arms. "Why don't we take these wet clothes off?"

She shivered, but not because of her damp clothing. She didn't bother to look around his house. Ben was with his aunt next door. In a dreamlike haze, she allowed Micah to peel off her dress while he guided her to his bedroom in the back of the house.

"I want you, Kat. I want to make love to you. Now," he growled in a low whisper. His declaration was a question that needed to be answered before he'd continue.

She didn't let herself second guess. She knew what she wanted in this moment, and nothing was going to stand in her way. "I want you, too."

MICAH STIRRED, WONDERING MOMENTARILY AT THE heavy weight of someone's arm draped over his. Ben wasn't able to crawl into his bed in the night. And Ben was at Aunt Clara's, he remembered.

His eyes cracked to see the blond hair cascading in front of him. *Kat.* He tightened his grip as he realized where he was. He'd just had sex with Kat Chandler—Ben's principal and his sort-of, part-time boss.

Details of the hours before he'd fallen asleep slowly crept into his memory. He glanced out the rain-speckled window, seeing that the storm was over, and checked the clock—midnight.

Kat stirred, appearing to go through the same motions. She dreamily looked around and found him lying behind her. "Micah."

She smiled briefly, then gasped and pulled the white sheet from his bed higher to cover herself.

"I guess we fell asleep," he said, wishing he could find something more charming to say. "Do you want some water?"

She nodded. "Please."

Happy to have something to do, he got up and walked to the kitchen. Sleeping with Kat hadn't been a mistake. He'd wanted her ever since the first moment he'd laid eyes on her. But he wasn't ready for a relationship, and one with her spelled disaster. He needed to focus on Ben, he reminded himself.

"I hope this is okay." Kat stepped into the kitchen a moment later, wearing one of his T-shirts that he'd folded and had meant to put away. It was long enough to be a dress on her, hanging loosely on her body. Even so, she was the best thing he'd seen this decade. Her hair was pulled back neatly in a clip, with a few stray pieces falling sexily around her flushed face. "My dress is still soaked," she explained.

"It's fine." He cleared his throat in an effort to clear his mind. "You okay?"

She took a step closer. "I was a more-than-willing participant, if that's what you're asking. And yes, I'm okay. Tonight was wonderful, actually."

"Perfect, I'd say. Here you go." He slid the glass of water across the counter instead, directing his focus to the window above his kitchen sink. "Looks like the rain stopped. I can show you my garden now. Unless you think it's too late. I could take you home if you need me to."

She shook her head, blushing as she looked up at him. He wondered which memory she was entertaining. There were several he could think of. "I'm not ready to go home quite yet," she said.

Which was good because he wasn't ready to let her go.

"Okay, then." Reaching for her hand, he led her outside beyond his deck. The damp air smelled like rain-soaked soil and he gulped it in. He hadn't shown many people his garden. Just Aunt Clara and Uncle Rick. His father had seen it a time or two in the beginning stages, but he'd always frowned and reminded Micah his career was with the military. His father always made sure Micah knew that.

This was the first garden that would be Micah's only and no one else's. He'd never had the luxury of growing roots in the past. All he'd had before was container gardening, where the roots grew shallow and the plant was never allowed to reach its full growth.

Here, though, there were no limitations.

Kat stopped walking for a moment and looked at what he'd created. He felt like he was seeing it for the first time, too, as he looked at it through her eyes. The wooden archways he'd built to walk under were no longer visible, covered by vines that twisted and tangled together, shooting off flowers where they fancied. Then there were the sectioned areas, where he'd created patches of gardens, like a quilt of many colors. Some squares of land were elevated and in wooden cases he'd built himself. Others were on the ground.

He'd purchased this home five years ago, knowing when it went on the market that this was the perfect place for him and Ben to live. Since then, whenever he'd gotten leave from the military, he and Ben had come here from whatever place they were stationed at the time, and Micah had worked in this garden. *His* garden. When they'd finally gotten stationed at Camp Leon, that's when the garden had really taken form.

Kat's mouth was open. "This is amazing."

And under the moon, with everything cast in a glow of pale white light, Micah felt slightly in awe, too. He never tired of being here. "Come on." He continued walking down a wooden plank path he'd built to allow Ben's wheelchair to roll through. "My aunt Clara would probably frown at me right now if she saw me wearing shoes."

"You can't wear shoes in the garden?"

"You connect better in bare feet," he said, catching her uncertain gaze. "I'll have to show you sometime, when the dirt isn't quite as muddy."

The corner of her mouth kicked up on one side. He'd noticed that she did that a lot.

"What kind of flower is that one?" She stopped and touched a bright pink bloom.

"You like it?"

She leaned in to smell the flower's gentle fragrance, her hair escaping from its clip and falling around her face as she did. "It's gorgeous."

"That's a lily. Their petals are thick. They're as beautiful as any flower out here, but a lot tougher. They could take ten times the storm we just had and still stand."

She considered his description. "A survivor. Sounds like a flower I could get along with."

Looking at her right now, he could swear he was falling in love with this woman. Which was ridiculous. They barely knew one another. And that was his problem. He didn't fall for women often, but when he did, he fell hard, and once that happened, it was nearly impossible to turn those feelings off. That's the way it'd been with Jessica. It'd taken her abandoning Ben to shut his feelings down for good. Right now wasn't good timing. Falling for Kat Chandler was a bad idea.

"This is a really magical place." She looked up at him with those angelic eyes as she continued down the path. "Thank you for showing it to me."

"Thank you for not saying it's stupid."

"It's definitely not stupid. You can really see how much love you put into your work."

And when he loved something, he was incapable of giving less than a hundred percent. That one hundred percent belonged to Ben right now. He was the only parent Ben had, and his son needed him.

Micah swallowed hard. "It's getting late. I should probably take you home."

Her smile wilted slightly. "You're right. My sister will be wondering where I've gone. Or, actually, she's probably guessed where I've been and she's stalking the living room, waiting up to hear all the details." Kat looked up with wide eyes. "Not that I would."

Micah smirked. "You don't kiss and tell. That's good."

"If word got out about us at the school, a principal and a parent . . ." Alarm continued to build in her expression.

"Don't worry. I don't kiss and tell, either. And it was never supposed to have happened. I didn't plan this when I invited you over tonight."

"You didn't?"

Micah shook his head, surprised that she'd even have to ask. "Of course not. I wanted to show you my garden. I have Ben. The last thing I need to be doing is . . ." He motioned toward his home and back to Kat, searching for the right words. "The timing is all wrong. I mean, you've told me yourself that you're not ready for dating."

"And I'm not," she confirmed.

"So what are we doing, Kat?" he asked, already missing the feel of her in his arms.

She didn't respond for a long moment. "We had sex. Val and my sister have both been telling me that I need to relax and have . . ." She wobbled her head from side to side, and if he wasn't mistaken, her skin was growing steadily redder. "They think casual sex is exactly what I need to push me back into"—she fidgeted with her hands—"*that* area of my life."

Tonight hadn't felt casual to him, but maybe she was right. Maybe he could reframe his thinking. It was just meaningless, feel-good sex. That's all. "Casual sex?" he repeated.

She nodded, her gaze uncertain as she looked at him. "Isn't that what it was?"

~

"RIGHT." MEMORIES OF THE WAY SHE'D LOOKED AT HIM when they'd been in bed flashed through his memory. And the way he'd kissed every bare inch of her body, cherishing her like the rarest of flowers. "Yeah. I'm surprised you're okay with that, though. You don't seem like the type of woman who does those things lightly."

She hugged herself, lowering her head to watch the ground as they walked toward his back porch.

Oh, no. He hoped he hadn't upset her. "No offense. You just seem more wholesome than that."

"This year is about moving on for me."

Micah watched her, loving how fidgety and cute she was when she was nervous. "So your goal this year is to make some changes in your life? And part of that involves a fling?" he asked.

She nibbled her lower lip. He had to say, he kind of liked the idea of being intimate with Kat with no strings, or guilt, attached.

"Do you intend to have flings with a lot of people, or just one person?" he asked, suddenly hating the idea of anyone else getting their hands on her.

They were back at the steps of his deck and she sat, leaving just enough room for him to sit beside her on the still damp wood. Their legs brushed against each other as he did.

"I'm not really the type to see more than one person at a time. I don't want to change that drastically. So most likely just one." Her gaze skittered toward him and she looked away quickly. "It's a good thing you have me, then." Because if there were no strings attached, maybe he could be a good father to Ben and keep seeing Kat.

She was looking at him again. "I didn't plan this tonight, either." Her cheeks were crimson now. "I should probably get home to sleep before I completely scare you off."

Micah reached for her hand. "I'm not scared." He leaned in closer, the smell of her body mixing with the scent of new fallen rain.

Her gaze fell on their interlocked hands. "We could have our own little club of two."

He lowered his voice. "You and your clubs. What would we call this one?" He turned in toward her.

"The Lovers' Club?" she suggested, with a small giggle.

His mouth brushed against her ear, kissing down her jawline. "Count me in. Just us. Any rules for this one?"

"Rules?" she asked, closing her eyes as he continued kissing her.

"Yeah. You know. The Friendship Club has rules." He kissed her neck. "One hour a day after school. Be good to others." He pulled her on top of him as they sat on the deck's steps.

"I guess . . ." she said through shaky breaths, "the only rule would be that it's just a casual thing, you and me. And when we want out..."

"Then we say so," he said, completing her thought.

THE NEXT MORNING, KAT PUSHED OPEN THE DOOR TO HER and John's room together and stared for a long beat. Then she walked to the small bedside dresser and sat. Ready or not, life was moving on. It'd been moving on since Micah had shown up this year with his broad shoulders and black hair. And those chocolate-colored eyes that made her knees liquefy. Good thing for those mirrored sunglasses he liked to wear. That kept her on two solid, walking legs most days.

Those solid, walking legs didn't feel so solid right now, however. The mission this morning was packing John's things so that Julie could have a more hospitable place to stay. If she were going to stay here for any length of time, the couch definitely wouldn't suffice.

His clothes were mostly gone, except for the ones that held special memories. Those still hung in the closet, and she guessed eventually she'd have to part with them. Today she'd tackle the dresser, though, which held things that took more time to go through.

She sat on the floor and pulled at the bottom drawer. It stuck a little, resisting being opened. It didn't want to let go of the memories, either. Finally, it gave way and she fell back on her bottom, coughing a little as a plume of dust flew toward her face.

Dipping her hand into the drawer, she pulled out an old Valentine's card first. It was one she recognized immediately. She'd given it to John the February before he'd left. As she opened it, a soft battery-operated tune sang "Burning Love" in a mechanical Elvis impersonation. She smiled, reading her words to her future husband.

The answer was always yes. And always will be.

He'd meant to ask her to marry him three times before he'd actually been successful. But all three times, they'd sparked an argument somehow, and fearing she'd say no, he'd opted not to pop the question. She never would've turned him down, though. She'd been ready to say yes to forever since their first date. That's when she'd known. Maybe from the first time they'd looked into each other's eyes. She'd also known that they'd spend their lives together forever. But they hadn't. Even though he'd made promises to her, he'd never come home.

Where did a Valentine's card go? Not to the Goodwill. Not in the trashcan. She slid it inside a shoebox and did the same with the next several mementos of their lives together. When the box was full and the drawer half empty, she stopped, drained for the morning. She'd do a little at a time, she promised herself, rising as she heard Julie come through the front door.

Glancing around the room, she decided all it needed for Julie to stay here tonight was a change of sheets and a new bedspread. That's all that had to be done physically. Emotionally, she needed a good glass of wine. Both could be arranged.

"Hey." Kat poked her head outside the bedroom door as Julie headed down the hall.

Julie's brows lifted in question.

"Just cleaning out your new room." Kat forced a smile.

"My new room?" Julie repeated, the tone a questioning one.

"Yep." Kat hugged the shoebox of old cards in her arms. "I'll change the sheets and you can sleep here tonight. As many nights as you need."

"Are you sure?" Julie asked, her shoulders relaxing a little.

"Because the couch is fine. Even though I've had a kink in my neck for the past two days. Nothing a little yoga can't fix."

"I'm sure." Kat sucked in a solid breath. "I'll, uh, work on cleaning out the closet for you another day."

Julie nodded, peeking into the master bedroom. "Thank you. I almost feel like you want me to stay."

Kat narrowed her gaze softly. "Of course I want you to stay. You're my sister. We're family. Now, go get your things and bring them in here."

Before I have a chance to change my mind.

Julie nodded and headed back to her suitcases in the living room. With one final glance in the master bedroom's direction, Kat forced her feet, and her mind, forward.

Chapter Fifteen

I t'd been a week since she and Micah had slept together for the first time. It hadn't been the last time, though. In that week, they'd somehow managed to meet every day, or night, to take advantage of their agreement. No strings. Just plain, feel-good pleasure.

Kat looked up from her desk and sighed at the image of Val.

"You're still going to tell me that nothing happened?" Val asked, hands on her hips, obviously not buying Kat's outright lie. "Fine, don't tell me. I know what's going on."

"You only think you do," Kat called to Val's back as she headed into the front office. With her friend gone, Kat smiled to herself. Yep, she was enjoying herself and no one else needed to know—that would only complicate things. Micah had a son that was his first priority, as Ben should be, and she . . . well, she still had one leg stuck in the past and he didn't seem to mind.

Kat stared at the ring on her finger and sucked in a deep breath. Then, she slipped it off. The band resisted a little, and she had to twist it and give a hard yank. When it was off, she set it on her desk and stared at it, remembering when she'd first seen it in the velvet box that John had presented to her. When her friends had gotten engaged before her, she'd pretended to fawn over their rings like they were the most special things she'd ever seen. They never were though. Not in her eyes. It was always just another diamond, maybe cut differently or shinier than others, but a diamond just the same.

But she'd understood when she opened the box from John and saw this one for the first time. Her heart had swelled in her chest and her fingers had shook as he'd slipped the ring on her left hand. She'd sworn at that very moment that she'd never take it off.

Kat unclasped the gold chain she wore around her neck and slid her diamond engagement ring on it. Before she could change her mind, she clasped the chain with the ring attached back in place.

There. She'd taken another tiny step forward.

Val cleared her throat, standing back in Kat's doorway with an expectant look.

"Still not talking," Kat said.

Val crossed her arms. "That's not why I'm back. Mrs. Burroughs wanted me to ask if the Friendship Club is meeting this afternoon."

Kat furrowed her brow. "Of course we are. We meet every afternoon. Why? And why didn't she come ask me herself?"

Val shrugged, rolling her eyes to the ceiling. "She said she was hoping to meet with you alone to discuss school matters."

Yeah, right. "What's wrong with right now? I'm free for the next hour or so."

Val lowered her voice. "That won't work for our lovely assistant principal. She's busy. And administrators are supposed to meet after school, you know? The school hours are for assisting students," Val said in a mocking tone.

"I'm the last one to leave every night. My door is always open. And we just met last week."

Val held her hands out to her sides. "So I should tell her yes, the club is meeting this afternoon and she can just kiss your—"

Now Kat's hands flew out in front of her. "No. No, don't tell her that." Dora Burroughs was an old-school administrator. She had ideas of how things should be run and Kat understood that. Kind of. "Tell her I'll meet with her right after the bell today. You can help Micah get the group started for the first fifteen minutes, right?"

Val dug a finger into her own chest. "Me?"

"I did give you that comfy office job. Even though you're not all that people-friendly. School secretaries are supposed to be nice."

Val frowned. "I am nice. Just misunderstood . . . Fine. I'll tell her. And I'll watch the little rug rats for you, because I'm so sweet. For fifteen minutes only, though. I'm timing it."

Kat steepled her hands in front of her. "Thank you."

In response, Val pointed a finger at her. "But I expect a full, detailed report on the wild sex you're having with Micah later."

Kat's mouth fell open. She hurried to the doorway and searched around the front office for anyone who might have overheard. Dora Burroughs stood at the end of the hall with her back to them. Kat really hoped her assistant principal hadn't heard that comment. Turning, she frowned at her friend and lowered her voice to a harsh whisper. "If you weren't my best friend, I'd fire you right now. You know that?"

"So you keep saying. The fact of the matter is, I'll always be your best friend, so you're stuck with me." Val's smile deepened. Then her gaze caught on the diamond engagement ring on Kat's necklace. She looked at Kat's hand and back up. "That's progress. Maybe you're having more than sex."

Kat's hand instinctively fidgeted with the chain as she laughed lightly. "How many times do I have to tell you? We're just friends."

Val nodded, with a knowing grin stamped on her face. "Okay. We'll continue this conversation later." She gave a little wave and headed down the hall toward Mrs. Burroughs's office.

Well, hell. Kat returned to her desk and plopped in her chair. Val didn't know what she was talking about. What she had with Micah was just sex.

She nodded to herself as her hand went to the ring dangling off her necklace. Because anything more than that would put a damper on things. A *big* damper.

"So you asked her out on a pre-ball date? And you've been having sex with her ever since?" Lawson grabbed a soda from Micah's fridge and sat down.

Micah felt his eyes widen as he scanned the room. "Lower your voice, man. Ben's down the hall doing homework."

Lawson laughed. "You did, didn't you? I can see it all over your face. Was it good?"

Micah glowered at him from the hot stove. "If you keep being such a jerk, I'll stop letting you come over for dinner every week. Then what will you do?"

"A man needs a home-cooked meal at least once a week," Lawson agreed. "I guess then I'd have to settle down and find a good woman." He shook his head and took a long drink of his Coke. "She'd have to be a good cook. Otherwise, I'd starve."

"You wouldn't starve. You could live off junk food for another decade or two before it caught up to you," Micah said. "Or you could just live at your sister's house."

Lawson scratched his chin, a look of heavy concentration weighing down his features as he considered this. "I feel like I practically live there as it is. If I ever see Beth's jerk of an ex, I'm going to introduce him to my fist. Who up and leaves their wife and little girl?"

"I don't know. Jessica didn't have any problems leaving her husband and son."

Lawson shook his head. "After I introduce Beth's ex to my fist, I'll introduce him to Jessica. A perfect match."

"Anyway, I'm not discussing my love life with you."

"Love life?" Lawson was grinning again.

Micah let out a deep growl. "Just cut it out with the s-word, all right? I don't want Ben to hear you."

"What s-word?" Ben asked, walking down the hall while keeping one hand on the wall to stabilize himself.

Micah startled at his son's voice, then nearly burnt his hand on the stove when he saw Ben standing. "Where's your chair?" His voice seemed to boom in the small kitchen.

"In my room. I can still walk, you know." Ben waved at Lawson, and Micah immediately understood why his chair had been left behind. It was another reason Lawson would be invited over no matter what he said or did. Ben loved him. He was the uncle that Ben didn't have by blood. Blood didn't matter, though. Micah knew that well enough. Family was made through the time people spent together.

"What s-word?" Ben asked Lawson.

Lawson's face turned serious. "Top-secret military stuff that can't be spoken in front of young ears."

Ben didn't buy it. He continued to take slow, deliberate steps to the table. "Hopefully we're not eating Dad's spaghetti again."

Micah's head dipped in mock insult as he turned to watch him. "What's wrong with my spaghetti?"

Ben made a face. "Green noodles are weird."

"They're spinach." Micah looked at Lawson to help him out.

"I agree with the kid. It's weird," his pal said with a shrug.

Micah pretended to brood as he brought the plates he'd prepared to the table. "Manwiches." He smiled proudly at his son and friend. "Dinner of men. Let's eat."

Micah and Lawson lifted the oozing buns to their mouths as Ben watched. "Dad, can we say grace?"

Micah's Manwich hovered in front of him. Clearing his throat, he set it down. "Grace?" He hadn't considered praying before a meal since his mother had passed away. She'd always insisted they bless the food before eating. "Who taught you about saying grace?"

Ben looked at the table. "There's a girl at school that says it before her lunch. I thought, you know, it might be time for me to get to know the big guy . . . so he'll protect Mom for me while she's in the war." Ben's gaze hung on his plate. "Never mind. It's not important."

"Sure it is, little buddy." Lawson folded his hands in front of him and cast a convincing look in Micah's direction. Micah was too stunned to think. If there wasn't enough for his little guy to worry about, now he was concerned about his mother dying, too.

"Aren't you going to eat?" Lawson asked, halfway into the meal. Micah shook his head. "Not hungry."

"Too worried about your big night out," Lawson asked, knowing good and well that wasn't it. "How do you feel about that, little buddy?" he asked Ben. "Your dad taking your principal to the ball? Kind of gross, huh?"

Ben shook his head with a large, heart-gripping grin. "All I want is for my dad to find someone who makes him happy."

Well, damn if the kid doesn't sound like a little adult.

"You make me happy," Micah said, getting up and clearing the plates. "And we're just friends," he protested. "She's my boss."

His objections were ignored.

"Well, what if they make each other miserable?" Lawson asked, passing his dish up to Micah.

Ben shook his head. "Scientifically impossible."

"There's science behind this, huh?" Lawson asked.

Ben grinned. "Just like magnets. Dad and Principal Chandler are polar opposites of each other. I have a list. Wanna see it?"

Lawson glanced in Micah's direction. "Sure, buddy. I'd love to see your list."

Micah dried his hands on a dishtowel and headed toward the table. He wanted to see this scientific evidence, too.

Ben walked slowly to his room, returning in his wheelchair with a handwritten list a few minutes later. He placed it in front of Lawson, who held it up and read it aloud.

"Dad likes trucks. Principal Chandler likes cars." Lawson's gaze slid toward Ben beside him. "That's a huge polar opposite."

"It gets better." Ben tapped the paper with his right arm.

"Dad is tall. Principal Chandler is short. Dad has black hair. Principal Chandler has blond hair. Dad is a Marine. Principal Chandler is a teacher. Kind of." Lawson chuckled under his breath. "Dad's wife left. Principal Chandler is alone, too."

Ben pointed at the list. "That's not really opposite, but it's important. They're both lonely for different reasons. Principal Chandler used to wear a ring, but now she doesn't. I'm not sure why, but it means she's available. And they both love me. So they have to love each other, too. Right?"

Micah swallowed. He could almost see the logic behind his son's rationale. "Why does it matter if I ever fall in love again, son?"

Ben took the list out of Lawson's hand. "It just does. It's my wish."

Micah stared at him.

"I know I can't make you fall in love by wishing, but if you spend time with Principal Chandler, it's going to happen. I know it will."

"Because of science," Lawson said, nodding his head agreeably.

Ben's smile was back, revealing a crooked top tooth. "Exactly."

Micah stood at the entrance of the school's courtyard and watched Kat with the group of after-school kids a few days later. He'd been running late today due to some wise guy Marine who needed to understand the value of doing a job right the first time.

Unfortunately, that added work to his own plate, and subtracted time from his son. And the Friendship Club.

Ben was at the picnic table with Kimberly again. They'd sat together a lot lately and, as much as he didn't want to, Micah liked her. She had spunk. And it wasn't her fault that her father was a complete jerk of a mayor.

Kat turned and caught his eye, giving him a quizzical look.

"Sorry I'm late. Work ran over," he said.

She nodded and looked away. Kat never wanted to talk about his day job. He knew she didn't like the fact that he was a Marine. She hadn't said as much, but he knew it. He'd connected the pieces of information he'd been allowed about her ex and understood. Marines went to war. Some didn't come home. He knew that all too well. Getting involved with a Marine was a risk that cost too many wives, or in Kat's case, fiancées, their happily ever after.

"It's okay," she said.

Micah scanned the new group of kids. "Looks like they're all sitting down on the job. What's going on?"

Kat chuckled. "Your son is giving them another science lesson this afternoon."

Now, Micah was the one giving the quizzical look.

"Did you know that you could change the color of a plant by adding food coloring to the water?"

He dropped his head in his hands. "Yes," he groaned.

"Don't worry, the kids are into it. They've been listening to him more than they do their own teachers."

Micah looked around. Kat was right. The kids weren't making fun of Ben. They were listening. "How the heck did he do that?"

Kat lifted one shoulder. "He's got a talent for science. And teaching. He even showed them pictures. Said his seedlings are bigger than yours because he reads to them."

"Already showing up his dad. My plants are some of the best in these parts, I'll have these kids know."

"And that's why it's so amazing that Ben's are twice as good. It's scientific proof," she said, sounding just like Ben.

Micah laughed. "I don't even want to tell you what other scientific proof Ben's been coming up with these days."

Her forehead wrinkled as she looked at him.

"Apparently, Ben is proving that you and I are the perfect match. He's got a list."

This made her laugh.

"Hey. Don't act like it's so funny. The list is pretty damn convincing," Micah said.

"Yeah?" Her gaze locked on his, and suddenly there was heat radiating between them. By the look in her eyes, he could tell she felt it, too.

"Yeah," he said. His gaze slid to her hand and hung on the barren ring finger.

She pulled a gold chain with the ring dangling from it from under her blouse. "Baby steps.

It's not because of you, though," she said quickly. Then she cleared her throat. "Or it is a little, but don't worry. No strings attached."

"Right." And he hadn't been able to think of anything other than what the strings weren't attached to for the past ten days. He resisted the urge to pull her to him and run his hands down her body. This wasn't the time or the place.

His attention on her broke at the sound of screaming children.

"Fight!" Ben pointed in the direction of Sam, one of the newest members of the club, and Jacob.

Micah took off running and threw himself between them, pushing them apart with his hands.

"What do you guys think you're doing?"

"He called me a wuss!" Sam screamed.

"No, I didn't!" the other kid, Jacob, insisted, his face red and dirty from the near fight.

Micah looked at Kat, who was standing beside him now, and then back to the boys. "All right. What exactly did you say?" he asked Jacob. "Not that it matters. Fighting is never the way to solve your problems."

"I said he was *acting* like a wuss. I didn't say he *was* one."

"You see!" Sam said. "He's not my friend."

Kat stepped up beside them. "We're all friends here."

Even to Micah, it sounded like a movie-of-the-week line. "You don't have to like each other, but you can't call each other names. And no more fighting. That's what got you here in the first place."

Sam stared at his feet. "What's wrong with here? I like staying after school and working in the garden."

Micah frowned. "This is supposed to be punishment."

"You could just beat him. That's how my dad punishes me." Now, Jacob was looking at the ground.

Micah exchanged another look with Kat. She'd be calling the school's social worker later about that comment, no doubt. "Well, then how about this? You can keep coming and helping out after school as long as you want. But if you call each other names or start another fight with anyone, I'll have to put you back in that classroom with Mrs. Burroughs, writing sentences on the blackboard."

The boys groaned.

"All right, you two," Kat said. "Apologize to one another."

Sam shrugged. "I'm sorry if you are," he told Jacob.

"I'm sorry if you are, too," Jacob said.

Micah nodded. Fair enough. "Back to work, boys. Fifteen minutes until your parents get here."

Sam started to walk away, then turned back to Micah. "Did you mean it when you said we could keep coming? Even when our time is up?"

Micah nodded. "I'd hate for you to feel like you had to cause trouble just to get yourself back in the group."

Sam's face brightened. "Thanks."

Kat touched Micah's arm softly when the kids had gone back to their tasks. "I think you missed your calling, Sergeant Peterson. You're awesome with these kids."

"Not to brag, but I'm pretty awesome at all my jobs." It was supposed to be charming, but her body stiffened, and her shoulders were suddenly tense.

Yeah. She hated the fact that he was a Marine. He could only imagine how she'd look at him on Saturday when he took her to the Marine Corps ball. She'd be surrounded by uniforms. Every place she turned, she'd be faced with a reminder of what she'd lost. So far, she'd only seen him in uniform once. Most of the time they were together, he wore holey jeans and a white T-shirt while riding a lawnmower.

Or he wore nothing while she was riding him.

Things would probably change between them after Saturday's date.

He swallowed. He wasn't supposed to care. They'd agreed to no strings attached. But the more time he spent with her, the more a newfound hope began to bristle up inside him where there'd only been an empty, robotic existence over these last few years, working full-time and being a single father to a child with special needs.

He felt like he was coming alive again, living for something other than his responsibilities. He was beginning to need Kat, and that felt really good. And really terrifying at the same time.

Chapter Sixteen

K at sat on her bed and stared at her reflection across the room. Why in the world had she agreed to go to the Marine Corps ball with Micah? She felt like shoving the silky black dress back in the closet and feigning sickness. She'd be surrounded by Marines. Memories of the events she'd attended with John would be everywhere.

"You okay?" Julie stood in the doorway, watching her.

Kat attempted a smile, but it fell flat. "I'm glad you're here. I've never been any good at getting dolled up."

Julie took a step inside. "Well, the first step is hair and makeup. *Then* you put the dress on." She lifted the dress from Kat's lap and hung it on the back of the closet door.

Kat turned at Val's voice in the doorway.

"Ladies." Her friend's smile was devilish as usual. "Shall we get started?"

Kat's hands folded on her chest. "I didn't know you were coming. I thought you had something else to do."

"Well, now I don't." Val plopped a large duffel bag on the bed.

"What's that?" Kat's eyes widened as Val pulled the zipper, revealing a host of beauty products. "Am I so ugly that I need that many cosmetics?" She looked up at her best friend, whose smile deepened, poking soft dimples in her cheeks.

"No. You're beautiful. But tonight is special. It's just like Cinderella going to the ball or something."

Julie nodded in agreement. "Definitely. And you of all people deserve a Cinderella moment."

Kat smiled sincerely this time. "You girls are wonderful. You know that?"

Val and Julie looked at each other. Since Kat hadn't known that Val was coming, Julie and Val must've conspired together to make this happen. They'd hated each other since high school, but now, maybe they could become friends. Especially since her sister was staying.

"Okay." Kat looked between them. "Anyone bring the Xanax?"

Val lifted a bottle of starter wine. "This'll have to do. Only half a glass before you go because you're wearing heels, and you're clumsy in heels." She angled Kat toward the mirror and started to work, brushing Kat's thick, blond hair off her face and pinning it to her head so that she could curl one piece at a time. In their reflection, Kat looked up to meet Val's eyes. "You're a good best friend," she said quietly. "I wish we'd been better friends growing up."

"You're the best best friend." Val's brush snagged on a knot of Kat's hair.

"Ouch!"

"Oops. Sorry." Val met her gaze in the mirror. "And me, too. Think of all the trouble we could've caused back in the day."

Kat shook her head. "I never got in trouble."

"All the more reason we should've been friends. You could've kept me in line, and I could've gotten you to walk on the wild side a little. A perfect match."

Right. Just like Ben had declared she and Micah were. *A perfect match.*

"What's next?" Kat asked after Val had fixed her hair and Julie had worked magic with makeup.

"The things that go under the dress," Val said, already walking toward Kat's dresser. She got lucky on the top drawer and held up a pair of granny panties. "Is this all you have?" she asked.

"Really?" Julie said, lifting up another pair. "This looks like something Mom would wear."

Kat snatched the undergarments and tossed them back in the drawer. "I have sexy underwear, too." It's just the sexy underwear were reserved for when she'd been with John. She couldn't wear them with another man. It wouldn't be right. It'd—

Julie held up a hand. "Stop right there. Your brain is working too hard. I'll be right back."

Julie left and returned a minute later, holding up a tiny, black thong with the tags still on it. "I bought these for myself the other day. They're brand-new and they're all yours. I certainly won't be wearing them."

Val smiled approvingly. "Those are exactly what that black dress needs underneath."

"The dress is staying on tonight," Kat said, only partially convincing. She took the thong anyway. Because her clothes never seemed to stay on when she found herself alone with Micah. He seemed to have that effect on her. And after the ball tonight, she would definitely need a distraction of the sexual kind. "Fine. I'll wear these," she said.

～

MICAH POINTED A FINGER AT BEN AS HE REACHED FOR Aunt Clara's doorknob.

"I know, Dad. Listen to Aunt Clara and Uncle Rick. In bed by nine-thirty." Ben looked at Clara with a small smile that Micah wasn't supposed to be able to interpret. Yeah, he remembered being a boy at Aunt Clara's house. She'd always let him stay up at least an hour later than he was supposed to. And she'd never made him eat his dessert after dinner—he got to have it first.

Micah pointed a finger at his aunt, whose eyes widened a little. "You. Thank you."

Her expression softened. "Anything for my favorite nephew. Stay out late. All night. I've got Ben until tomorrow after breakfast."

"Yay!" Ben squealed from the kitchen table where he was supposed to be doing his homework. Micah knew the pen would stop moving as soon as he closed the door, though.

He nodded, slipping on his dark navy jacket. It was adorned with golden medals that he'd earned during his three tours in the desert. "How do I look?"

Uncle Rick entered the room as he posed the question. Pulling off his John Deere ball cap, his uncle nodded. "You look like a man who's been wrapped so tightly around a woman's finger, you can't hardly see straight." He chuckled under his breath, eyeing his wife. "I know this from experience." He pointed at his glasses. "I haven't seen straight since her."

Clara tsked. Then she shooed Micah out the door. "You look great. Just remember what I told you."

Micah nodded, even though he didn't need his aunt's advice in the dating arena. "Yes, ma'am." Glancing at Ben, he said, " 'Bye, son." Shutting the door behind him, he headed toward the Jeep. Kat should be ready by now. He didn't want to keep her waiting too long. But if she wasn't ready, he didn't mind. Tonight was about her, not him. Kat deserved to be treated right. What had Aunt Clara said? Treat her like one of his roses? Not that he planned on watering her, but he understood what Clara meant. Handle Kat with care. Admire her.

Micah smiled to himself. He'd always liked the idea of having family nearby. Being a military brat, he and his parents had moved throughout his childhood. He'd never gotten to know his cousins. Not really. And he'd never had a friend long enough to want to buy a school yearbook.

He sat behind the wheel and drove the short distance to Kat's home. He noticed two other cars as he pulled into her driveway, recognizing one as Val's. She always parked next to Kat in the school parking lot. He guessed the other car belonged to Kat's sister, Julie.

Great. There would be three women greeting him when he rang that doorbell. He sucked in a deep breath, reminding himself that the night was about Kat. That was his mantra. If she was happy, the date would be good. But Kat deserved better than good. Going to a military event wouldn't be easy for her, and agreeing to be his date was above and beyond her principal duties. At this point, if she had backed out of going to the ball, he'd still be helping with the after-school program. He liked the kids and it was something he wanted to continue doing after he was out of the Marine Corps.

He pulled on the collar of his dress blues jacket, making sure it was in place, then pressed the doorbell, hearing a scurry of female commotion inside.

The night is about Kat. About Kat. About—

She opened the door and his mind went blank. She was all he could see. All he could think about. Yeah. He definitely wouldn't have a problem following his aunt's advice. The night was definitely all about Katherine Chandler.

"You, um . . ." Words stuck in his throat. Julie and Val were staring at him. That didn't make this easier. "You ready?" he asked again, getting his thoughts out this time. All three ladies nodded, which brought a smile to his face. He was only taking the one. His gaze moved back to Kat. Whatever her female posse had done tonight, they'd somehow improved upon perfection.

She stepped forward and turned as Val stuffed a glittery clutch bag in her hand. "Have fun. *A lot* of fun."

Emphasis on "a lot." Micah reached for Kat's hand. Yeah. He was going to take his aunt Clara's advice on revolving the night around Kat. He couldn't divide his attention at this moment if he tried.

"You look amazing," he said as he helped her get into the Jeep.

She pulled her dress safely inside, then looked up. "Thank you. But it's not me. It's Julie's and Val's handiwork."

"It's you," he said, closing the door and walking around to the driver's side. As they drove, he listened to Kat's nervous chatter about her sister's and friend's efforts to get her ready for the ball.

"I've never been good at dressing up," she said. "I skipped my high school prom."

"Yeah?" He glanced over. "Why is that?"

She shrugged. "No guy. No dress."

"I find it hard to believe you couldn't find a guy to be your date."

She laughed. "I didn't say that. I just couldn't find one that I wanted to spend an entire night with."

They entered Camp Leon and the conversation suddenly lulled.

"You all right?" he asked, wondering for the millionth time if this was a bad idea. Yes, he'd needed a date for tonight, but asking Kat to be here with him was asking a lot. His gaze went to her hands, wringing absently in her lap.

She looked over and nodded unconvincingly. "Yes."

"I can turn around. We can leave and just go have fast food."

"In this?" She gestured toward her fancy dress and heels, forcing a laugh. "Really, Micah. I can do this. It'll be fine." The small smile stayed stamped on her lips, as if trying to convince him, and maybe herself, too.

She was tough. He'd give her that. It was one of the things he admired about her. He wasn't buying her tough girl act, though. Inside, she was terrified. He could see it in her eyes. It was the same fear he'd glimpsed when she'd first seen him in uniform at the school.

He was about to make the call and just turn the Jeep around. There was no way he was letting Kat go through with this for his sake. It was idiotic of him to let it get this far. "Listen," he said, lifting his foot off the gas pedal.

She reached over and placed her hand on his, as if reading his thoughts. "This is something I want to do. I need to do. I want to prove to myself that I'm strong."

He divided his attention between her and the road. "You don't need to convince me. I already know that."

A real smile, not forced, bloomed this time. "I can do this."

After a long moment, he nodded. "Okay then."

The parking lot for the Pavilion Center was crowded as they pulled in, and more vehicles spilled in behind them. He parked the car and reached across the seat to squeeze Kat's hand.

"You say the word and we're out of here, though. You promise? Leaving wouldn't make you any less strong."

She focused on their interlocked hands and then squeezed back. "Promise."

They got out and began to walk among the other couples, the women wearing fancy gowns of every color. Kat bumped up against him as they walked. He suspected it was the heels, but maybe some part of her enjoyed staying close to him, too. Or maybe, being here just made her need to be closer, which he was happy to oblige. He protected the people he cared about, and he cared about Kat.

"Hey." Micah stopped before leading her inside. "Thank you for coming with me."

She arched a brow. "Like you couldn't find a number of women to volunteer for the job."

His mouth quirked. "I'm usually the type to come alone. Easier that way."

Tilting her head, she revealed the long curve of her neck. "But not this time?"

"This time, being with someone, with you, feels right. So thanks." He faced the building again, then slid a glance in her direction, holding out an elbow. "Shall we?"

She released a wobbly breath and straightened. She was tough, just like the pink lily in his garden. Compared to everything she'd been through in the last two years, attending the Marine Corps ball was a cakewalk. "Ready," she said.

The breath whooshed out of Kat's body as she stepped through the entrance of the Pavilion Center. It was like stepping back into the past, only John wasn't with her.

Micah's grip tightened on hers. Okay. She could do this. *Maybe.*

"Just say the word," he reminded her.

She nodded and forced another smile. Her face was already starting to hurt from all the fakery. But someone had once advised her to "fake it until you make it" and she'd found that to be good advice. It'd gotten her this far.

Micah's gaze hung on hers for a long second, his dark eyes revealing that he wasn't buying her brave act for a second. "Do you want some punch?" he asked.

She nodded, hoping to God it was spiked.

"It's not spiked if that's what you're thinking," he said with a sexy smile.

Her mouth fell open. "How did you know?"

An easy laugh escaped his lips as he pulled her toward the table of treats. "Because I wondered the same thing my first time at one of these events."

This wasn't her first ball, though, she wanted to say, taking the cup he offered her. She took a timid sip and then gulped it, hoping the sugar would cause a kind of euphoria that would make her forget where she was. She glanced around at all the couples in their dress blues and sequined dresses. She'd never really enjoyed an event like this, even before John's death. It'd always felt like a lot of pressure to look just right and to make sure you said hi to all the right people. Heaven forbid you forgot someone's name or got his or her rank wrong.

She took another sip and looked at Micah. "So, who are we supposed to be mingling with?" she asked.

He shrugged, tossing his cup in the trashcan nearby. "I'm supposed to be mingling with you. That's all."

She narrowed her gaze, loving his smile and the way, when he looked at her, everyone else in the room seemed to fall away. "You don't care about appearances?" she asked.

"Sure, I do. I care that I'm exactly who I represent myself to be. Nobody different." He wobbled his head. "Now, if you'd asked who my father would prefer I be mingling with right now, then it's that crowd against the wall. Don't worry, though. I'm the CO's son. They'll all come to me."

Kat leaned in to hear him better over the crowd, and to get a better whiff of his cologne. "Why is that?"

"Because I'm the one they think they're supposed to be sucking up to. It's like a game. Not the military. The military is a noble profession. But the politics here are a game to some people, and I don't want to play."

"Then why did you bring me?" His scent begged her to touch him. She curled her fingers at her side to keep from doing so, knowing that people were watching them.

"Whatever my original reasons, they've changed. I brought you tonight because I like being around you. How's that for a motive?"

She chewed her lower lip. "I might enjoy your company, too, Sergeant Peterson." They were flirting, and she loved every second of it. Maybe being here tonight wasn't such a scary thing, after all. Not with Micah beside her.

His arm slid around her bare back, making her spine straighten. She could think of other places she'd rather be with Micah right now, though. Less formal places, where fitted dresses and high heels weren't allowed. Where no clothing was allowed and she could touch him all she wanted.

"I apologize in advance," he whispered in her ear, startling her from her thoughts.

"Apologize?" Her brows lowered. "For what?"

"For the conversation we're about to endure." He straightened and reached out his hand to the man walking toward him. "Colonel Peterson." Kat's eyes widened. *Peterson*.

The older man had the same dark brown eyes as Micah. His face was sterner than his son's, though, with his mouth set in a hard line under a crooked, eaglelike nose. The man smiled, the gesture not quite meeting his eyes, and offered a hand to Kat. "And who is this lovely lady you've brought tonight?" he asked with a rigid smile.

Micah pulled Kat even closer to him. "Katherine Chandler. She's the—"

"Principal of Seaside Elementary School," his father finished for him. "Your reputation precedes you, Ms. Chandler."

Kat's body stiffened. "Thank you. I think." She glanced, unsure, at Micah. "Nice to meet you, Colonel Peterson."

"Likewise." He straightened and studied Micah. "Have you thought about what we discussed?"

Kat watched Micah's body language change. Scanning the room, he avoided his father's eyes. "Yep."

The older man's face grew almost imperceptibly harder. "Good."

Micah's jaw ticked on one side.

Then, after a long, awkward second, Colonel Peterson's attention returned to Kat. "Have a lovely evening, Ms. Chandler. I had just taken command of Camp Leon when I first heard your name. I'm so sorry for your loss."

She swallowed, lowering her gaze from his. *That* was the reputation that had preceded her. "Thank you, sir."

"And what an honor to have you with us tonight. It's a testament to your strength." He glanced at Micah. "That's something we value here in the Corps. Strength and commitment. Perseverance."

Micah's jaw continued to tick as Colonel Peterson nodded and moved on to another couple across the room. "I'm sorry," he said when his father was out of earshot.

"You said that before he walked up."

"It's worth saying again," he said, his mood notably darker. "Are you okay?" He pulled her toward him, guiding her to look into his eyes.

"I'm fine."

"I had no idea he'd bring up—"

"It's fine. Really." She mustered a smile for Micah's sake. He looked more taken aback from the conversation than she did. "What was that other stuff about anyway?" she asked, wondering at his drastic change in demeanor. If Micah and his father hadn't resembled each other so closely, she might've guessed they were enemies rather than family. She hadn't seen her mother in several months, but when they met, it was usually with a hug. "What did he want you to think about?"

Micah shook his head, his gaze scanning over the room. "It's not important. He wanted me to think about my future in the military, and there's nothing to think about anymore. My father just doesn't know it yet."

Two hours later, after dinner and dancing, Kat wobbled on her heels as Micah pulled her through the crowd. They'd been forced to make small talk with an unfathomable number of people, but now Micah seemed to be on a mission.

Yeah. Kat wanted to ditch this place and go back to his house, too. Wanted him to touch her with those hands that had hung heavy on her back all night. Wanted him to lay her down and do all those marvelous things he'd done the last time they'd been alone together.

"Any way you can drive faster?" she asked as he drove through the military base.

His gaze slid over as a smile curled on his lips. "There's strict speed limit enforcement here. Trust me, if I speed and get caught, it'll take us a hell of a lot longer to get home."

She nodded. Right. She just needed to occupy her thoughts with something other than how good Micah looked in his dress blues. And how delicious the side of his neck had smelled when he'd held her close tonight. "So, isn't your father going to blow a gasket when he finds out you're not reenlisting?"

Micah laughed. "Are you trying to kill the mood?"

"No." She shook her head vehemently. "Sorry."

He nodded. "Yes, the good colonel is definitely going to have a tantrum worthy of a two- year-old." His smile grew bigger. "And that's my icing on the cake. The old man is going to learn that there are some things that can't be controlled. That's what he's always hated about being a father, I think."

"The lack of control?" she asked.

Micah nodded. "And I loved using that knowledge against him when I was growing up."

Kat pushed her heels off and folded her legs under her in the seat. "I think it's great that you're molding your own path, not staying in the Marines because that's what you're expected to do."

"Ben needs more stability. Maybe having a permanent home will alleviate his insistence that I need a wife."

"Can't you have both?" As soon as she said it, she knew it'd sounded like a proposition.

He cocked a brow in her direction. "I get what you mean. And yes, maybe one day. I don't want anything to take away from caring for Ben right now, though. If his own mother couldn't handle the responsibility, how can I expect someone else to?"

Kat started to answer. Ben was a great child. Any woman would be lucky to be his mother. She knew it'd only sound like she was nominating herself, though, and she wasn't. As much as she loved the little guy, she wasn't prepared to take on a ready-made family.

Instead, she touched Micah's shoulder, the desire between their bodies reigniting immediately.

He glanced over and groaned. "Hold on," he said as they drove off the base and into the cozy town of Seaside. The Jeep lurched forward as he pressed the gas. Ten minutes later, he pulled around the back of his house so that no one would know he and Kat were hiding inside. "I think that's the fastest I've ever gotten home from work."

She laughed as nervous energy bubbled up through her body like carbonation in a bottle of champagne. "Let's see how quickly we can get inside."

"Have I told you how much I adore the way you think?" he asked.

She shook her head, stepping outside and pulling her heels off to hold as she ran toward his back door. The only place he was going to catch her tonight was in his bed.

He unlocked the door and their bodies meshed together as they peeled each other's clothing off, leaving it on the floor as they continued toward the bedroom. Kat reached for his belt and started to unfasten it as he pressed her against the wall in the hallway. He kissed her until it was hard to breathe, but she didn't care. She needed the kiss more than she needed oxygen right now.

"Mmm. You feel so good," he said in a low growl that rumbled in her lower parts.

She clutched the fabric of his shirt, pulling him to her. Then she felt something else rumble.

"You're vibrating," she said, looking up at him.

He planted kisses along the side of her jaw, pressing into her even harder. "I know," he said, reaching her ear.

"No, I mean your phone is vibrating. In your pocket," she said breathlessly.

He pulled back a little and reached for his phone, glancing at the screen. His hooded eyes immediately widened and he quickly pulled it to his ear. "Uncle Rick? What's going on? Everything okay with Ben?" The rasp in his voice was suddenly gone, replaced with efficient military speech.

Kat watched his features tighten, making him look more like his stern father, as he listened.

"I'll be right there," he said, looking at Kat. He clicked a button on his phone and started collecting his clothing off the floor. "Ben's on his way to the emergency room. He fell and hit his head. I can drop you off at home and—"

She shook her head, a loose curl bouncing on her shoulder. "No. I want to come. If that's okay."

Micah hesitated and then gave a nod. "I think that'd make Ben happy." He gathered up her clothing and handed it to her, watching her as she slid back into her dress. Then they hurried back to his Jeep and raced toward Seaside Medical. It was a smaller hospital that had recently been established to meet the locals' needs. Its mother hospital was over an hour away, but the doctors at Seaside had good reputations. Many were retired military who just so happened to enjoy living a simple life on the coast.

Micah glanced over. "Thank you."

"For what?" Kat gripped the scaredy-cat handle overhead. They hadn't gone nearly this fast when they'd been rushing to his house.

"I usually go through this alone. Aunt Clara is older and she'll end up going home in an hour or so. It might be nice to have someone by my side for once."

A smile curved her lips. "You're welcome."

They took another sharp curve and she shrieked unintentionally as she fell against the window. This was not the way she'd planned on spending her night with Micah, but she was happy she could be here for him and Ben. It made her feel like she was part of something again—part of a family. Gripping the overhead handle even tighter, her heart raced along with her thoughts.

Being a part of something also meant there was more to lose.

Chapter Seventeen

The hospital smelled of disinfectant tinged with a light citrusy odor.

Kat followed Micah briskly through the halls, feeling people's eyes on them as they walked. "Aren't you going to get in trouble for wearing your uniform?" she asked.

He shrugged. "My son is in the hospital. I don't give a damn."

Right. She struggled to keep up in her heels as he held firmly to her hand and navigated past nurses and patients, past carts full of medical supplies. Ben was on the fourth floor—the children's unit. They'd skipped the ER and admitted him immediately because of his cerebral palsy diagnosis.

They stepped into an elevator and Micah pushed the button for the fourth floor. His whole body appeared tense. Even his jaw, which had been relaxed in a smile most of the night, was tight, the bulky muscle along his cheek clenching and releasing.

"He'll be okay," she whispered softly, rubbing her hand along his arm.

Micah turned to her. The heat in his eyes was gone now. To an outsider, he might look calm, cool, collected, but she knew better. He had pushed his emotions aside, like a good Marine. He was on a mission, going through the motions. "I know. This happens several times a year," he said.

"Several times a year?"

He nodded. "More when he's on a growth spurt. His bones are growing longer, but his muscles remain tight, restricting his movement. He tries to do more than he should and his muscles won't let him. Then he falls. I shouldn't have left him tonight."

"He was with your aunt, though."

"Who doesn't know his limits like I do. If I'd been there, this wouldn't have happened." He ran a hand through his cropped hair.

When the elevator stopped, she followed Micah down the hall, stopping at room 407.

"Hey there, buddy." Micah's smile was back, but the thick bulk of muscle in his jawline was still knotted. "Looks like you and the wall got into a fight."

Ben grinned, lying on his back in a white hospital bed, looking smaller and more fragile than Kat had seen him. "Actually, it was the railing of Aunt Clara's deck. I was trying to stand and look at her flowers."

"Yeah?" Micah walked up to the bed.

"She has a rabbit that's been chewing on the leaves. I was keeping a lookout for it." Ben's gaze jumped to Kat. "Did you have a good time with my dad? I'm sorry I ruined it."

"You didn't ruin it," Kat insisted, stepping closer. "We had a wonderful time."

Ben's smile stretched, making her heart ache in her chest. He was such a sweet kid. He didn't deserve his plight in life. No one deserved to have a body that didn't listen to its brain.

"I was hoping you did. I think you and my dad are perfect for one another," Ben said.

"Perfect?" she asked.

"I made a list. It proves you two should be together."

From the mind of an eight-year-old.

"Buddy, I'm more concerned about you right now." Micah sat

down on the chair beside him and pushed a hand through the boy's matted hair, revealing a bandage along his forehead.

"Stitches, huh?" Micah shook his head. "You're going to look like Frankenstein if you keep trying to stand."

"Dad." Ben's grin faded. "My legs still work. I want to use them."

"And I don't want you to end up here all the time."

Clara had been quiet since they'd entered. "It's my fault." She was seated in a chair against the window. "I told him to keep watch for me. He was glued to the window, watching for you two to come home, so I thought it'd be better if he kept a lookout for my critter instead."

The knot of muscle in Micah's jaw was pulsing again. "It's my fault. I shouldn't have left him."

"Dad." Tears formed in Ben's eyes. "You can't stay with me all the time. I'm not a baby. Tell him, Principal Chandler. You told me that I could do whatever I set my mind to. That my disability shouldn't hold me back. Tell him."

Her mouth fell open. "I . . . You *can* do what you want, Ben—when you're an adult. But right now you have to listen to your father."

"Why? He doesn't listen to me." Ben folded his arms at his chest.

"Ben—" Micah started.

"No. It's true. You treat me like a baby. I'm eight. I'm not a little kid anymore."

"Right now, you're still a child." Micah's voice grew stern, the knotted muscle in his jaw ticking harder, faster.

Kat's heart ached as she watched Ben's lower lip quiver.

"I just want you to be happy." Ben's voice was as fragile as his bandaged body.

Okay, Kat thought. She should leave. She was Ben's principal, not family.

"I'm happy with you," Micah said, taking Ben's hand. "It's just you and me, kid. Isn't that enough?"

Ben looked away, staring off past the tinted hospital windows. "No."

Heart breaking, Kat took a tiny step backward. This was a private family moment and she didn't belong, even if she'd relished the idea of being part of this group of people on the way here.

She started to back away and then her heel caught on the foot of the mobile table that held Ben's food. *Damn heels.* With a high-pitched squeal, she started to fall backward, landing with a hard thud before she could even try to catch herself. All the attention turned to her, splayed on the floor in a fitted black dress, pain shooting up her body from an indistinguishable place.

"Ma'am, are you all right?" A nurse who'd witnessed the fall hurried to Kat's side.

"I'm fine." But that was a lie. She wasn't fine. Her ankle had twisted in her high-heel shoe as she'd gone down. And her heart was more than a little shattered at the father-son moment she'd just watched play out. Her ego was a little damaged now, too.

She tried to stand. "Ouch, ouch, ouch!"

Taking hold of her hand, Micah helped her as she wobbled on one good leg, maneuvering her to the seat where he'd been sitting. "You two are trying to kill me tonight, aren't you?"

"I'll see if I can find a doctor to take a look," the nurse said, hurrying out of the room.

Kat clutched her ankle. "I'm sorry. I don't know what happened."

"You were trying to leave," Ben said. "I scared my mother away and now I'm scaring you, too."

"No." Kat shook her head. "That's not it. I thought you and your dad could use some time alone." She swallowed thickly, the ache in her chest overriding the pain in her ankle.

The door opened and a doctor wearing a white lab coat and a stethoscope walked in. "Two patients in one room, huh? Are you Ben's stepmother?"

Kat shook her head quickly. "No."

"Not yet." Ben was smiling again. "But I'm working on it."

The doctor nodded, the skin between his eyes slightly pinched, but he was too busy to ask. He grasped Kat's ankle, causing her to flinch in pain. "Sprained," he said efficiently. "We'll have the nurse wrap it and get you some ice. No high heels for a few months."

She laughed lightly. "That's fine with me." She might never wear high heels again. Her gaze caught on Micah's as the doctor headed out the door. Worry replaced the hunger she'd seen in his eyes earlier in the night. A deep, impenetrable worry that she knew too well. She didn't have children, but she worried about them. She took their fears and burdens home with her every night.

If her ankle wasn't swelling to the size of a small grapefruit right now, she would have walked over to him and placed her hand on his shoulder.

"Did you guys at least get to kiss?" Ben asked, looking between them. "I didn't ruin the good-night kiss, did I?"

Micah looked between Kat and his son. "You must've hit your head pretty hard to ask your principal a question like that one."

Ben's laughter was light. "I have a hard head, Dad. You should know that by now."

Micah leaned forward and ruffled the boy's dark hair. "Yeah. I know that. Just like your old man."

"Sooo?" Ben flashed another toothless smile. "Did you?"

KAT'S CHEEKS BURNED AS SHE REMEMBERED THE MANY kisses they'd had in the hallway right before the call from Micah's uncle. And if not for Ben's little fall, they'd be in bed on round number three right about now.

She stood on wobbly legs. "I'll just go sit outside." Before she could embarrass herself any further tonight. "I'm glad you're all right, Ben," she said.

"You, too, Principal Chandler," Ben called back.

MICAH WAITED UNTIL BEN WAS SLEEPING BEFORE slipping out of the small hospital room and dialing his father's number. He'd missed three calls in the hour he'd been in Ben's room.

"Hey, Dad? You called?"

There was a long pause.

"It's two o'clock in the morning. Don't tell me you're just now getting your lady friend home," his father finally said, a tone of disdain evident.

Micah ground his teeth. "We're at the ER. Ben had a fall."

Another long pause.

"He okay?" his father asked.

"Yeah. Just an overnighter." Not that his father really cared. "Why'd you call, Dad?"

"I didn't realize you were seeing that Chandler woman."

"Just friends. Is this the reason you called? To interrogate me on my love life? Because I have better things to do right now."

"I don't think it's wise of you to connect yourself to that woman, sad as her story is. There'll be talk, and it won't have anything to do with you. I don't see how that can be a positive thing for your reputation."

"I don't care about my reputation, Dad. You know that."

His father took his time answering. "Do you care about hers? I happen to know she's working hard to polish her own image. Word has it that if she doesn't, she'll be out of a job next year, thanks to a few unfortunate incidents at the school."

Blood was drumming in Micah's ears. How did his father even know about Kat or what she was going through at the small elementary school? He shouldn't be surprised, though. His father knew everything that was happening in this town.

"Being seen with the father of one of her students, a man who *works* for her, that might not be too glowing for Ms. Chandler's image, wouldn't you agree? And, really, son, hasn't the poor woman been through enough?" There was a fake air of concern in his voice.

Micah knew the truth, though. His father was only pointing

any of this out because he hated the fact that Micah took "menial" jobs around town. It wasn't the Marine way—not if he expected to get anywhere in his career. Far be it from his father to understand that maybe Micah wanted something different for his life. Maybe he wanted a job that didn't take him away for months at a time. Maybe he wanted his son to look at him with admiration rather than the wariness that Micah had grown to have around his own father.

Or maybe, just maybe, Micah wanted a wife who didn't cry herself to sleep at night the way his own mother had done when his father stayed out too late "working," or whatever the hell he'd been doing back then.

A wife?

"Dad, Kat's personal life is none of your business," Micah said through tight lips.

"*You* are my business, son." His father's voice hardened, like a commander talking to his infinite inferior. "And whether you like it or not, what you do affects my career, too. Make sure whatever you have going on with that woman doesn't pull our family name down. Understand?"

Micah forced himself to take a calming breath, and not to punch the wall beside him. He couldn't help being bullied by the old man when he was a child, but now things were different. "If that's all, I have a son who needs me."

"I see." A long beat hung between them. "We'll speak tomorrow," his father said. Then the phone clicked and an empty dial tone replaced the silence.

Micah growled low in his throat, stuffing his phone back in his pocket. "You okay?" Kat was leaning against the wall, watching him.

His gaze flicked to her ankle. "I could ask you the same."

"Just a sprain. I'll be fine."

Which was what she was always pretending to be with him. Fine.

"The bandages look nice with your dress." He attempted a smile, but the night had been too long.

She limped closer. "You looked angry just now."

He nodded and tapped his pocket, where his cellphone was. "My dad, the control freak."

Her lower lip puckered slightly. The movement made him wish they were back at his place, doing what they should have been doing instead of spending the evening here in the ER. This was his life, though. It wasn't his every day, but Ben had medical issues that other children didn't. And anyone who was going to be in their lives needed to know that.

His gaze moved to Kat, assessing her. "You disappeared for a while."

"I thought I'd give you guys some privacy."

"You didn't have to leave. Ben missed you." He stared at her. He'd missed her, too.

"I checked in on him just now," she said, taking an unsteady step closer. "I'm glad he's feeling better. He gave us quite a scare, didn't he?"

"He does that from time to time." His gaze held hers, and some part of him waited for her to run away. To tell him that she couldn't do this anymore, whatever this was. That's what Jessica had done. It's what Nicole had also done.

Instead of running, though, Kat took another step closer to him. "I don't scare easily," she said, standing in front of him now. "And Ben's worth it."

Something in his chest shifted as she said those words. This was more than sex between them. He'd known it, deep down, but part of him had been waiting for Kat to realize what she was getting herself into. This was what any woman he dated seriously would be getting herself into, and they needed to know that.

She reached her hand toward his. "Come on. I'll go back to the room with you," she said.

"Are you sure?" He stood, pulling her against him. "I can take you home. He's resting now." Shaking her head, she beamed up at him, looking more beautiful than he'd ever seen her.

"I'm not going anywhere."

～

Kat closed the front door quietly behind her the next morning, not wanting to wake Julie down the hall.

"All night long?" a voice said behind her.

Kat screamed and whirled around, her hands flying to her chest. "What—?" Her brows furrowed. Val and Julie were crumpled together on the couch, bleary-eyed and waiting for her. "Are you guys trying to kill me?" she asked, attempting to catch her breath.

"No. Just get you laid. Which, judging by the hour, you did in spades." Val waggled her eyebrows.

Kat set her purse on the coffee table and plopped down on the couch between the girls, still wearing her gown from the ball. "Wrong. We spent the night at the ER."

Julie's gaze dropped to Kat's bandaged ankle now. "What happened to you?"

Kat waved a hand. "We didn't go to the ER because of me. Ben had a fall."

Now Val was gasping. "Is he okay?"

"Yes. Just a bump on the head and some stitches. No concussion, but they're keeping him overnight just in case. Micah is heading back to the hospital to be with him."

"Of course," Julie whispered, frowning disappointedly. "So, you were there all night?" she asked, lifting a brow. "No juicy details at all?"

Kat shook her head. "None to speak of."

"The kid has some timing, huh?" Val said, puckering her lower lip.

"But it's okay. He's worth it," Kat said, repeating the words she'd said to Micah earlier at the hospital. And she'd meant them. She adored Ben. He was a good kid with a good heart. She was lucky to be a part of his and Micah's life.

Julie and Val exchanged a glance.

"What?" Kat asked, looking between them. "Why are you guys looking at each other that way? Did I miss something?"

"You're drooling over the guy. The ring on your finger has suddenly moved to your neck. And now you're talking about the kid as if he were your own." Julie pointed a finger. "You're falling for him."

This made Kat laugh. "Love? No way. I like him. A lot. And I'm a principal. I happen to enjoy children. It's my job."

Val and Julie exchanged another knowing look that made Kat squirm, because they were more right than they were wrong. Her feelings for Micah had definitely deepened over the past few weeks, and even though she hadn't thought she was ready, her heart didn't seem to care.

She yawned forcefully, hoping the girls would buy it. She couldn't talk about this with them. There was nothing to talk about. Not right now, when she was still figuring things out for herself. Val's lips puckered. "I want to hear more details about the naked part. How early can I wake you?"

"You're staying the night?" Kat asked, noticing the extra blankets arranged on the couch now.

"A regular sleepover. And don't think for a moment about skipping any of the details," Val said.

Kat started down the hall, her ankle immediately reminding her of what a klutz she was.

"Don't wake me before noon. It's Sunday."

When she got to her room, she dropped her dress on the floor and climbed into bed in just her black thong underwear and lace bra, too tired to shuffle through her dresser drawers for a pair of pajamas. She lay there, eyes wide open, thinking about what her best friend and sister had just said.

She was falling for Micah—another Marine.

But he was getting out of the Corps and making Seaside his forever home, which meant that maybe falling for him wasn't such a bad thing. In fact, maybe falling in love with Micah was one of the most right things she'd done for herself in a very long time.

Chapter Eighteen

The three women sat at the kitchen table the next morning and stared at each other over their coffee mugs, none of them saying a word. Kat's phone lay at the center of the table, where she'd placed it after playing the voice message on speakerphone.

"What are you going to do?" Val finally asked, her hair sticking up around her face from sleep.

That was the big question. While Kat had been out at the Marine Corps ball last night, falling in love with another soldier, her late fiancé's mother had called and left her a voicemail, asking her to call her back. Saying they needed to talk.

Kat shook her head, holding her coffee mug close to her lips. "I'm not sure," she said. "I haven't seen Rita since the funeral." Which was crummy in and of itself. She should've been there for the woman who was set to be her future mother-in-law. Seeing Rita had seemed too hard, though. She'd needed to stay strong, the way John would've wanted her to be. Except now, looking back, avoiding Rita had been weak.

Julie reached for one of the cheese Danishes that Val had made earlier in the morning and took a bite, her eyes rolling back in her head as she did. Licking her lips, she agreed. "You have to call her back. That's the only thing to do."

Kat nodded numbly. The right thing was always the harder thing. It'd be so much easier to pretend like she'd never gotten the message. She was moving on, getting stronger, falling in love—the last thing she needed was to get dragged back into the past. "You're right." She looked between her friend and her sister. "Rita sounded good, right?"

"Oh, yeah," Julie agreed, licking her fingers now, too. "Cheerful even. She probably just wants to make sure you're okay."

"You think?" Kat asked, hearing the hopeful lift in her tone of voice. "After two years?"

"Or she wants to make sure you're still pining over her son. Make sure you're not sporting the after-sex glow." Val's brows waggled. "Which you are, by the way."

Kat's heart dropped. "The after-sex glow?"

Val snickered. "You've been sporting the look for the past couple weeks. Did you think no one noticed?"

Julie nodded again, reaching for another Danish. How did her sister get blessed with such a good metabolism, and Kat didn't?

"It's true," Julie said, between chews. "I'm kind of jealous, actually. I have to do an hour of yoga for my skin to look that way."

Kat didn't protest this time. The jig was up. She had been sporting the after-sex glow, and a completely different kind of glow that she hadn't even recognized. She was happy. Not just surviving and proving to everyone around her that she was strong. No. She was doing well in her job as principal of Seaside, no matter what a handful of people might argue. Her sister was home and getting along with her best friend. And she was dating a man who could possibly turn into something more.

"Why are you smiling?" Val asked, waving a hand in front of her to get her attention. "Did you decide what you're going to do about the voicemail?"

Kat blinked and looked at the phone again. "Julie's right. The only thing to do is call Rita back and find out what she wants. It's probably nothing."

Val picked up the phone and handed it over. "No time like the present. And we've got your back. Do it right now. It'll be just like ripping off a Band-Aid—quick and easy."

At this, Julie nodded again. Kat frowned at the two of them. From sworn enemies to practically clones, minus the fact that one was endlessly perky and the other eternally sarcastic.

Kat sucked in a deep breath and smiled at the support system sitting around her kitchen table. She could do this. She could totally do this.

Her insides twisted as she looked at the phone. "I can't," she said, standing and moving away from the kitchen table. "Not right now." She forced a smile and looked at her sister and friend again. "But I will. Later. Right now, I promised Micah that I'd meet him and Ben for pizza after Ben is discharged from the hospital. I need a shower and clothes, and . . ." Courage, like the scarecrow.

"You're stalling," Val said, matter-of-factly.

Hell, yeah, I'm stalling. But it'd been two years. What was another few hours? She'd call tonight, Kat promised herself. She wouldn't sleep until she'd returned that call. With a nod, she excused herself to go get ready to meet Micah and Ben. They were her future. Her past could wait.

∾

BEN WAVED AT HIS OCCUPATIONAL THERAPIST, A YOUNG woman with long blond hair and milky white skin. He hadn't minded this woman stretching his left arm, whereas he usually put up a fight with Micah.

Micah pushed his wheelchair down the hall toward the elevator, ready to say goodbye and good riddance to the hospital for now. It'd been a long twelve hours.

"Where's Principal Chandler?" Ben asked, craning his neck to glance at Micah behind him. "Shouldn't she be with you?"

Micah grinned as he pressed the down arrow for the elevator. Just hearing her name these days was enough to make him smile.

And it felt good—damn good. The doors to the elevator opened and he pushed Ben inside. "Why would she be with me?" he asked.

"Because you guys fell in love last night, right?"

Micah's heart clenched. "It takes a lot more than one date to make two people fall in love, son."

"I know that," Ben said with an exaggerated tone. "But you guys have spent time together at the Friendship Club. And this was actually your second date. The first one was to the Veterans' Center."

"Are you keeping tabs on me?" Micah once-overed Ben as the elevator jerked to a stop. "We had a nice time, okay? And Principal Chandler called this morning to see how you were doing. We're having lunch with her when we leave here. How's that? Satisfied?"

Ben's right arm punched the air as he cheered. "I knew the Marine Corps ball would seal the deal. Women like dancing. It's very romantic."

Tousling his son's hair, Micah laughed. "They also like know-it-all third graders, apparently. Or at least Kimberly Flowers does." Micah bent forward to watch Ben's cheeks redden, and smiled to himself.

"She's cool, that's all. Even if she did draw those pictures of me. I know that's just how girls flirt."

Micah pushed the wheelchair out of the front entrance of the hospital and stopped, walking around to meet Ben's face. "Kimberly drew those pictures?" he asked, not sure he understood his son correctly.

Ben nodded, his gaze dropping a little. "Don't worry, Dad. She said she was sorry. She even drew one of me wearing a superhero cape to make up for it, so . . ." He shrugged, swiping at his unruly hair and meeting Micah's gaze again. "Don't say anything to her, okay? We're . . . friends now."

"Friends?" Micah studied Ben's face. Ben had a friend. He nodded and returned to pushing Ben's chair, navigating through the parking lot toward his Jeep Cherokee in the back. No wonder Ben hadn't ratted out his bully. He had a crush on her. And she apparently had one on him, too. Which was good news, despite the tightening of his gut. His son was growing up.

After helping Ben into the Jeep, Micah started the engine and pulled out of the hospital parking lot. The ride was unusually quiet, considering Ben's mood. Micah's gaze jumped to the rearview mirror. "Everything okay back there?"

"Did you . . . tell Mom I was in the hospital?" Ben finally asked.

Micah gave his head a hard shake. "She's in the desert, buddy. I tried, but . . ." He didn't need to finish his sentence. "I'll try again later. Just to let her know you're okay."

Ben shrugged, his right shoulder going higher than his weaker left arm. "No big deal. I'm fine now."

Micah watched from the rearview as Ben stared out the back passenger window. He was fine physically maybe. But emotionally, Ben's mother was across the world and unavailable to even know what was going on with her only child. That wasn't fine.

Pulling into the parking lot for Kirk's Pizza House, Micah said, "What do you say we go see Principal Chandler and have pizza?"

A slow smile crawled across Ben's pale face. "The hospital food wasn't good. I am kind of hungry. And I'm sure Principal Chandler wants to see for herself how I'm doing today."

Micah nodded. "I'll bet she does." He scanned the crowded lot for Kat's car, hoping she'd remembered. Their conversation had been rushed this morning and it would be easy for it to slip her mind. Spotting the black Mazda, a small rush of adrenaline shot through him. She'd come, just like she said she would. That was Kat, true to her word, dependable, and . . . his.

She waved as Ben wheeled his chair toward her. Ben didn't beg Micah to push him when Kat was around. He was Mr. Independent. In fact, since school had started, he'd gotten to value his independence a lot more.

"Well, you look like you're feeling much better this morning," Kat said, meeting Ben's high five.

"One thousand percent better." Ben took his place beside her and rolled up to the front entrance of Kirk's Pizza House, leaving Micah to walk behind them, watching the two together, as casual as a mother and child would be—something Ben had never truly experienced.

Micah's heart gave a hard squeeze.

Don't mess this up, his mind growled. *For you or Ben.* Because from where he was standing, things were working out perfectly.

~

AN HOUR LATER, KAT WALKED OUT OF KIRK'S PIZZA House feeling better than she had this morning. "You're sure you can't come to our house?" Ben asked, his honey-colored eyes pleading with her as he wheeled beside her.

She shook her head. She had things to do, like stare at her phone and try to muster her courage to return Rita's call. "I can't. But I'll see you at school tomorrow, okay?"

"Ben needs to be resting anyway. Doctor's orders. Right, buddy?" Micah's gaze moved from Ben's to hers, and her whole body warmed. She'd much rather be spending the afternoon with him. They'd been interrupted after they'd left the ball last night, and her body was begging to finish what they'd started.

"Right," Ben said, the enthusiasm drained from his voice.

No kid wanted to be told to rest.

Kat laughed lightly, feeling compelled to lean in to the sexy man in front of her. To kiss him.

They were in the awkward stage of going public with something that had been their own little secret for the last few weeks. Micah was still a parent of one of her students and some people would undoubtedly talk. Those people were talking about her anyway, though. About her past and how they thought she was doing as the school's principal. She might as well give them something juicier to talk about.

"I hope you're not going to the school," Micah said, stepping closer to her as they stood beside her car. "All work and no play," he teased, reminding her of when they'd first met. They'd definitely advanced beyond that point.

She smiled, looking up at him now. "No. Just a little work at home in my bed tonight. Principals need their rest, too," she said loud enough for Ben to hear.

Micah nodded, then angled Ben's chair away from them and took yet another step closer to her. "Close your eyes, little man," he called behind him, soliciting a whine from Ben.

"Aww!"

When Ben had dutifully obeyed, Micah bent and softly kissed her lips, cradling a hand behind her head.

In public. For all of Seaside to see.

"You guys are kissing. I know it," Ben said, desperately trying to turn and see them. "I can hear the kissing sounds."

Pulling back, Kat laughed, her insides lit up like one of the Christmas trees of her childhood.

Micah smiled at her, slow and easy, seemingly unbothered by their public display. Yeah, screw anyone who wanted to talk. Kissing him had felt good—too good for it to ever be bad. "Get your rest. I'll call you later," he said, holding her gaze for a long moment. His was a phone call she'd look forward to. The other one she needed to make—not so much.

Stooping beside the wheelchair, she kissed Ben's cheek, making a loud smack with her lips just to tease him. "You need to get your rest, too. Principal's orders."

A dimpled grin replaced his frown. "I will. I'm helping out after school tomorrow, so it'll be a long day," he said, sounding like a little adult.

"That's right."

Micah reached for her hand, sweeping his thumb along the back and sending shivers up her spine before stepping forward and opening her car door for her. The gesture felt different than any he'd ever done. The kiss and the way he was looking at her felt different, too. *No strings attached* was definitely turning into something more. It'd turned into something more a long time ago.

"'Bye," she said, pulling her car door shut as girlish excitement bubbled up inside of her. She'd expected that last night would change things between them. Expected that being at another military event with Micah would make her see him differently, that it'd remind her that he was something she never wanted to be a part of again.

Watching him with his son now, though, she definitely wanted to be a part of his life. Marine or not, it didn't matter. What mattered was the man.

Later that night, after staring at her phone with her finger hovering over the redial button, Kat tossed it on the pillow beside her and reached for a stack of papers for work. She couldn't very well call Rita with Micah on the brain. Much better to have a brain dulled by paperwork for that conversation.

A knock on her door made her look up from the papers. "Come in."

Julie opened the door and leaned against the doorway. "Hey. Just checking on you. Making sure you're all right."

"Of course I am. Why wouldn't I be?" Kat asked a little too quickly, a telltale sign that she wasn't okay. The weight of Rita's phone call was gnawing at her.

Julie gave her an assessing look. "Oh, I don't know. John's mother called you last night."

Kat shrugged, wishing she felt as nonchalant about it as she tried to pretend she was. "I'm sure it's no big deal."

Julie's gaze moved to the phone beside her. "Which means you haven't called her back yet." Kat shook her head. "Nope. Not yet. But I will. Just as soon as I finish this stuff up."

Julie's eyes narrowed. "It's already past nine."

Checking the watch on her wrist, Kat grimaced. "I guess you're right. Tomorrow then. I'll call her tomorrow."

Julie's gaze told her she wasn't buying it. "Val said you've been invited to a support group at the Veterans' Center. That might be something to think about."

"Why?" Kat asked. "You haven't been here, Julie, but I'm fine.

Better than fine. You're sleeping in the master bedroom that John and I shared. And this ring has moved off my finger." Kat pulled the chain around her neck to show her sister. "There is absolutely no need to worry about me, okay?"

"There never is," Julie said flatly.

"What is that supposed to mean?"

Julie took a step inside the room. "It just means that you're always so in control. So together. It's human to fall apart sometimes, sis."

Kat tilted her head. She knew her sister was just trying to help, and she appreciated the concern. But she was fine—most days. Softening her voice, she said, "I have fallen apart, and I've pieced myself back together. Truly. I will call Rita back tomorrow. Time just slipped away from me today."

Julie nodded. "Okay." She started to walk out and then turned. "I'm about to watch a movie on TV. Want to join me?"

"A black-and-white romance?" Kat asked warily.

"Yeah, so?" Julie asked, feigning insult as she crossed her arms at her chest.

Kat laughed. "Maybe next time. Thanks, though. I'm really glad you're home."

Julie smiled. "Me, too."

"And next time I fall apart, I will definitely call you."

"You've put me back together so many times. I'd love to pay you back one day. Good night."

She winked, and then shut Kat's bedroom door.

"Good night." Kat stared at her closed door for a long moment. She hadn't lied. Everything was going perfect right now, better than perfect. And she was fine. She didn't need to go to a support group to handle her issues, because she didn't have any that she couldn't handle on her own.

So, why hadn't she called Rita back? And why was there still an unopened box of John's things sitting on top of her dresser?

Chapter Nineteen

Aunt Clara tapped Micah's plate with her long wooden spoon. "Eat," she demanded, gesturing toward his roasted vegetables, fresh from her own backyard.

Ben was already halfway through his meal, barely stopping to breathe.

"Chew or you'll choke," Micah warned, tapping Ben's plate now.

"And we certainly don't want to make another visit to the emergency room tonight," Clara said, lifting a brow. "I swear you took ten years off my life last night, child." Ben looked up from his plate.

"Sorry," he said through a mouth full of food.

This made Clara laugh. "Don't be. Just don't ever do that again, okay?"

"I promise." Ben smiled widely.

Micah wanted to add that Ben shouldn't make promises he couldn't keep, either, but with the way things were looking up these days, maybe it was true. He stabbed at a stalk of broccoli on his plate. "Where's Uncle Rick tonight?"

"Oh, he's got a newcomer's car to work on. She broke down at the fire station."

"Sounds like him."

Clara offered a wobbly smile. "You have to love a man who loves to help others. It's one of the things that made me fall in love with him." She sipped from her glass of sweet tea. "So, you and your lady friend seem to be doing well." Her brows lifted as she looked at him, silently soliciting details.

Details he didn't want to spill in front of Ben.

Micah glanced over at his son. "How about you go eat the rest of your meal in front of the TV, buddy?" he said.

Ben's eyes widened and his fork stopped in midair. "We don't eat in front of the TV in this family. Ever. And I want to hear whatever you're going to say. If Principal Chandler is going to be my stepmom, I want to know."

Micah sighed heavily. "Go eat. And take slow bites." He pointed toward the living room.

With a groan, Ben backed up his wheelchair and began rolling forward, careful to keep his plate balanced on his lap. "I want you to know that families aren't supposed to eat in front of the television. That's what the school counselor says," he called behind him without looking back.

"Yeah, well this'll be our family secret then, okay?" Micah waited until Ben was out of the room. "And turn up the volume really loud," he shouted after a few minutes, glancing back at his aunt, who was frowning at him. "He already thinks Kat and I are the perfect match. And now he's talking about stepmoms. I just don't want him to get his hopes up any more than they already are."

Clara's knowing eyes softened. "Because it might not work out between you two?" she asked between chews.

"I haven't exactly made the best choices for my family in the past. Jessica. Nicole." He shook his head. "Kat is wonderful, but she might not be ready for something so"—he hesitated, tossing another glance in Ben's direction—"complicated."

Setting her fork down, Clara shook her head. "Seems to me that Kat is stronger than most. Look at what she's already survived. And your life is no more complicated than her own."

Micah moved his food around on his plate, knowing his aunt was right. Aunt Clara was always right.

"I wouldn't have pegged you as a coward, Micah Daniel Peterson," she said then.

His gaze jumped up. "A coward?" Few people in his life had labeled him as such. Actually, no one had ever accused him of cowardice to his face. "I'm not. I'm just being cautious. Ben is fragile and, as his father, I want to protect him."

"Just him?" she asked.

He didn't answer.

"You're only alone if you choose to be, son. But making that choice for Ben, well, that's what your father did to you. It takes more than one person to raise a child. Especially one like Ben."

Meaning a child with special needs. "That's why it's important to only put people in his life who'll stick," he said.

"And what makes you think Kat won't stick?"

The question made his throat and chest tighten. The thing was, he was pretty damn sure that Kat *was* the kind of person who would stick. She was loyal to the core. And she seemed to adore Ben as much as he adored her. She worked with kids for a living, and knew exactly what kind of responsibilities came along with caring for a child with cerebral palsy.

So maybe Aunt Clara was right and he was having a moment of cowardice. Seeing Kat and Ben act so close earlier in the day at Kirk's Pizza House had been wonderful. And yet slowly, for the rest of the day, he'd let doubts settle in. What if this didn't last? What if Ben got his heart broken yet again? What if he did?

Needing some air, Micah pushed his chair back from the table and stood. "I'll be at home. Call me when you're ready for me to walk over and get Ben."

"He's fine here." Clara's hand covered his. "I want to help you take care of him. Let me."

The words tightened around his heart, squeezing it so hard that he couldn't say anything. His five-foot-one aunt had already called him a coward. The last thing he needed was to be called tenderhearted or some other sissy label right now. Instead, he kissed her forehead and walked next door to the house he planned on growing old in. The question was, would he grow old alone here? Or would he trust his heart, and his son's, to love one more time?

⁓

KAT HURRIED TOWARD THE BACK OF THE SCHOOL THE next day. Her parent conference had run longer than expected, making her late to the Friendship Club. Today was Kimberly Flowers's last day, which should've been a relief, but Kim wasn't who she'd pretended to be. She was a sweet girl, and over the last couple weeks, she'd become a good friend to Ben.

Kat stepped up beside the school's counselor, Liam Blakely, and nudged him softly. "Thanks for covering. Any problems?" she asked.

"Not one." The young counselor looked at her. "A lot of these kids frequented my office last year, but my room has been eerily quiet over the last couple months. I'd say this club is making a difference."

This made Kat smile. "Don't give me any credit. Micah Peterson is the one who put these kids' hands in the dirt. And Ben taught them to talk to the plants."

Liam's brow lifted. "Talk to the plants?"

"Oh. I thought you knew. Apparently, there's research behind it." She giggled lightly, realizing how silly it sounded. "Some of these kids didn't feel like they could talk to anyone. But they do talk to the plants."

His head wobbled back and forth. "We could just fill my office with a bunch of ferns, and I'll go on vacation."

Kat eyed him playfully. "You're full of great ideas, Mr. Blakely. And where would you go if I let you escape this place for a second?"

He shrugged. "Anywhere with waves."

"The waves in Seaside will have to suffice because we need you too much here. A potted fern could never take your place." She surveyed the group, and then her breath caught when she saw Mayor Flowers walking through the grass to come pick up his daughter. "Crap," she muttered, tugging on her blouse.

"What?" Liam followed her gaze and he instinctively straightened, also.

"Mayor," she said, meeting him halfway and forcing her best smile. "I didn't expect you here."

The mayor didn't smile. "Kimberly is done today, is that correct?" he asked with unabashed irritation.

Kat nodded. "Yes, sir. She's served her time and, I have to say, I think she's enjoyed it."

He narrowed his beady gaze. "I understand why she had to stay, Ms. Chandler. And I respect the fact that you didn't give my daughter a free ride. But if I'm going to continue to support you, then you need to clean up your act."

Kat's brow lowered. *Clean up my act?* "I'm sorry?"

The mayor gestured toward the children. "You have these kids working on school grounds, I hear? I also hear that you're dating an employee now, too? That you two were seen kissing in a public parking lot like a bunch of hormone-ravaged teens."

News travels fast in Seaside.

~

KAT'S BODY STIFFENED. "WHAT I DO IN MY PERSONAL time is none of your business, sir. And Micah . . . um, Sergeant Peterson, is the school's groundskeeper, which is a position contracted and paid for by the county." She was also paid by the county, but she hoped Mayor Flowers wouldn't get technical. "So, he's not really an employee directly under my supervision." At least not one that worked inside the building.

The mayor shook his head, looking disappointed. A few months ago, that look would've shattered her to the core. Her goal had been to prove to everyone that she was the right person for the job. To make a difference at SES, so that everyone would know she was capable.

And she had made a difference this year. She knew it in her heart, which was all she really needed.

"Kimberly," the mayor called, soliciting the young girl's attention. Kimberly looked back and frowned. Then she grabbed her book bag and reached inside to give Ben a folded piece of paper before running toward her father.

"Let's go," he said to his daughter, returning his gaze to Kat. "I want to support you because I believe in you. I always have. But public appearance is just as important as what's inside your heart, Ms. Chandler. More important when it comes to staying put."

She wanted to argue that the mayor's reputation wasn't the shiniest, but she held her tongue. She was better than that, better than the way he dealt with things. "See you later, Kimberly," she said instead, flashing the girl a genuine smile and watching them walk away. When they were out of range, Kat blew out a breath and let her shoulders relax.

"Yeah, I wouldn't want your job for a second," Liam said, stepping up beside her. "Why don't you head out early? I can handle the rest," he offered. "Even principals need a break every now and then, right?"

She stared at him. A lot of people had told her that lately. The business card that'd been burning a hole in her purse, and her thoughts, especially since Julie had brought it back up, came to mind. The Veterans' Center's director had handed Kat the card two months earlier, telling her to stop by sometime.

Kat had put off going, telling herself she didn't have the time or the need to go. But ever since receiving that phone call from John's mother, the support group for Marine widows had been at the forefront of her mind. A strong woman would've called Rita back by now, so why hadn't she? Maybe she needed to go and talk to other people who'd experienced the same kind of loss that she had.

"You sure?" she asked, glancing over at Liam.

"Gotta earn my keep somehow, don't I? See you tomorrow, Principal Chandler."

She nodded. Okay. She'd go to the support group. And maybe it wouldn't be the worst thing in the world.

A half hour later, Kat stared at her watch, hesitating behind the closed door. She was five minutes late. Being late was a pet peeve, and a perfect excuse for turning right around and going back to her car.

Deciding to come here had been a temporary moment of insanity. She didn't need to be here. And, really, how would talking about John's death help anything? People had been telling her to move on and stop talking about it for the last two years.

Right. So she'd just be leaving now.

"Kat. You came." Allison Carmichael, the Veterans' Center's director, seemed to appear out of nowhere. "I thought your schedule wouldn't allow you to be here at this time."

Yeah. That had been the excuse. And it would've worked if she hadn't had a lapse in judgment. "Well, it looks like I'm late anyway, so I'll um . . ." She rolled her lips together, glancing past Allison's shoulders to the glimmering beacon of hope right above the facility's double doors—the exit sign.

"Nonsense. The group is just about to get started. They like to kick off by having coffee and refreshments. Here." She opened the door and gently pushed Kat inside. "I'll introduce you to everyone."

It was nearly as bad as walking into the Marine Corps ball the other night. All eyes suddenly turned to watch her, as she walked in with feet like lead. She wanted to turn around and walk right back out, but something about the eyes staring back at her . . . haunted and full of hope . . . lured her to continue forward. "Hi," she whispered, swallowing hard.

The woman at the center of the circle stood and smiled warmly. "Katherine Chandler. We're glad to have you."

Kat nodded, the words sticking in her throat. "Please, call me Kat." Conveniently, there was one empty seat, welcoming her to sit down. She did, and then something else happened—she started talking. And even if her story had been heard before, people listened and they understood because they'd all been through the same unspeakable horror of losing a loved one to war.

"He's never coming home. I know that." Kat's hand went to the ring she wore on her neck. "And I need to let go. Really let go, if I ever want to move forward."

When she left the meeting, she felt like a weight had been lifted. A big, oversized weight that she hadn't even realized she'd been carrying. And just like releasing a balloon, she left her story in the support group. It didn't define her, even if it'd always be a part of her.

"Will you come again?" an older Hispanic woman asked as they walked out into the front room together.

Kat hesitated and then nodded. "Yes. I think maybe I will."

"Good. See you later then." The woman waved and walked into the parking lot.

Kat planned on following just as soon as she made one very important phone call that couldn't wait another second. Pulling out her phone, she ignored the green blinking light that signaled about a thousand voice messages, scrolling through until she found Rita Cruise's contact number. With a steady hand, she dialed.

Chapter Twenty

The next afternoon, Seaside Park was full of children—happy, carefree children who were oblivious to Kat sitting at a bench just beyond the playground, her stomach a bundle of twisted, knotted nerves.

Whatever Rita had to say, she was ready to hear it, she reminded herself. And actually, after hearing Rita's voice, she was kind of excited about seeing the woman she'd once loved as dearly as a mother.

A red car pulled into the parking lot and Kat's breath caught; she recognized the woman who stepped out immediately. Rita's hair had grown silver in the two years since they'd last seen each other, and her body thinner, but there was no mistaking the way Rita carried herself, with confidence and assurance. She was a strong woman, the kind of woman that Kat had always hoped to become.

Spotting her, Rita waved and headed over.

"Kat, how are you?" Rita's warm voice asked as she drew closer.

Kat met Rita's eyes, eerily similar to those of the man she'd once been engaged to. She looked happy. There was a glow about her—and not the kind that Val and Julie had accused Kat of having. "I'm good." She scooted over for Rita to sit beside her, then they both watched the children play for a long moment. "And you?" Kat asked finally.

"Better." Rita's hand patted Kat's lap. "Kat, I am so sorry that I didn't call sooner." Her voice broke as she said it. "I just—" Shaking her head, she sniffled while pulling a tissue from her pocket.

"You?" Kat angled her body to look at Rita. "I'm the one who should've called. I should've stopped by. I should've—"

The skin beneath Rita's warm eyes crinkled. "You were grieving."

Kat's eyes suddenly burned. "Yeah, but you were, too." It'd been a long, hard road, but they'd made it. They'd survived, just like John would've wanted them to. "I've missed you," she said, allowing Rita to take her hand. Rita had been like a second mother to her at one time. They'd been closer than Kat ever remembered being to anyone outside her own family. And after John's death, they'd simply stopped interacting.

Rita squeezed her hand. "You're just as beautiful as you were back then. Have you found someone? A man?" There was no judgment in her eyes as Kat met them. Instead, she seemed eager to hear Kat say yes.

"I have," Kat said, her chest immediately swelling as she thought of Micah. "A really good one."

At this, Rita smiled. "I am so happy to hear it. John would be, too, honey. You deserve a happily ever after."

Kat sniffed back the tears waiting just behind her eyes. She didn't want to cry. This was a happy moment. They were two women who'd been dealt a hard hand, and here they were smiling. No tears were allowed today. "And Billy?" Kat asked. "How is he?" John's brother had still been in high school after the helicopter accident. He'd be in college now, or working a job somewhere.

Rita took in a slow breath, looking out among the children in the park again. "He's one of the reasons I wanted to meet with you. He's found someone, too." She was beaming again. "He's going to ask her to marry him."

Kat's lips parted as Rita looked at her again. "That's wonderful." And sad at the same time. It meant she was getting old. "John would've been so proud."

"Yes. He would have." Rita hesitated, clasping her hands in her lap. "Kat, I hate to ask you this, but . . ."

The hesitation made perspiration rise on Kat's skin. "But?"

"Billy would like to give Lindsay, his girlfriend, the ring."

"The ring," Kat repeated, waiting for the connection to form in her mind. *My ring?* Her hand immediately flew to the chain around her neck, where the gold band hung. "My ring?" she asked, hoping she'd heard Rita wrong.

"It's been in our family for three generations. John was the oldest, so naturally he got to have it, but now that he's . . . well, you understand, don't you, dear?"

Kat glanced around at the children again, her heart beating so loudly that she could barely hear their laughter anymore. It was just a ring, but it had once symbolized so much. It was a promise that John had made her—one that would no longer come true.

She pressed her eyes closed for a long moment. Then with a deep breath, she slowly lifted her arms and unclasped the chain that held the ring close to her heart. Rita didn't say anything as she waited.

Kat held the band of gold in her palm for a long moment, memorizing it, loving it, and then, when she was ready, letting it go. "I don't need his ring to remember him," she said, her voice quivering slightly. And she didn't need a constant reminder of her past around her neck either— not if she expected to move forward with Micah.

The two women talked for another half an hour, in which time Rita insisted that Kat come to Billy and Lindsay's wedding when it happened. She also insisted that Kat stop by and see her from time to time. Then, with a tight hug, Kat got back in her car and left the park. She'd been intent on not returning to work this afternoon, but going home with so much work hanging over her head would only lead to a restless night. Just an hour, she promised herself, pulling into the school's parking lot.

Everyone was gone at this time, except for the lone Jeep parked along the side with a trailer attached. *Micah.* Opening her car door, she heard the distant hum of his mower around back, which conjured all sorts of images. Him sweaty, dusted with dirt, his T-shirt clinging to those rippling abs. Yeah, she couldn't wait to lay her eyes on that. That would definitely improve her mood. But first she had work to do.

She flipped the lights of the school's front entrance as she headed toward her office, stopping when a noise erupted from the other side of the building. It was late. No one was supposed to be here right now, which meant only one thing. Vandals.

Walking quickly down the hall, she silently thanked God that she hadn't worn heels today. Instead, she had on fast-walking flats. The vandals had already blasted the school and her, and come hell or high water, she was going to catch them this time.

She started running.

Click, click, sheeeeee.

When she got to the end of the hall, she realized the double doors that led out to the playground were propped open with what looked like a skateboard. Then she heard the kids' laughter. There were two of them. Maybe three.

Click, click, sheeee.

She pushed through the heavy doors and turned toward the noise and the two boys she recognized all too well. Then she turned to look at the wall. "What do you boys think you're—?"

The bottle of spray paint in Donald Williams's hand pointed directly at her and gave another *sheeeeee* as it sprayed all over the front of her dress.

Kat let out a small shriek and started to chase after them. "Wait! Get back here!"

After a solid minute, she stopped and groaned in frustration. The kids were fast and it was hard to breathe through the thick smell of paint currently burning her nostrils. Maybe she should put up a reward for anyone who caught these guys, because at this point, she was willing to give just about anything to get her hands on them.

~

MICAH TURNED OFF THE LAWNMOWER AND WIPED HIS brow. It took a second for the buzzing in his ears to stop. As soon as it did, it was replaced with a shrill scream.

Kat.

He jumped off the mower and started running toward the side of the school, adrenaline pumping through him like it did anytime there was trouble. He responded the way the military had taught him to. Quickly. Cautiously.

His stride ate up another ten steps and then he turned a corner, nearly plowing over two boys. "Whoa!" With one quick scan to see that the kids were okay, he understood exactly what the situation was. One of the vandals still had a can of spray paint in his hands.

Grabbing them both by the arm, Micah avoided the spray paint directed at him.

"Let me go!" the kid on his left yelled. It was Donald Williams. And Micah recognized the other kid as Luis Grant. He was in Ben's class.

Micah gritted his teeth. "What are you two doing out here anyway?" He noticed more cans on the ground and also . . . "Kat?"

The same color paint that speckled the boys' hands and clothing was sprayed across her mid- section.

He dragged the kids toward her. "You okay?" he asked, scanning her body with his eyes, assessing every scuff and bruise—and luscious curve.

"I think so." Her eyes narrowed and she folded her arms at her chest, giving her that principal look that he had to admit turned him on. "We're calling your parents. And you'll be cleaning this wall after school next week," she said, pointing a finger.

"I ain't joining your stupid Friendship Club," Luis said, keeping his gaze low. "I've heard what they do and it sounds lame."

"I don't think you're in a position to be making demands. Let's go." Micah ushered the boys inside, letting Kat take the lead toward the office. He hoped these vandals' parents came fast because he was ready to help her out of those spray-painted clothes. Time had been limited over the last few days, partly due to work obligations and his need to spend extra time with Ben. But he had nothing pressing to do right now, except get his hands on the woman in front of him.

As if hearing his thoughts, Kat turned back and raised a brow, a small smile lifting at the corners of her mouth.

She pointed at two chairs in her office and waited for the boys to sit. "Do you guys have any idea of the trouble you've caused this year?" She dragged a chair to sit in front of them and waited for their answer. Only a few weeks earlier, Micah would've wondered why she wasn't screaming bloody murder at them. Now, though, he respected her style of discipline. She was calm and nurturing, and it seemed to work.

"It's just paint. Don't we get freedom of expression in this country?" Luis asked, evoking a chuckle from his fellow delinquent.

Kat's gaze met Micah's, then returned to the kids. "Sergeant Peterson fights for your freedoms in this country. Did you know that?"

The boys lowered their eyes.

"I don't think your expressions are exactly what he has in mind when he puts his life in danger. Do you?"

The boys didn't answer, but they weren't laughing anymore.

"You've written a lot of things about the school." She paused. "And me. If you tell me what you don't like, maybe we can work together to fix it. I think that's a better action than vandalizing the school and running away."

Donald finally met Kat's eyes. Micah couldn't see him directly, but he heard the boy sniffling. Yeah, Kat was a good principal. Better than he ever realized. Not only that, she was a good person. She cared about these boys' futures.

"I'm sorry," Donald said, sniffling. "I don't really think you suck, Principal Chandler."

Kat smiled. "But if you did, you could tell me why and I'd try to do better."

"And thank you for fighting for our country," the boy said, turning to Micah. "For keeping us free."

Micah nodded at him. He wasn't a bad kid at all, and he guessed no kid was, really. "You're welcome, buddy."

"Yeah, I guess I'm sorry, too," Luis said with a shrug. "So, since we apologized and all, do we still have to do that lame after-school thing you got going on?" he asked.

Kat laughed softly. "Afraid so."

Kat released a breath as the two boys were picked up by their parents. When she turned around, Micah was watching her.

"You okay?" he asked.

She nodded, but her insides were still jumping from the scare, and from the look that Micah was giving her. Glancing down, she groaned at her spray-painted clothing. "It would be my luck that the mayor is somehow waiting outside when we leave."

He sat on the corner of Val's desk and watched her as she locked up. Thanks to the vandals, she'd gotten exactly no paperwork done tonight. And reading the heated gaze that Micah was giving her, she wouldn't be doing any now, either.

She grabbed a key that hung just below Val's desk and went to lock the file cabinets on the other side of the room. She could already feel her sprained ankle from the night of the Marine Corps ball swelling back up after chasing the kids outside. Limping, she tried to put as little pressure on it as possible.

"That bad, huh?" Micah stood and wrapped an arm around her waist, helping her hobble over to Val's swivel chair. "Sit," he said. Then he crouched in front of her, holding her ankle in his hands—his hands that she remembered could do a lot of dizzying things.

She swallowed. "It's, um, okay." Her head was spinning from his touch, innocent as it was.

"It's swelling pretty badly." He ran a finger over the large pocket of purple blood puffing up around the bone.

She flinched under his touch.

"Did that hurt?" he asked, his face serious, but his heated eyes telling her exactly what was on his mind.

She shook her head quickly. "Not much." The truth was, she was surprised there was any blood left in her to pull to her ankle. All of her blood seemed to be warming other places. Places he'd made very happy not too long ago.

"Good," he said, slowly lowering his mouth to brush his lips against the swelling ankle. "Did that hurt?" he asked, his voice low and deep, tickling up her body.

"No," she managed to say, throat tight, mouth dry.

His eyes stayed locked on hers for a long moment.

They both turned toward a creaking sound. It wasn't the sound she'd grown to know was the vandals at work. No, this was one of those mysterious sounds that buildings made for no apparent reason.

They both straightened.

"Yeah, an elementary school is probably not the best place to be doing this," he said, his hand still running over her legs.

"Do you have to go get Ben?" she asked. Her heart was knocking around in her chest. It wasn't just his body that made her feel feverish. It was him, all of him. His smile. His low laugh. The way he touched her so delicately at times, seeming to cherish her, and at other times he pulled her to him just as hungry as she was.

"He's with my aunt."

"My sister is out tonight," she said. "She and Val are going to this thing outside of town."

"I see. You didn't want to go?" he asked, his lips curving. He could tell where this was leading, and judging from his growing smile, he liked it.

"I told them I have too much work to do."

"You work too hard." He leaned forward, pushing his way between her open legs, and crushed his mouth against hers, making her moan as he kissed her. Pulling back, he kissed his way toward her ear and whispered, "All work and no play, Kat. That's very bad."

She nodded, loving his hands as they rode up her waist. She bit down on her lower lip, distracting herself from her needy desires. This wasn't the time or place.

He grinned at her, seeming to read her mind. "We'll take my Jeep. You shouldn't drive with that ankle. Your place?"

She nodded, ready to agree to anything at this point. "Perfect. Let's hurry."

Chapter Twenty-One

Kat stumbled into her front door and called Julie's name, just in case. The house was dark. Quiet. Perfect.

She pulled Micah in after her, pressing her mouth to his. They kissed, maneuvering down the hall, leaning against the wall, and pressing against each other's bodies as they traveled.

"Which room?" he asked. His hands continued to move along her sides, traveling higher, flirting with the clasp of her bra.

Kat closed her eyes. "This one." She turned the doorknob to her bedroom and back-stepped toward her bed, fitted with a pink flowery spread that screamed sweet, not sexy. She'd just have to make sure he focused all of his attention on her and not her décor.

Sometime in the night, Kat rolled over and reached out for Micah before opening her eyes, and finding . . . no one. Where did he go?

Turning her neck, she looked at her bedside clock. It was midnight. They must've fallen asleep. Rolling over, she heard a paper crinkle beneath her. She reached for the pull of her lamp and light flooded the room, causing her to wince and shut her eyes.

After a moment, she found the paper and read the scrawled hand-writing.

Had to go home to Ben. Thanks.

She stared at the note for a long moment. *Thanks?* Thanks for what? She bit her lower lip, knowing she shouldn't feel insulted, but *thanks?* Really? She'd thought they'd moved past being just friends with benefits. Although neither of them had said as much.

Her stomach growled as she pondered what it meant—or didn't mean. She hadn't eaten dinner before getting hot and naked with Micah. Dropping her legs off the bed, she winced as fresh pain shot up her swollen ankle, a reminder of the spray-painting incident.

"Ouch, ouch, ouch!" she whispered to herself, limping across the floor. It hurt like a bitch, but she wouldn't have it any other way because this sprain had been the culprit behind a most enjoyable night of nakedness. Those boys should get promotions, she decided, as she limped down the hall. Skip third grade and go directly to fifth.

The lights in the kitchen were still on. She headed straight toward the fridge, and then stopped cold, staring at the two women leaned against each other on her couch, fast asleep. This was starting to become a regular thing, and she didn't mind it one bit. The TV was still on, flashing some horror flick that she tried not to look at as she turned it off. That would completely sway her dreams from sexual to scary.

She stared at Julie and Val for another moment, then her stomach snarled as she spotted the container of popcorn between them.

Perfect. Sitting beside her sister, she grabbed the bucket and shoveled several handfuls of popcorn into her mouth, still thinking about the note. Once she was satisfied, she snuggled into the cluster of people she held dear, and closed her eyes.

Micah lay in bed, unable to sleep. Ben was with his aunt next door, so he guessed he could've stayed with Kat tonight, instead of leaving her an awkward thank-you note and heading home. Why the hell had he left a thank-you note? That wasn't at all what he wanted to tell her. He wanted to say he liked her. Liked her a whole damn lot.

He got up and paced the room, deciding to put his hands where they belonged—in the dirt.

Or up Kat's skirt, but they'd already had that pleasure tonight. He grabbed his spotlight and loaded several tools in the back of his Jeep, where Ben's wheelchair usually sat. Then he loaded several of his offspring plants that needed a new home. And he knew the perfect place to put them. He'd caught sight of Kat's yard this afternoon. Or really, it couldn't justifiably be labeled a yard. It was a large square of land behind her house. A yard was meant to be a sanctuary. Kat didn't have one of those. She spent every waking moment at that school, and she deserved a place to kick up her heels, preferably flats since she wasn't that graceful with women's footwear, and relax.

He revved the engine of his Jeep and headed back in the direction he'd retreated from a little over an hour ago. Kat would be asleep by now, so he wouldn't wake her. He just wanted to leave an expression of his heart. Something that said more than thanks for the great sex.

He flinched because that's probably how she'd interpret it.

Ten minutes later, he pulled past her driveway. Val's and Julie's cars were both parked out front now. He drove through the grass toward the back of the house and stopped beside a five-foot wooden privacy fence. After a military-style fence jump, he unlocked the gate and let himself in, deciding to work on the far back corner, where the sunlight hit the yard best in the mornings. In the late evenings, when Kat would most likely enjoy the garden, the sun would be down, and she'd be shaded. It was too late in the season for anything to bloom right now, but the bulbs he intended to plant tonight would produce vibrant flowers for her to admire come spring. And every time she saw them, she'd think of him.

After unloading the supplies, he started working, losing time like he always did when he was landscaping. Two hours later, he stood back and surveyed the small square of plowed earth where he'd planted the flower bulbs. Parallel to the side fence, he'd placed a lattice that roses would overtake next spring. There was a stand-alone swing in the center of the garden that he'd picked up earlier in the week with Kat in mind. She was the first woman he'd seriously considered allowing in his life since Jessica. She was special, and deserved a beautiful place where she could sit and think. This was a good start.

Maybe he'd add a small fountain and motion-detecting flood lights. It was unsafe for her to be living practically alone without them, although their lack served him well tonight he thought, as he wiped a hand across his brow. But right now he was tired. He packed up his stuff and headed home with a smile set on his mouth. He'd liked doing that for her, liked imagining her face when she woke up to his surprise. The thought made him want to find other ways to make her happy. That's what people in love did. They found ways to show each other how they felt. Better ways than leaving a thank-you note by someone's bed.

SOMETHING WET STROKED THE INSIDE OF KAT'S EAR. SHE snapped awake and then tumbled off the couch. "What the—?" Her eyes shot open and she clutched her ankle as it hit the carpeted floor. "Oww!"

Val's eyes widened as she looked at Kat's foot. "Oh, crap. Did I do that?"

Kat's gaze slid over. "Give the wet willy to my ear? Yes, you did. And it was very gross, by the way."

"No." Val pointed. "That. Your ankle looks like something from a sci-fi movie."

Julie yawned, then gasped, too, pulling herself back into the cushion of the couch.

"It's not contagious," Kat teased, lifting her leg and waving her ankle in her sister's face. Julie's face scrunched. "What happened?"

Kat rested her leg back on the couch. "A couple of vandals at the school attacked me with spray paint last night and I lost my footing a little bit. I guess it aggravated my sprain from the hospital."

"What?" Val shook her head. "For crying out loud, how many times have I told you it's not safe to stay there alone?"

"I wasn't alone."

Julie and Val stared at her.

"The vandals?" Val asked. "The ones who did that to you?"

"And Micah. He caught the boys who have been vandalizing the school. Then we called their parents. It's fine." Kat nibbled on her lower lip as the two women continued to stare at her, waiting for more.

"And then what happened?" Val asked, a wicked smile spreading along her sleep-creased face.

"And then . . ." Kat's cheeks burned at just the memory. She tried not to look at them. "Then he took me home," she said, opting for truth. It was the truth. And if she could avoid eye contact until she veered the subject in another direction, no one would need to know about the encounter in the school's front office. Or what had happened in her own bedroom afterward—not that her sex life was a secret from the two these days.

"See." Val gestured toward Kat. "It's in her eyes. That far-off, glassy look. That's how I know she got some."

Julie nodded. "At least a kiss."

Val shook her head. "Oh, no. It was way more than a kiss. I'd be willing to bet—"

"Whoa! You guys. I'm sitting right here," Kat said, pretending to be insulted.

Val cocked an eyebrow. "And why is it you needed a ride from Micah anyway? Your car isn't in the driveway. Where is it?"

Kat nibbled her lower lip, remembering how she'd left it in the school's parking lot in order to stay with Micah. "He didn't think I should drive with my ankle like this," she said, which was the truth. "Maybe you can help me get it from the school later today?" she asked, looking at Julie.

"Sure." Julie shrugged.

"Thanks." Getting up, Kat squeaked as her body weight hit her ankle like a dozen tiny, sharp knives.

"Are you going to get that looked at?" Julie moved toward it and sat on the floor, poking at the pocket of swelling. "Does that hurt?"

"Ouch! Yes, it hurts."

"I think I saw an elastic bandage under your bathroom sink. I can fix this." Julie turned back to Val. "Guest bathroom. Do you mind?"

"I guess not. You sisters seem to like ordering me around." Val pointed at Kat. "But don't think you're off the hook. I want details."

Five minutes later, Julie had Kat's ankle wrapped in a fancy pattern intended to push the swelling out.

"I did this for my clients at the health club that I worked at. When someone would get a sprain, I'd wrap them. It seemed to help," Julie said.

"Yeah. It feels better already." Kat took a few steps. "And to think I thought you were just watching all the hot men flex their oversized muscles up in Charlotte."

"That, too." Julie got up and headed toward the kitchen and the coffee machine. "No more freebies until I get my first cup."

A few minutes later, they all sat around the kitchen table and sipped quietly.

"So, it's your turn to spill some details." Kat looked at her sister. "What happened with that guy you were dating?"

Julie's smile faded. "We broke up. That's all."

"Why? What'd you fight about?" Kat asked, wondering if Julie would tell her this time.

She'd asked several times in the last few weeks. It had to be over something major to send her sister running back to the town she swore she'd never come home to.

"Nothing really." Julie shifted uncomfortably.

There was an invisible shield that seemed to come up with just the mention of Julie's ex. "Well, I'm glad you're back. I'm dating for the first time since John died. I need your sisterly expertise."

"I thought you hated having me here." Julie hugged her legs as she sat in the kitchen chair.

"We're family." Kat reached for her hand. "And friends. Right, Val?"

Val didn't move a muscle.

"Val?" Kat urged.

"I'll agree to friendly acquaintances," Val said, her gaze meeting Julie's. Then she stuck her hand over theirs at the center of the table.

"Aww! I wouldn't have pegged you for the sappy type," Julie said, causing Val to roll her eyes.

"Your sister does that to me, okay? I can't help it. And now there's two of you, heaven help me." Val shook her head. "And before I get any sappier, or before it's my turn to spill the deets about my nonexistent love life, I'll be going." She pulled her hand away and headed toward the back door.

"'Nonexistent'? What happened to Doug?" Kat asked, following her.

Val's steps slowed. Her shoulders pulled back as she took a breath. "Apparently, not all Marines are sex-deprived on deployment."

Kat grabbed her arm, turning Val to face her. "Are you okay?" She knew that Val had really liked this guy, as opposed to all the guys from her father's church she usually dated. She'd practically beamed every time she'd spoken about Doug.

"I'm fine. I don't want to talk about it, okay?" Val shrugged, making light as she always did of the things that hurt the worst. Her gaze skittered past Kat and she cleared her throat. "Anyway, I stepped in dog poop on the way in last night, so I left my shoes on your back deck."

Kat's face scrunched now as they continued walking down the hall. "I keep telling Mr. Dailey to keep his dog out of my yard. It's part of the reason I put up that fence. But the dog just digs his way inside."

Val swung the door open and grabbed her shoes, holding them as far away from her body as possible. "Disgusting. Can I wear a pair of your old shoes home?" she asked.

"Of course." Kat turned to go get a pair. She froze with Julie's gasp.

"What is that?" Julie pointed out the door.

All three stared at the corner of the fence where they saw a perfect square of land. In the middle was a stand-alone swing with a tin roof on top.

Kat swallowed. "Where did that come from?"

Val elbowed her. "From that *kiss* you and Micah shared last night."

He had to have done this last night after writing her the thank-you note. "What does it mean?" she said, more to herself than the two women beside her.

"It means he's in love," Julie said, smiling thickly.

Chapter Twenty-Two

K at's mouth went dry and her chest tightened as she walked toward the picnic table where Micah was sitting on Monday afternoon. The two newest club members were already hard at work, one looking sullen and not a bit remorseful over his acts of vandalism this school year. The other seeming to enjoy himself.

"Hey," she said, soliciting Micah's attention.

He was wearing mirrored sunglasses against the late October sun, but she suspected his gaze was washing over her, remembering what her body looked like without the iron-pressed blouse and long skirt. Remembering the other night when they'd devoured each other's body in a heated frenzy, after which he'd left her a thank-you note and apparently created a garden in her backyard.

"I haven't gotten a chance to say thank you yet. For Saturday night," she said.

He raised an eyebrow. "Which part?" he asked, lowering his voice.

She pulled her lower lip into her mouth, scanning the campus and making sure there were no little ears to overhear them. "All the parts, but the swing and the flowers is what I was referring to."

He nodded. "I thought you could use a place to relax."

He was her place to relax. She'd been very relaxed in his arms as she'd fallen asleep on Saturday night. "Well, thank you. It's beautiful. How are our vandals doing?"

"They have an attitude as big as Texas, but a little work in the earth should do them good." Since the beginning of the school year, the flat piece of land behind the school had transformed into a large expanse of green sprouts and leaves, its delicious colors rising from the dirt. It was amazing, and the kids had done it with Micah's help. And hers.

Micah gestured toward the boxes of handpicked vegetables. "A home-cooked meal will do the wounded warriors good. A lot of them won't be going home for the holidays."

She smiled. "The Veterans' Center agreed to let us have the facility on Saturday, so we'll be able to treat our heroes right. Do we have cooks for Saturday's feast?" she asked.

Micah rubbed his chin between his fingers. "I have a few good men. Lawson owes me."

"And Val and Julie offered to help. Probably more to look at the guys, but"—Kat shrugged—"whatever works."

Micah's attention turned to the tall, lanky man walking toward the back of the school with a notepad in hand. Glasses framed his angled face.

"He's a reporter from the *Seaside Daily News*." Kat stood and smiled.

"You're smiling?" Micah asked.

"He's here to do a story on our club. A real story. I invited him." She extended her hand as the reporter approached. "Mr. Todd. Thank you so much for coming."

The man shook her hand and then took Micah's. "Wow. You were right, Principal Chandler," he said, directing his attention to the after-school group.

"Please, call me Kat."

"Kat. This place is amazing." The Gumby-like man pulled a pen out of his chest pocket and started writing feverishly as Kat and Micah told him about the club, and how several of the kids who'd been assigned time after school were still here, because they wanted to be. They told him how the kids' efforts would be feeding the wounded Marines this weekend to show their appreciation to them for serving their country.

When they were done walking the premises, the reporter stopped and stared at the wall of latest graffiti. Stanley had been home sick over the last week and couldn't get to it. She wished she'd removed the paint herself.

"Kids will rebel everywhere," she said, turning to Mr. Todd. "It's what you do to handle it that makes the difference. No kid wants to misbehave. They want to be loved. They want to know they're worth something. That they're worth a lot." Kat was getting all misty-eyed and tight-throated just talking about the Friendship Club. This was something that mattered, and it made a difference. She knew it did.

Micah's hand squeezed her shoulder. Then he pushed his mirrored sunglasses up on his head and shook the reporter's hand. "I can't wait to read the article." There was a tone laced in the comment. A tone that said it better do the school, and its principal, justice.

The reporter nodded. "And I can't wait to write it. When I spoke to your assistant principal about the club the other day, she led me to believe this would be more of a sidebar article."

"Mrs. Burroughs?" Kat queried.

"I ran into her at church on Sunday. Can't hardly go anywhere in a small town without running into someone you know. I asked her about the club."

"And what did she say?" Micah asked, still standing beside her. Kat could almost hear his muscles tightening in her defense, and she loved that about him. Even though she didn't need rescuing, she liked the fact that he had her back.

The reporter shrugged. "I believe she said your little club was temporary. That traditional methods of punishment were more effective in changing kids' behaviors."

It was no secret that Mrs. Burroughs thought Kat was too young and inexperienced to be the principal at this school. But she never thought that Mrs. Burroughs would intentionally undermine her efforts to help the kids. This club wasn't temporary and it had made a difference. Dora Burroughs was supposed to be her partner here.

The reporter placed his pen back in his front pocket. "After seeing it for myself, this is definitely front page material. The town will eat this up."

"Thank you." Kat shook his hand one more time, then watched him walk away.

"What are you going to do?" Micah asked, when their interviewer was out of earshot.

She shook her head, watching the kids maneuver a water hose to spray the plants. "I don't know. It seems like my assistant has resisted every decision and action I've made since I became the principal here last year."

"I can talk to her if you want me to," he said.

This made Kat smile. Yeah, she'd love to see how Micah would handle that confrontation.

But it was her battle, not his. "I don't think so," she said, resisting the urge to lean into him. "Maybe it's just like with the kids. Maybe no adult wants to rebel, either." She chewed her lower lip. "Maybe we could force her to dig holes and drop seeds. Perhaps that would fix her."

Micah laughed softly. "Adults are a whole different story. I think your assistant doesn't like the fact that someone half her age is telling her what to do. And I think that some part of her might want to see you fail."

"So what do I do?"

He wrapped his arm around her shoulder and squeezed. "You're already doing it. You're standing up for yourself, showing the world how wonderful you are. And you're not failing."

"Right."

"I know I'm proud of you," he said.

Kat tilted her head and looked up at him. "You are? That means a lot to me." They held each other's gaze for a beat, and then she shrieked as cold water drenched the front of her blouse.

The kids in the Friendship Club roared with laughter.

"Water the plants, not the adults," Micah said, feigning temper. She knew him better than that, though. Under his tough Marine exterior, he was gentle. The kind of guy who'd make her a backyard oasis in the middle of the night.

She watched, laughing as he pretended to chase the kids for the hose.

"I'm going to get you guys," he said playfully, moving much slower than she knew he could. Even Ben was wheeling his chair across the ground as fast as his right arm would push.

So the group still had a little rebellious streak. At least they'd kept up their angelic appearances for the *Seaside Daily News* reporter. She wouldn't have wanted this water fight to end up on the front page tomorrow morning. Although that probably would've made Mrs. Burroughs happy. An assistant principal who wanted to see her boss fail wasn't good for anyone, and the school couldn't thrive with that kind of leadership.

Micah finally grabbed the hose and pretended to turn it on the kids, who shrieked with delight.

She'd talk to Mrs. Burroughs tomorrow, and try to come to a truce. If that didn't happen, then she had a decision to make: continue being undermined or let her assistant principal go.

The following Saturday, there were more than enough fresh vegetables to feed an army on the table in front of Micah. Or a crew of hungry Marines.

~

"How long did it take for your aunt Clara to clean and cut all these things?" Lawson asked, dropping the last box on the table.

"I didn't ask, but she's a saint." Micah glanced over the food proudly. "A hot, home-cooked meal is good for the soul. And after what these guys have been through, they deserve it."

Lawson nodded, and they both grew quiet a moment. They both knew good men and women who'd lost far too much in the desert. They'd risked their lives, all of them. Some came home with wounds that couldn't be seen—some called those "lucky". And others had wounds visible for the entire world—the not-so-lucky. PTSD and physical injuries couldn't be compared though. Both were equally disruptive and devastating in Micah's opinion.

"Put us to work," a broad-shouldered Marine, Donny, said as he walked into the room. "We might be Marines for life, but we'll be damn good cooks for a day."

Lawson grinned, giving him and the other Marine who'd walked in a shove. "I don't think so. You're on cleaning duty."

Donny's smile faded. "Seriously? I thought I'd get some action behind the stove."

"Have you *ever* had any action behind a stove?" Micah asked, tossing a glance over to the tall, lean Marine with a blond buzz cut and a California tan.

"Not exactly," Donny brooded.

"That's what I thought. We cook it and you serve it. The pretty ones always serve," Micah said.

This comment spawned a deep frown from Donny. "Men aren't pretty."

"Tell that to Chris Hemsworth," the other Marine, Mark, said, patting his buddy's shoulder.

"Well, if I'm pretty, then you're a damn Playboy bunny," Donny told Mark, waggling his eyebrows. "Let's call Hugh Hefner."

When they were gone, Lawson dropped some chopped vegetables into a pan of hot oil, stepping back when it hissed loudly. "Don't think I forgot about ribbing you on that spring in your step. I'm planning to finish that up later," he teased.

Micah's gaze trailed out into the banquet hall where Kat and Julie were walking in, lugging jugs of sweet tea. He smiled to himself. "And I'll be ribbing you about checking out Kat's sister later, too. Whether you admit to checking her out or not."

Lawson straightened. "I'll admit it. I'm a man and I do have eyes in my head. She's hot."

Micah pretended to glare at him. "You better keep your eyes and thoughts to Kat's sister," he growled. Because Kat was his.

He walked down to the center of the room and helped the two sisters with the jugs. "Hey, beautiful," he said to Kat. "Beautiful day to feed some Marines." He bent and brushed his lips against hers. She tasted sweet, like she'd just taken a sip of that tea she'd lugged in.

"Ben's not coming?" she asked, looking around the room.

"No, he's with my aunt. He'd get bored with us old folk, and I wanted to focus on the guys today. And you. I thought I might focus on you."

If he wasn't mistaken, her cheeks turned a deeper shade of rose. He liked that about her, how she blushed too easily. It made him want to say more things to make her body flush. But Lawson was in the room, and Micah had no doubt he was taking notes so he could tease him mercilessly about it later.

"I promised Ben a father-son day tomorrow, so he's happy about that."

Kat met his eyes and smiled. "That's sweet. Who'd have thought? A big, tough, sweet Marine."

Frowning, Micah shook his head. "Don't throw that word around too loudly. The guys are already teasing me."

Val stepped up beside them and unloaded a box of homemade pies.

"Did you make those?" Micah asked, peeking inside. Lawson and Donny were beside her now, too.

"Those look like my grandmother's used to," Donny said, staring up at Val, who waved a dismissive hand.

"No big deal. There are three pineapple and two pecan in there."

"Pineapple pie?" Donny and Lawson both said at the same

time. They looked at each other. A frown settled on Donny's lips. "My grandmother never made pineapple pies."

Val shrugged, looking uncomfortable with the attention. "I have to get the rest of my stuff out of the car."

"I'll help you," Donny said, stepping up beside her, and causing Micah and Lawson to laugh.

Donny didn't volunteer for menial jobs. He usually had to be coaxed into doing jobs that no one else wanted to do—like serving instead of cooking.

Val ran her gaze over him and released a tired sigh. "Fine," she said and started walking toward the door.

"That's how she treats people she likes," Kat said, when they were out of ear range.

"Charming," Micah said, then howled when Kat's elbow tapped his rib cage.

An hour later, there was a long line of men and women snaking through the room, stopping at each table to put a healthy serving of real, home-cooked food on their plates. Some were in wheelchairs, others limped or showed evidence of their wounds some other way. Then there were those with mostly invisible wounds that cut just as deep. They all sported a smile today, though, and for that Micah was proud. The Veterans' Center had a volunteer band made up of veterans who liked to play at the community functions, and their music filled the room as people ate, laughed, and enjoyed the day.

"A success." Micah nudged Kat, who'd been standing behind her table and watching the contented crowd for several minutes. A small smile played on her lips. "Another success for Kat Chandler."

"Thanks to you. It was your idea," she said.

"I don't think you give yourself enough credit. You made this happen. And the Friendship rebels, of course."

"Friendship Club," she interjected playfully.

"Right. Maybe now that they know they did something to make a difference, they'll want to do more. That's how you change the world. One good deed at a time."

"There you go being sweet again." Kat leaned in to him. "How about doing a good deed for me, Sergeant Peterson?"

Hooking his eyebrow, Micah didn't need to ask. He knew exactly what she wanted, and screw being teased by his guys. He didn't care. "Yes, ma'am," he said, dipping to brush his lips against hers. "That's the sweet version," he said, pulling back. "You get the dirty version later," he promised.

Chapter Twenty-Three

T he next morning, Ben was already dressed and seated at the table with a bowl of cereal in front of him when Micah emerged from his bedroom.

Micah glanced around, half expecting Aunt Clara to be nearby. She wasn't.

"I did it myself, Dad," Ben said, seeming to read his thoughts. "It wasn't that hard."

Micah smiled. "When did you get to be so big?"

Ben shrugged, scooping Frosted Flakes cereal into his mouth. "You said it would be just you and me today. What're we doing?" His eyes were wide with excitement, no doubt expecting nothing less than the grandest of adventures.

Micah hadn't even thought this far ahead. He scratched his chin, then rubbed a hand over his unshaven face. The fresh growth was definitely against military regulations, but it was his day off.

"Dad? We are having a father-son day, right?" Ben asked, concern lowering his shaggy brows.

"Yeah, buddy. Of course we are. We're, uh, going fishing."

Ben's expression dimmed as he clutched his spoon. "Fishing?"

In all their time together, they'd never been fishing. And fishing was the one thing that Micah's father had ever done with him that hadn't involved preparing him for the military.

"How am I supposed to go fishing? My chair—"

"If you can get yourself dressed and fed, you can go fishing," Micah said, convincing even himself. It'd be easy. Ben's chair had locks on the brakes. They'd settle down on the banks of one of the creeks and toss their lines in. He could adapt the pole to hook onto Ben's chair, that way he only needed one hand to reel when he got a nibble. "It'll be great." Just thinking about it made his chest lighten. He hadn't been fishing in one of North Carolina's spindly creeks in ages.

Ben bounced in his chair. "Cool. Can we eat what we catch?"

"Well, what would be the fun of catching if we couldn't eat 'em?"

Ben squealed with delight, making Micah's heart lift a little higher. He'd do anything for this kid. Including getting out of the Marines and breaking his own father's heart. Not that he was fully convinced that the elder Peterson actually had a heart to break.

Micah gestured toward the laundry room. "Let me go get the supplies and we'll be on our way." He squeezed his son's shoulder as he walked past, resisting the urge to tell him to take smaller mouthfuls. Ben was growing up and needing less supervision, which meant that Micah would have to start stepping back.

Half an hour later, father and son were in the Jeep and heading toward a spot that Lawson had told them about. A secret, magic spot, Micah told Ben, adding to the spirit of adventure. He scoped out the flattest area of the creek's bank and settled there to prevent Ben's chair from rolling toward the water. It was shaded by pine trees, and a gentle breeze carried around them, reminding Micah of his childhood days. Not all of his memories with his father were bad. There were times when he'd actually looked up to the man. The memories ached in Micah's chest.

He rigged up Ben's wheelchair with the reel positioned right beside his good arm, and gave a thumbs-up sign. "Let's catch us a big one." Then Micah tossed his own line in the water and smiled to himself as he watched Ben from the corner of his eye. Ben's eyes were wide and his little body leaned slightly forward, as if he was sure that something was going to launch out of the water and swallow his line any minute. They watched and waited for nearly half an hour before Ben said anything.

"Dad?"

"Yeah, bud?" Micah started to reel his line in, deciding to toss it in a different location.

"Why hasn't Mom called me since she's been gone?"

Micah paused for a long second, then continued reeling his line and tossed it further out. "I'm sure she's been busy, little man." He offered what he hoped was a relaxed smile. Ben didn't need to worry that Jessica couldn't take care of herself out there. She damn well could. It was taking care of others that was her weakness.

"Don't you guys get phone calls over there? You were able to call me all the time when you were deployed last year."

Micah nodded. Yeah. He'd made Ben a priority, whereas Jess had never considered her son anything more than a burden. There was no good answer to give. "She'll be home in eight months." This was just a guess, because she'd never actually told him when she was coming back. Or if she intended to see them at all when she did.

There was another long beat of silence. "Dad?"

"Yeah?" Micah focused on the red and white bobber in the water, praying for a distraction.

Grab the bait, little bastards.

"Do you think Principal Chandler will stick around?"

Micah's eyes slid over, as he remembered his discussion with Clara earlier in the week. Kat was loyal. He could trust her with his son's heart. "I'm not sure, son. But if she doesn't, it means your dad screwed something up. Dads do that from time to time."

Ben considered this, still watching him intently. "Even your dad?"

Micah glanced over. "Uh-huh. Even Grandpa."

"Well, why don't you like him very much? I hear you and Aunt Clara talking."

Birds chirped in the background as Micah tried to find yet another hard answer. "I do like him. It's just hard to be around him sometimes."

Ben returned to watching his bobber. "I'll always want to be around you, Dad. No matter how much you mess up."

Well, damn. Leave it to a kid to say just the right thing to kick you in the balls and make you want to hug them at the same time. "Yeah? Thanks, bud."

Ben nodded, that wide grin that Micah loved spreading through his cheeks.

"I can learn a lot by spending time with you. You know that?"

"We should do a lot more of it then. And maybe Principal Chandler can come with us next time. I like her a lot."

"Me, too." He hadn't wanted to like her a lot, but he did. He'd moved past just liking her a long time ago.

"You should try really hard not to mess things up with her, Dad," Ben added, glancing over again. "But even if you do, I think Principal Chandler is a lot like me. I think she'll keep wanting to spend time with you no matter how much you mess up."

"I'll try, little man." Micah pointed to the water. "I think you got a bite. Better reel it in."

Ben hurried to wind the reel backward with his good arm. The motion was uncoordinated, but Micah prayed the entire time that the fish would hold on. *Just hold on.* They needed this moment, this fish. Then the line lifted out of the water and there was a ten-inch bass.

"I did it! I caught a big one!" Ben bounced, and Micah had to keep the chair from tipping over on the uneven terrain, while also reeling the line in faster before the fish flopped itself off.

"Yes, sir. It'll make a fine dinner. Big enough to feed a squadron, I'd say." Micah grabbed the fish's mouth and reached for the hook.

"Can we show it to Grandpa?"

Micah's gaze narrowed. "Show it to Grandpa?"

"You said he used to fish with you. Wouldn't he be proud of me?"

Micah laid the fish in a cooler of the brackish creek water and watched it flop. "I'm sure he would be, son. I know I am." He rebaited Ben's line and cast it again, contemplating Ben's question and his son's desire for his grandpa to be proud of him. Micah had that desire, too. He'd always wanted to make his dad proud. Telling him he wasn't reenlisting wouldn't bode well on that front. But maybe his father, commanding officer of Camp Leon and all, would surprise him if he gave him half a chance. Or disown him. Micah wouldn't be surprised by either outcome.

They caught two more good-sized fish, then packed things up. When they were back in the Jeep, he glanced at his son in the rearview mirror. He knew he'd regret even posing the question, but he asked anyway. "Do you want to stop by Grandpa's and cook the fish?"

Ben nodded enthusiastically. "Yeah, Dad. Let's do that!"

It was the big house, Micah reasoned. Kids loved big houses. And his father had a fondness for model trains, which Ben went crazy over. He wasn't a kid that could rampage a house. He didn't have the motor skills for that, so his father had always been very good about letting Ben mess with the trains. That got him a lot of brownie points.

Micah turned the vehicle south toward the water, where his father lived alone. It seemed a sad existence. He doubted his father saw it that way, though. His father enjoyed the kind of order that only living alone could provide. His mom had been a saint to keep the house's order when she was alive. No other woman could ever live up to that.

Micah parked and helped Ben back into his wheelchair, then got the cooler out of the back. The front door opened as they approached the front steps.

Micah stopped and stared at him. "Hey, Dad."

His father smiled tightly. The older Peterson was a compact man with stern features. "I didn't know you were stopping by," he said in a low voice that rivaled John Wayne's.

"We went fishing!" Ben announced excitedly, his smile fading as he looked at the steps and turned back to Micah. He couldn't get up, not without help.

Micah had told his father to get a ramp a thousand times. Any other grandfather would've done so if they had a disabled grand-child that they expected to visit. "We thought we'd fry some fish tonight, if you're up for company. Just like old times."

His father's smile relaxed a notch. "You're getting sentimental on me."

Micah's throat constricted. "Nothing wrong with good memories."

"Nothing at all," his father agreed. "Come on in. Ben, I have a new train for my set."

Ben was smiling again. Micah picked up the back of the chair and lifted it to the top of the steps, giving it a push to get him rolling toward the front door. When Ben was safely inside, he went back for the cooler of fish. They'd eat fish, drink a few beers, and then he'd tell the old man what he probably didn't want to hear. He was getting out of the Marine Corps.

He'd never intended to be a career Marine. He was landscaping for Seaside Elementary and the local cemetery already. A few other locals had contracted him as well and last week, out of nowhere, the mayor's assistant had called to tell him that Mayor Flowers was interested in hiring him for their home. Landscaping was becoming a full-time job, and it was something he enjoyed.

Micah stood in the doorway and watched as Ben's face lit up. His father pushed a button on the remote control in his hand and the model train's lights flickered on and off.

"Let me try! Let me try!" Ben begged, taking the remote from his grandfather.

Okay, so maybe the old man had an appreciation for happiness, too, somewhere in that icy heart of his. Maybe he'd understand.

And maybe the Queen of England would show up for their fish fry tonight.

Micah headed toward the kitchen to start filleting. Five minutes later, the kitchen door swung open behind him. "He okay?" Micah asked, recognizing the heavy sound of his father's footsteps.

"He's with my trains. He's fine." His father started digging through the cabinets and pulled out some seafood seasoning. "I'm glad you came. I was beginning to wonder if you were avoiding me."

Micah gave a hard shake of his head. "Not avoiding you. Just doing my job."

"Speaking of which." His father glanced over his shoulder at Micah.

Micah watched from the corner of his eye, keeping his hand steady and continuing to fillet.

"What?"

"There's a promotion with your name on it, but it would mean moving to Fort Goodman. I told Colonel Hampton you'd gladly go."

Micah set his knife down now, keeping his gaze low and bracing his hands on the granite countertop in front of him. "I don't want it."

His father turned and leaned against the counter, folding his arms stiffly at his chest. "I know you like it here. You have that woman friend and—"

"The answer's no, Dad," Micah said through tight lips.

His father stood erectly and pointed a finger. "Don't forget, I'm also your commanding officer. If I think this is what's best for your career, then I can say yes and send you the damn- hell where I want to send you."

"You can't force me to reenlist, though." Micah faced him now, working hard not to smile as he said it.

His father was as hard as a statue, revealing no emotion in his face. "You are reenlisting," he said coldly. "You're not just going to throw away your life over some hobby. Is that what this is about? The landscaping thing?"

Micah shook his head. "I'm not throwing away anything. This is my life, and I'll do with it what I want. It's not my problem if you think it's a waste." He headed for the kitchen door. There was no way he was going to stick around with his father's oversized ego filling the room. They could talk about his later, when his father had calmed down. *If* he ever calmed down.

"Where are you going? You're not leaving while I'm still talking to you," his father barked.

When Micah was a kid, his old man would've pushed him against the wall. He'd never hit him, but Colonel Peterson believed in force. *Not this time.* "Come on, Ben. We'll cook our fish at home."

Ben's eyes widened as his mouth fell open. "But I want to eat with Grandpa."

"Another time, bud. It's our father-son day, remember?" Micah started pushing Ben's chair forward, feeling his father's eyes behind him, boring into the back of his skull.

Well, that had gone as well as could be expected.

When Ben was strapped in the Jeep, Micah got behind the wheel and started to pull away.

"Dad?"

Micah's gaze flitted toward the rearview mirror. "Yeah?"

"Grandpa looks sad."

They both looked at the colonel, standing on the front porch with his arms folded and his chin lifted high.

"He doesn't get sad, Ben." It wasn't in his father's emotional repertoire. Sad would imply that the man had feelings. Nope. Micah was willing to bet that look on his father's face was more disgust than anything.

And he hated himself for caring. His father's actions never said they cared about what he wanted.

"Dad?" Ben said again.

Micah's gaze lifted to the rearview again, meeting his son's eyes. "Yeah?"

"Thanks for taking me fishing. This was the best father-son day ever."

And that was all that mattered—being a good father to his own son. "It's not over yet, buddy. Let's go fry our fish."

~

KAT YAWNED AND CONSIDERED GOING TO BED. IT'D BEEN a long, boring Sunday, which she used to think was the best type—until a certain tall, dark, and handsome groundskeeper had come into her life. She'd missed him today, but she understood. Spending time alone with Ben was important.

Her phone buzzed on her nightstand table, signaling a text. He must've been thinking about her, too. Hopefully missing her as much as she missed him. She glanced at her screen and read:

Are you awake?

She typed "Yes" and waited to see what he'd say next, hanging on his every word. Or she would've been hanging on his every word if he texted her again. The phone was quiet. No buzzing. No beeps.

Her doorbell rang across the house and she jumped. Getting out of bed, she hurried toward the door, hoping it was Micah. She went up on her tiptoes to look through the peephole and got a rush of excitement. "Who is it?" she called, loud enough for him to hear her, teasing him. Her phone buzzed in response.

I know you're alone. I've come to take advantage of that fact.

She giggled, preparing to open the door when her phone buzzed again.

Don't open the door unless you want me to take you to bed.

Well, she had planned on going to bed. She doubted Micah had sleeping in mind, though, which was just fine with her. She opened the door and met his ready gaze.

"I told you not to open the door unless you wanted me as much as I want you."

She grinned. "I know."

He wasted no time walking in, closing the door behind them, and scooping her up into his arms.

Kat laughed. "What has gotten into you tonight?"

"I told my father the good news this afternoon," he said, his face turning serious for a moment.

"Oh. Wow. How did he take it?" she asked, bracing her hands against his chest.

"He didn't."

She surveyed his demeanor. "Then why are you smiling?"

"Because there are no more secrets. I want to celebrate by touching you. Is that okay?" His voice dropped to a low, sexy growl.

"Um." She swallowed, her entire body responding to his request. "I guess that's okay."

"Good." He placed one hand on each side of her face and gently led her mouth to his.

If the kiss was any indication of how the "touching" was going to go, then she couldn't wait for him to get her to bed. "Julie comes home in one hour."

"So we better get started," he said, already lifting her shirt.

Monday morning came too fast, as it always did. The weekends were never long enough, especially when Kat had barely gotten to spend any time with Micah. The time they had spent together, however, had been quality.

Val rapped on Kat's office door and stepped inside without waiting for her to answer.

"What are you smiling so cheerily about?" Kat asked, taking in her friend's demeanor. Val looked as giddy as a child with a secret to tell. And knowing Val, she probably did.

"Have you seen the morning paper yet?" Val asked, stepping further inside.

Kat shook her head. She usually avoided the paper until she'd had her second cup of coffee. "What's in there? Anything good?"

"Oh. You know. There's a nice write-up on Seaside Elementary, talking more about you than anything else."

A sick feeling usually crawled through Kat's stomach when she heard people were talking about her, but judging by the look on Val's face, she didn't need to worry this time.

Val flattened the paper in front of her. "Front page, baby."

Kat's gaze sharpened on the bold letters topping the newspaper: *Seaside's Favorite Principal Leads the Path to Success*

Her breath caught in her throat as she skimmed the first few paragraphs.

The Friendship Club, created to help troubled students increase their self-esteem, is also working to care for Seaside's local soldiers who are in need of a home-cooked meal and a show of appreciation . . . Principal Chandler believes every child wants to succeed. They want to do well at something, even if it's doing well at stirring up trouble in the classroom, she says. The Friendship Club shows these children that they are capable of working together as a team to create something beautiful.

Kat finished the article and smiled up at Val. "This is amazing."

"We'll have to make sure *everyone* sees it," Val agreed, glancing in the direction of Dora Burroughs's office. Then she lifted the paper off Kat's desk and hooked her head with a wicked grin. "No time like the present." She winked and walked out the door, closing it behind her.

Kat grinned ear to ear. Not that she wanted to rub her good news in anyone's face. *Much.* She'd have to call and thank Mr. Todd for writing such a flattering article about the school and Friendship Club later.

Another knock sounded on her door. This one was softer than Val's had been. "Come in."

The knob turned and Ben pushed his wheelchair inside. "Hi, Principal Chandler," he said in a sullen voice.

"Ben." Just seeing him made her heart squeeze. She loved that disheveled hair. And that large, toothy grin he usually wore, stretching through his freckled cheeks. He wasn't grinning today, however. "Everything okay?" she asked.

With his right arm, he rolled his wheelchair closer to her desk and stopped, keeping his head down.

"Are you sick? Do you need me to call your dad?"

He shook his head. "No. Miss Hadley sent me here."

"To my office?" Kat straightened as she made the connection. Ben had been sent to the principal's office. "Oh. Well, what happened?"

He lifted one shoulder, keeping his eyes planted on the floor.

"Can you at least look at me?" She lowered her voice. "Please." As he slowly lifted his head, she saw the tears shining in his eyes, and her heart nearly broke in half.

"I'm s-sorry. Please don't tell my dad."

She quickly moved around her desk, grabbing some Kleenex and crouching beside him. "Tell him what? I don't even know why you're here yet."

He sniffed, wiping quickly at his tears. "A girl in my class said that moms aren't Marines. She said my mom didn't really go to war, she just left me."

Kat sucked in a breath. "You know that's not true, though. Your mom is a Marine."

"And she left me, too." His eyes flooded over. "So I called the girl a stupid idiot."

"A stupid idiot? Ben, that's not very nice." And it wasn't like him to call people names.

His lips quivered. "I didn't mean it. I was just . . ."

Large tears spilled down his cheeks. Kat dabbed them gently with a tissue in her hand.

"I just want my mom to want me," he said. "And I don't want her to die. And I don't want you to leave me and my dad, either."

She squeezed his hand. "I'm not leaving you, honey. Don't worry about that. Have you talked to your dad about how you feel?"

He nodded, but she was willing to venture that Micah hadn't heard all of it. "Listen, I have a friend. Mr. Blakely. I'd like you to talk to him, too. Would that be okay?"

"The school counselor?" Ben asked, looking up.

Kat nodded. "He's been dying to hear about how you got the kids to talk to their plants this year."

This made the corners of Ben's mouth curve. "Okay." He hesitantly met her eyes. "Are you going to tell my dad what I did?"

Kat pressed her lips together. "I might. But you're not in trouble. As long as you apologize to the stup—"

Ben's mouth fell open as she started to repeat the names that had gotten him sent to her office. And yeah, it was probably in bad principal form, but seeing his little eyes light up, she'd make the exception. "And promise me that you won't call anyone else names."

He nodded slowly. "Promise."

Then she watched as he wheeled out of her office. Why did that little boy have to struggle so hard, without a mother to tell him everything would be okay? It wasn't fair. Life wasn't always fair. That was a lesson she'd learned in spades, but she was tougher for it and Ben would be, too.

Another loud knock sounded on her door and then Val grinned as she pushed through.

"Dora about choked on the doughnut she was eating. Then she said how nice it was that someone was trying to throw you a bone."

Kat's eyes narrowed. She just might land herself in her own Friendship Club by the day's end because she was going to walk down that hall and have a heart-to-heart with her dear assistant principal.

"What are you doing?" Val's smile was replaced with concern, and with good cause.

"I'm going to stand up for myself. Dora is a bully, and I'm going to teach her to be nice, damn it." Kat marched down the hall toward Mrs. Burrough's door. It was open, so she waited in the doorway for her assistant to look up.

"Yes," Dora finally said, with that plastic smile that Kat wanted to call her out on. This woman was supposed to support her. She was supposed to back up her efforts and help her make the school a better place.

"Why don't you like me?"

"Excuse me?" Dora's plastic smile grew wider.

"You don't like me. You've been pretending like you do, but it's all a big, fat lie and I want to hear the truth now."

If at all possible, the color drained from the elder woman's already pale face. "Principal Chandler, what on earth are you talking about?" She released a shrill laugh.

"You told Mr. Todd that the Friendship Club wouldn't work. You've been against it from the beginning. Against me since I came on board as principal last year."

Dora straightened and sighed dramatically. "All right. I don't believe you're doing a good job leading the school. You're too young, Katherine. Too inexperienced. Honestly, I feel it was a mistake to put you in this position. Don't get me wrong. I think one day, you might make a very good principal."

"That day is now." Val stepped up beside Kat.

Kat stopped her with a raised hand. This was her fight, and by golly, she was going to fight it. "I'm a damn good principal, Mrs. Burroughs. Do you want to know what I think?" Not waiting for an answer, Kat continued. "I think you're jealous. I think you wanted this position and you think you could do a better job than me. But you're wrong. Because a true leader would never undermine a member of her team. A true leader has the best interest of everyone in mind, not just her own interests."

Dora's frown deepened. "I'm sorry you feel that way."

"And I'm sorry we won't be able to work together any longer."

Now, the older woman's eyes widened. "You can't fire me. You don't have that kind of power."

"No, but I can have you transferred to another school. I have that kind of power, and I'll use it. Not to get back at you. I don't care about revenge. I care about this school's reputation. I care that parents feel good about sending their children here. And what you've been doing to undermine my authority has been hurting our students. That's unacceptable."

"Katherine, please." The woman's voice shook a little.

Kat held up a hand. "That's all. I hope we can end this relationship professionally." She turned and started walking back to her office, feeling weak and shaky. And pretty damn good.

When she plopped behind her desk, Val was already leaning in her doorway with one leg crossed in front of the other. "You've changed."

"What do you mean?"

"The Kat I grew up with never would've done that. She'd have complained and moaned about wanting to do that, but she never would've actually gone down there and told that prude off."

Heat moved up into Kat's cheeks. "Was it too much?"

"Hell, no. It was perfect. I just wish I would've gotten it on video. Your sister would be proud."

"Yeah." Kat smiled to herself. "It felt good. I can see why men pick bar fights. I feel like going in for round two."

Val shook her head. "Stay, lady, stay. I think you've done enough. And I plan to personally head up the farewell party for Dora."

Kat chewed her lower lip. "It's not too mean to threaten to transfer her?" she asked.

Val cocked a brow. "That wasn't a threat. It was a promise, and you better make good on it or I'll take back everything I just said about being proud of you."

"You didn't say you were proud of me."

Val's mouth quirked to one side. "I didn't? Hmm."

Kat smiled as she watched her best friend walk away. Then she leaned back in her office chair and laughed a little, feeling good. *Really* good. And she couldn't wait to share this moment with one person, the man who'd helped her find her way this year—Micah.

Chapter Twenty-Four

M icah slowed the Jeep as he approached his home, seeing the stiff figure sitting on his front porch rocker. What was his father doing here? His father had been perfectly clear over the weekend on how he'd felt about Micah's decision to "quit" the military. Or actually, his father had said that he was throwing his life away.

Micah's jaw tightened. It was a good thing Ben was next door with Aunt Clara. At least he'd be spared his grandfather's dramatics. The last thing Ben needed right now was another example of how dysfunctional his family was.

"Hey, Dad." Micah approached the older man seated on his front porch. When his father looked up, it struck Micah for a second how old the man suddenly looked. His hair had always been a distinguished gray, ever since his late twenties. But now his father's skin looked wrinkled, and the twinkle of his eyes seemed dull.

"You're making a mistake." His father's voice was low, unlike the other night.

Micah stopped walking. "I've heard your opinion on the matter already. The decision is made, so if you came here to talk me out of it, you can go home."

Colonel Peterson folded his arms across his broad chest. Old or not, he was in shape. "What is this about, Micah? Me? Are you getting back at me because of your mother? You never forgave me for not being there when she got sick."

Micah shook his head. "I forgave you." But he'd never forget. It proved his father's character. The man didn't care about anyone but himself. His father's only concern was that Micah was a reflection on him and, as a reflection, he needed to climb the military ranks and surpass all that his father had done in his own career.

"I push you so hard because I know what you're capable of, Micah. You're capable of a hell of a lot more than gardening."

Micah ran a quick hand through his military-regulated hair and laughed under his breath. His father *would* call it gardening. He started to unlock his front door, but it was already open. Ben must've come home already, which meant Aunt Clara was likely inside, too. She should've given him a heads up that his father was waiting here for him. Maybe he'd have driven around back and avoided him altogether.

Colonel Peterson stood, his chin lifting high as he looked at Micah, who was a good inch taller. "I'm still your superior."

"For another six months. Yeah. I get that." Micah pushed the door open and glanced inside, seeing Ben coming his way in his wheelchair. "I'll see you at the base, Colonel Peterson," Micah said, ready to slam the door in the good colonel's face.

"Micah." His father's commanding tone barked, making Micah turn. "You're deploying."

Micah's mouth fell open. "My squadron isn't scheduled to leave until next year." And schedules didn't change that fast, not in a profession that made you wait for everything, starting with entry onto the military base every morning.

"Things changed. You're leaving next month. I approved it. It'll be good for you to remember where you belong, Sergeant."

Blood hammered in Micah's ears. Hot, loud blood. "I belong in Seaside with my family. That's where the hell I belong."

"It's done." If his father had any emotion, it was kept in a safe with no evidence as to its existence.

"Dad?" Ben was suddenly in the doorway with tears clouding his eyes. He swiped a lock of hair out of his face and looked at Micah. "Dad? You're leaving, too? Who's going to take care of me?" Ben's gaze moved to his grandfather. "You can't send my dad away, too!" he cried.

A decent grandfather would've had some words of comfort. This one averted his gaze and descended the wooden front porch steps, not bothering to look back.

"You can't make my dad leave!" Ben yelled between sobs. "You can't!"

Colonel Peterson didn't turn, didn't so much as flinch as Ben's angry, pleading words followed him all the way to his polished SUV. Then he got in, calmly closed the door and robotically buckled his seatbelt. Standing on the front porch, Micah, Ben, and Clara watched the colonel drive away.

"Ben, let's go inside. We'll figure things out," Micah said, knowing there was nothing to figure out. Until next spring, he belonged to the military.

"Mom's already gone. I need a dad. This isn't fair!" Ben's freckled face was a mottled red color now. He wheeled himself toward his bedroom, slamming the door behind him.

Yeah, Micah felt the same way.

Aunt Clara folded her arms under her chest as she shook her head. "Can he do that do you? You're getting out."

"He can do it. And I have no choice in the matter." Micah plopped down in a chair at the kitchen table.

"You know I'll take Ben while you're gone. He's no problem."

Micah felt as if his entire life had just been suddenly twisted and rearranged with the efficiency of a tiller to solid earth. He was never supposed to leave his son again. "Thanks, Aunt Clara." He stood, needing to work. "I'm going outside. I'll come back and talk to Ben in a little bit. He needs some time to calm down right now."

And so did Micah.

"Sure. Micah?" Aunt Clara waited for him to face her. "If it's any comfort, I think my brother does believe he has your best interest in mind."

Micah shook his head. "It's no comfort." He closed the door behind him, forcing himself not to slam it. He'd forgive his father later, when it didn't hurt so badly. He wanted to believe his father was a good guy. When he was a child, he'd thought his father was the biggest hero, braver than Superman and Batman put together. Now, his father was just a man who'd let him down one too many times.

Grabbing his shears, he growled in frustration and then started hacking at an overgrown bush.

He'd go on one more deployment and then nothing, and no one, would stop him from being there for his son for the rest of his life.

～

VAL NODDED IN SATISFACTION. "YOU DID GREAT."

Kat lifted her mitted hands off the hot cherry pie that had just come out of the oven and stood back to admire it. "I hope everyone is right, and food really is the way to a man's heart."

Her friend arched a brow. "I think you're already in his heart, my friend. But a little pie might be incentive for him to spend an extra long time devouring your body later."

Kat laughed. "One of these days you're going to make some pie-loving guy very happy."

"In the meantime, my pies serve as good deeds and they make Preacher Hunt less likely to disown me as his daughter."

"You're a great daughter. And a great friend, in case I haven't told you lately."

Val held up a hand. "That's my cue to leave before you go all Pollyanna on me." She winked.

"I have to change clothes anyway." Kat slipped her cherry-stained apron off.

"I'll see my way out." Val gestured to the door. "My father has a mile-long list of things for me to do for the church anyway. I've run out of excuses not to do them."

Kat made a point of looking at Val's attire—a fitted blouse and too short skirt, perfected with knee-length black boots. "I hope you're going to change clothes first, too. That's not exactly an angelic image."

"I never claimed to be an angel." Val grinned. "I'll see you later," she called, walking out and closing the door behind her.

Kat left the pie to cool and retreated to her bedroom to change into something fresh. Something that said rip my clothes off later, because she kind of liked Val's promise that the pie would make her body a second dessert.

When she got to Micah's house an hour later, Kat found Ben sitting on the porch. "Hi," she said as she walked up, her heart swelling at the sight of him.

He kept his head down, his gaze just barely bouncing up to acknowledge her. She knew the look. It was the same one he'd had when he'd been sent to the principal's office the week before. Something was wrong, and she worried that maybe he was thinking about his mom again.

After setting the pie on the porch railing, she walked over to sit on the wooden swing. It creaked as she wiggled back and pushed the swing off with her feet. "Wanna talk?" she asked.

His left arm was coiled tightly across his waist. "Dad is leaving," he muttered.

Her heart gave a pause. Marines left all the time. They had weekends in the field, month-long trainings in other parts of the United States. "Leaving? What do you mean he's leaving?"

Hopefully, Micah was just going away for a few days because that was as long as she could endure without him lately. Her body was completely addicted to his.

"My mom doesn't want me, and my dad is leaving me to go to the war just like her," Ben said.

Kat's feet scuffed the ground to make the swing come to an

urgent halt. "Going to war? But your dad is getting out of the Marine Corps."

Ben sniffled as huge tears rolled down his already red and swollen cheeks. He must've been crying for hours already. Poor kid. Obviously, he'd misunderstood something he'd heard because there was no way Micah was deploying again. No way.

She turned and saw Micah standing at the front door, looking nearly as forlorn as Ben. Her heart sank like lead in her stomach.

"Guess he told you," Micah said, stepping toward them.

Her lips parted, but no words came. They were stuck in her throat and choking her. There was no way this was happening. It was a nightmare—a horrible one that she needed to wake from right now.

"It's a six-month deployment, so it'll take up the rest of my time in the Marine Corps. I can't get out of it," he said.

"Who will keep Ben?" she asked, quietly. *And who will make me laugh? Help me with the Friendship Club? Hold me at night? Love me?*

"Aunt Clara and Uncle Rick will keep him. They've done it before." Micah's gaze moved to his son and he offered a weak smile. "Six months will fly by. Then I'll be home and I'll never leave you again. I promise."

"You said you'd never leave me again after the last time," Ben croaked. "You make promises and don't keep them, just like Mom."

Micah crouched in front of him. "I'm sorry, little man. It sucks. That's all there is to it. If I had a choice, I'd choose you every time. But I have a duty as a Marine. Do you understand that?"

More tears rolled down Ben's quivering cheeks.

Kat realized she had tears of her own. "I shouldn't be here. You two should be alone." She stood and headed toward the porch steps, stopping when Micah grabbed her gently, pulling her to face him.

"I'm sorry," he said softly. "I don't have a choice."

Rolling her lips together, she blinked heavily through burning eyes. "Right. Of course." He didn't have a choice. He was leaving and, *damn him*, he was taking her heart with her.

She stepped back, just wanting to escape, and knocked the pie that she'd set on the railing, sending it falling to the ground. "Oh!" She hurried down the steps to get it as red cherry filling spilled out of its tinfoil cover. "It's ruined," she said, biting the inside of her cheek to keep from bawling.

"You made me a pie?" he asked, his gaze lifting to meet hers.

There were those cocoa-colored eyes she'd grown to love staring into. "No. Yes." It hurt to breathe. "I have to go." She took another step backward, tears blurring the image of Micah and Ben staring at her. She could hear Ben's soft cries, though, and her heart ached. She wanted to go to him, but she couldn't—not now. All she could do was leave. She left the pie. Left the man she loved, and his son on the porch, and ran to her car as quickly as she could. Then she drove blindly through thick tears of anger and confusion, heartbreak and despair, to the only place she knew to go.

Kat sat in her car and stared at the shaded cemetery for a long moment before getting out of her car. Blinking through the tears that refused to quit falling, her eyes burned against the wind that seemed to blow constantly through this little town. She hadn't visited this place much since he'd been gone. He wasn't in that grave, she knew that. His body may be, but John wasn't a man who could be caged in. That was one of the things that had surprised her when he'd asked her to marry him. He was willing to bind himself to her forever.

Their forever had been too short.

The gate to the cemetery creaked loudly as she entered. She wasn't even sure why she was here. She just didn't know where else to go to feel his presence anymore. She'd felt him with her when she'd worn his ring. But that was silly. She knew that in her head.

Now everything was so confusing. Her heart was starting to love someone else, and she was beginning to forget pieces of John, molding his memories with those of the man she was in love with now. How could she do this all over again? Love a man who was deploying to a foreign country, to put himself in danger?

She stood in front of John's granite headstone. Being here

always felt surreal. A few feet below her was the body of the man she missed snuggling into at night. She missed talking to him, telling him how her day was, and how she felt.

"Hey." Her voice cracked as she knelt on the soft grass. "It's me. I'm sorry it's been so long." A sob escaped as she spoke, and she wiped at her tears. Her nose was running now, too. "I wanted to tell you that I met someone. He's strong like you." Strong the way she had tried to be, and she'd almost succeeded until now. "I should be there with him right now, but I'm scared. Losing you was—" She swallowed hard, shaking her head and pressing her eyes shut. "I can't go through that again, John. I can't risk everything for something that might not work out. What if he doesn't come home? What if I'm left all alone?"

Her shoulders shook as she waited for an answer she knew wouldn't come. John was dead. He couldn't tell her what to do. But if he were here, he'd be arguing her out of these fears. That's what he'd done when she'd nearly backed out of applying for the principal job at Seaside Elementary. Anytime John had faced something that scared him, he'd run toward it head-on. Fear was like a personal challenge to him, and he'd never backed down from a challenge. That's what made him an incredible leader. A hero. The man she'd loved.

She loved another man now. Micah.

She sat there for a long time. Then she got up and starting walking on shaky legs. The wind was blowing harder now, seeming to push her toward her car as she walked away. It was as if John were telling her to go. Telling her what she knew she had to do.

But he was wrong. Maybe he'd always been wrong. She wasn't as strong as him, chasing down her fears and defeating her challenges. So, instead of going back to Micah, she went home.

MICAH'S ARMS WERE SORE FROM THE SHEARING ATTACK he'd declared on the first tree he'd come in contact with after his run-in with Kat. Limbs lay on the ground all around him as if a storm had shaken the tree within an inch of its life.

It'd grow back thicker and more beautiful than before, though. He knew that. And he and Ben would do the same once he returned home from his last deployment. He and Kat would not, though. She'd made that crystal clear and, in doing so, she'd also sent another devastating blow to Ben.

He hacked another branch, cursing under his breath. This was his fault. He'd known deep down in his gut not to get involved with another woman. Ben needed stability. That had been the whole theme for the year, giving his son a place to grow roots, to get strong.

Branch after branch fell to the ground. He was in a frenzy and he knew it, but it didn't felt good to release all the emotion storming inside of him.

"Just what on earth do you think you're doing, Micah Daniel Peterson?" Aunt Clara's voice snapped over the string of words coming out of his mouth. The moment reminded him a lot of that first summer afternoon when she'd found him doing something similar in her backyard.

"I'm trimming the bushes. What does it look like?" he growled, not meaning to get short with his aunt.

"It looks like a grown man having a temper tantrum, if you ask me."

He dropped his shears and looked at her, wiping the back of his hand across his brow to keep the sweat from pouring into his eyes. "She left. She couldn't even pretend like she wasn't going to run as fast as her legs would possibly carry her for Ben's sake. No. She just took off." He ran both hands through his hair. "I knew better than to get involved. I knew it. And if Ben takes a downturn because of this . . ." He shook his head.

"Then he'll bounce right back," Aunt Clara said slowly, stepping closer and bracing her arms over his. "He's a strong kid, Micah. You've raised him well, and you should be proud of yourself."

The words made his throat tighten, which isn't what he wanted.

He wanted to be mad. He wanted to tear something up, to punch something.

"And don't pretend this is all about Ben's hurt feelings."

Micah's gaze sharpened on her, but her eyes only warmed in response. "Your feelings are hurt, too. Kat walked away from both of you."

His chest ached. "Yeah," he finally said.

"Give her time. She's been through a lot."

Right now, he didn't care what baggage Kat had in her past, though. She'd come along for the ride, knowing he was a Marine. Knowing he had a kid that was fragile. She hadn't come into this relationship blind. There were risks, and if she wasn't strong enough to face them, then he couldn't afford to give her time, and hope she stuck if and when she decided to come back.

"How's Ben?" he asked, changing the subject.

"He's resting in his bedroom," Clara said.

With a nod, Micah picked up the shears again. "I need to be alone. Can you stay with him awhile?"

"As long as you need."

Which was exactly what Micah needed in his life. Someone with staying power. Someone who would be there for his family when they needed them. He'd hoped Kat was that kind of person, but he knew now that she wasn't.

"Thanks. I've got a few more bushes to trim," he said.

Chapter Twenty-Five

"You look sick," Val said when Kat walked in on Monday morning.

Kat plopped down in the chair behind her desk, catching a few loose papers as they flew

toward the floor. She felt sick, but not the kind that would allow her to stay home in bed, which is what she'd done all weekend after running out on Micah.

"And you didn't answer my calls yesterday. Julie said you were depressed." Val cocked an eyebrow, folding her arms at her chest.

"I plead the Fifth," Kat said miserably. "But I really hate the word 'depressed.'" Even though that's exactly what she was. So depressed that her bones literally ached and it hurt to move from one side of the room to the other.

"You want to talk about it?" Val asked.

Shaking her head, Kat pressed her lips together. If she spoke, she might get all teary-eyed, and this was where she worked. She was good at her job. At least she still had that.

Val came a little closer and laid a plate of fresh-baked muffins down. "Here. These are for you. I eat when I'm depressed. And you said my baking was good, so . . ." She shrugged.

"Thank you, Val. You're the best secretary ever."

"And you're a very bad liar," Val said with a smile.

"I plead the Fifth," Kat said again, smiling for the first time in the last forty-eight hours, and making herself laugh a little.

"Mrs. Burroughs wanted to know if you could help her set up for the book fair this week. She's in the media center right now helping the PTO unload boxes."

Kat reached for a muffin, peeling off its wrapper. Last week, she and Dora had a heart-to- heart, and Dora had apologized, humbly asking for another chance to be a better assistant principal. And everyone deserved another chance—Kat truly believed that. People deserved as many chances as they were sincere in asking for.

Kat took a bite, moaned, then set it down on the paper plate for later. "If you need me, I'll be in the media center," she told Val, who chuckled.

"Good luck."

As Kat walked in that direction, her heart pained seeing a familiar wheelchair in front of her.

Ben. She hadn't just run off on Micah over the weekend. She'd left Ben, too. Poor kid.

"Hey there, buddy," she said, walking up beside him, fully expecting him to look up at her with those large, adoring eyes that were always so happy to see her. He didn't.

"Ben?"

He pushed the wheel of his chair with his right arm harder, attempting to go faster.

"Leave me alone, okay?" he said, his words slurring together.

"I'm sorry about the other day. I shouldn't have run out the way I did."

He shrugged, not stopping or looking at her. "You're just like everyone else. I'm used to it."

"I'm not like—"

He looked at her. "Yeah, you are. Just go, Principal Chandler. I have to get to class."

She stopped walking and watched him wheel away. Biting the inside of her cheek, she begged herself not to dissolve into tears.

"Eating muffins is better—way better," she mumbled. Then she turned to go do exactly that and came face-to-face with her assistant principal.

"Kids don't hold grudges long. I had three boys and one girl. I have six grandchildren. Do something special for them and they're like putty in your hands."

"Like what?" Kat asked numbly, surprised that she was actually having a human conversation with Dora. Maybe things really would change between them.

"Saying 'I'm sorry' goes a long way with kids. Especially over a bowl of ice cream."

Kat swallowed a small laugh. "Thanks. I'll remember that. Do you still need help with the book fair setup?"

Dora waved a hand. "I heard you babbling about some muffins. Go eat your heart out. You can come help me later."

Kat laughed and nodded. "Sounds good." She wished saying sorry was as easy between adults. Of course, if she were to run into Micah right now, she wouldn't know what she was apologizing for. For falling in love with him? For not being stronger? For turning her back when he needed her most?

For all of the above, she decided, plopping behind her desk and finishing off that first muffin, then following it with a second.

Micah watched Ben and Lawson laugh across the table at each other. They usually had their weekly meal with "Uncle" Lawson at home, but tonight, the best that Micah could do was offer to pay for pizza, which Lawson readily agreed to.

Worth every penny, too, because Lawson made Ben smile.

"It's the cowboy hat," his friend tried to say earlier in the night, as Micah rolled his eyes. Micah was almost considering buying his own cowboy hat these days.

"So, this Kimberly girl has invited you to her birthday party, huh?" Lawson was saying as Ben's pale skin darkened to a deep red. "That's serious business." Lawson nodded. "When a girl invites you to her party, it means she likes you. Boys don't often get invited to girls' parties. Better make sure you buy a good gift."

Both Ben and Lawson looked at Micah, who just shrugged. "I'll take you tomorrow," he said, unable to muster any enthusiasm. "How's that?"

"I was thinking I might need to borrow your hat," Ben said, returning his attention to Lawson.

"You don't need a hat, little man. Not when the girl is drawing you pictures and begging you to come to her house. Your charm is natural."

At this, Micah finally smiled. It was short-lived, though, because his gaze caught on the three women walking into Kirk's Pizza House. Kat, Julie, and Val. He groaned, and Lawson immediately looked back to see the source of his misery.

"You could go talk to her," he said.

Micah shook his head. "I've got nothing to say."

She invited me to her office for ice cream yesterday," Ben offered, causing Micah's brows to lift.

"You didn't mention that," he said.

Ben shrugged. "I thought you might get jealous, or something."

Jealous? Well, yeah, maybe just a little.

"Ice cream and, let me guess," Micah said, tapping his finger on his chin. "She's now your favorite principal again?"

"She said she was sorry, Dad. And I believe her."

Micah leaned forward and ruffled Ben's hair. "You are a great kid, you know that? You're also a sucker for ice cream. Was it chocolate?"

"Chocolate fudge." Ben shrugged. "So?" He looked at Micah expectantly. Lawson did, too.

"So what?" Micah asked. "She didn't apologize to me, and she didn't invite me to her office for chocolate fudge ice cream, either." Although that was never exactly his treat of choice when it came to Kat.

"Maybe you should apologize first," Ben suggested, grabbing a third slice of pizza.

"Me?" Micah drew back. "I didn't do anything wrong."

"Doesn't matter." Lawson shook his head. "In my vast experience, the guy always has to say sorry first. It's a law or something."

Micah shot him a look. "Let's just eat and get out of here. I'm not saying sorry for something I didn't do." He glanced back at Kat, sitting with the other two women. At least she'd made amends with his son. That was something. But it wasn't enough, so pondering going over and saying anything to her right now was out of the question.

An hour later, Micah turned the lights off in Ben's room and stared at him from the doorway. In one month's time, he'd be gone, and this was one of the things he'd miss the most. He loved tucking in his son and telling him goodnight. Boys didn't get tucked in forever. By the time Micah got home from deployment, Ben might be too big for such things. He was already in the third grade, too big by most kids' standards. Ben hadn't pushed him away yet, though, and Micah was going to hang on to every opportunity to be a father to him that he could.

"Dad, stop staring at me," Ben said sleepily.

Micah couldn't resist. He crossed the room and bent to kiss his son's forehead. "Don't grow up while I'm away, okay?"

"Okay," came Ben's sleepy reply. "I'll try not to."

Micah walked down the hall toward the kitchen, not ready for sleep himself. Instead, he brewed a pot of coffee and started working on a new landscaping design for the azalea festival that would take place in early spring. He wouldn't be around in the spring, but someone else could work with his designs. He'd spoken to a guy named Trevor, who was interested in overseeing things while Micah was away. And when he returned, he'd hopefully be back in the same position as he was now. His father had tried to ruin things for him, or help him as Aunt Clara always insisted was his real motivation, and he'd failed. The only thing Colonel Peterson had ruined was Micah's relationship with Kat.

Which was probably for the best anyway.

At a quarter past midnight, Micah finally turned off the lights and headed to his room, hoping for more than another night of tossing and turning.

~

SHE COULDN'T SLEEP. KAT TOSSED ON THE BED AND READ the clock again. Almost midnight. Sitting up, she blew out a breath, and then reached for the pull on her bedside lamp. Her gaze immediately caught on the shoebox across the room—the one she'd been avoiding since cleaning out the master bedroom for Julie.

She was tired of avoiding things, though. Facing them head-on seemed to be working well lately. Although she hadn't had the opportunity to face Micah. Not yet at least. He seemed to be avoiding her, going so far as to hire a fill-in lawn guy named Trevor to take care of the school's campus.

Kat retrieved the shoe box and carried it back to her bed. Lifting the top, she stared for a long moment at the contents, which were mostly paper products. Cards. Love notes. Handwritten vows that never got recited. Surprisingly, she found herself smiling at the bunch. Coming to the bottom of the box, her hand paused on one crumpled envelope. It was unopened, and across the front, it simply read KAT. She'd never seen it before, but instinctively she knew what it was. A gasp caught in her throat.

~

JOHN WAS A MAN WHO LIKED TO PREPARE FOR THINGS. IT was his way. And before going to war, it only made sense that he'd prepare in case he never returned.

She ripped the top open, her heart speeding up as she pulled the thin paper from inside. She hesitated before unfolding it, wondering what he'd written, contemplating if she was truly ready to hear his last words to her. Then, taking a breath, she unfolded the paper carefully and started reading.

Dear Kat,

If you're reading this, it means I won't be coming home. I'm sorry for that. I know I made a lot of promises to you, and I meant every word. I love you. I always have.

Kat, you inspired me to be a better man. Did you know that? You inspire everyone around you just by being who you are. That's how I knew you'd be good at the principal job you applied for. You're one of those people who can change the world just by smiling. You changed my world, that's for sure.

If I don't come home, it's not because I didn't want to, or that I didn't try my best. I would've moved heaven and earth to get back to you. But sometimes things don't work out the way we want them to. I'm sure they turn out the way they're supposed to, though. Keep being who you are, Kat, because that's who I fell in love with. And if I don't come home, that's who some other lucky guy will one day fall in love with, too. Don't be afraid to love again. Remember, there is never loss with love, only gain.

Until we meet again. I love you. John

Her cheeks were wet. Shakily, she slid a hand down each cheek, smearing her tears. These were John's final words to her, and she was pretty sure he just told her in no uncertain terms to get up and fight for love.

There is no loss, only gain.

John was right. She would choose him again if given the chance, knowing exactly how things had ended. And she'd choose Micah right now, not knowing.

"Crap." She sprung up off the bed and pulled on the jeans that were draped over a chair in her room. Hearing the beating of the rain on the roof, she also grabbed her hooded raincoat and slid her feet into a pair of rubber boots.

"Where are you going?" Julie asked, meeting her in the hallway.

"Why are you still up?" Kat countered.

"Touché. I've been watching black-and-white movies again. Secret addiction."

Kat shook her head. "I've got to tell you, it's never been a secret, Julie."

"Your turn. You've finally come to your senses?" Julie asked, smiling. "It's about time, sis."

She glanced at the clock. "Or past time, actually. Won't he be sleeping?"

Kat's heart was thundering in her chest. Not answering the question, she called behind her, "Don't wait up!"

"Go get that sexy hunk," Julie cheered, seeing her out the door. "And it's raining. Lover reunions are always best in the pouring rain," she called.

Kat made a mental note to ban Julie from those sappy romances just as soon as she returned. Or join her, depending on how tonight went.

Chapter Twenty-Six

M icah's eyes snapped open. The room was dark, illuminated only by the moonlight streaming in through his bedroom window. Only, it was raining and the sky was overcast, so . . . the light wasn't coming from the moon.

He sat up quickly and moved to the window, hearing the noise again—a soft ping against the glass. Squinting through the glare, he saw the flashlight first and slowly made out the image of a woman outside, standing in the rain and tossing small rocks at his window.

"What the hell?" He pulled on a T-shirt and grabbed his umbrella, then headed toward the front door. Opening it, he stepped out into the night, not worried that the noise would wake Ben. His son was a sound sleeper.

"Kat?" he called, walking around to the side of his house where his window was. He spotted her as she tossed another stone. "Kat, what are you doing out here?"

Whirling around, she gave a little shriek. "Getting your atten-tion," she said, dropping the pebble in her hand.

He stood there, sheltered under his umbrella, thoroughly confused. Was he dreaming?

Because no way was Kat Chandler standing outside his bedroom window in the pouring rain.

"What do you want?" he asked.

She was wearing a light blue raincoat, the hood doing a piss-poor job of sheltering her face. She pointed her small flashlight at him, making him squint. "Oh. Sorry." She pointed it down at her feet instead. "I want to talk to you."

"I'm listening," he said, roughly, staring at her. If this was a dream, he had a mind to either drag her to his bedroom and make love to her all night, or give her a piece of his mind, which he'd been biting at the bit to do since she'd scared off so easily the other day.

"Right." She nodded, her face drenched from the rain. "Can we maybe . . ." She nibbled her lower lip and his groin jumped to attention. The first fantasy sounded good. ". . . go inside?" she asked, shining the light at him again. "Sorry. It's dark and the rain is in my eyes."

He moved closer, placing his umbrella over her, also, which was more than his mind told him she deserved. His heart wasn't listening, though. "Come on," he said.

They didn't go inside. Instead, he turned to face her on his front porch. "I'm listening," he said, tossing down his umbrella and bracing his hands on his hips.

She nodded. "Okay." Nervous laughter bubbled up through her. "I thought I knew exactly what I wanted to say, but now that I'm here . . ."

More nervous laughter escaped her mouth, and then she looked at him with those eyes that had captivated him since the first day he met her. There was more on the line than sexual attraction now, though. A lot more.

"I came here to tell you that I can't lose another man in my life." Her hair hung in solid, wet strands down by her face as she pulled her hood off. "It was too hard losing John. Harder than anything else I've ever gone through."

He nodded, keeping his distance as he watched her. Part of him wanted to wrap his arms around her as she spilled her feelings out in the open. She'd lost someone close to her, and he could relate to that. Jessica hadn't died, but he'd lost her. And he'd lost his mother. "I get it," he said, cutting her off. "It's fine, Kat," he said sharply.

She blinked. "I couldn't bear to lose another man that I'm in love with."

His whole body stilled. Was she breaking up with him and telling him that she loved him at the same time? Because that was a double blow. "You don't have to explain anything to me, okay? We can just part ways and pretend like the last few months never happened. In fact, I've already wiped them from my memory."

A frown settled on her lips. "I don't want to forget they ever happened. Micah, I'm telling you that I don't want to walk away from us. I don't . . . want . . . to lose you."

There was pain in her expression and hope in her eyes. The conflicting emotions speared through his heart. But he had to remember the other spear she'd staked through him recently. Ben was just getting back to normal. And in a few weeks Micah would be gone. He needed to know that Ben would be okay when he left. Which meant there was no room for error.

"We're done, Kat. It was good while it lasted, but it's over now." He watched her shivering body standing before him, and did his best not to pull her in and comfort her. He couldn't. Not this time. "Go home and get warm," he said, as the rain fell even harder, making his words hard to hear even to his own ears. Judging by the expression on her face, she heard them loud and clear. He reached down for the umbrella and offered it to her. "Take this."

She stared at it for a long moment, and then, ignoring his offer, she headed back out into the rain, leaving him as he'd asked her to.

"Come on, buddy. Get up." Micah stood in Ben's doorway, waiting. "It's Monday morning. You have school."

Ben's head peeked through the covers, cracking an eye at Micah, and then he reluctantly moved to sit up. "Eggs?" he asked.

"Only if you're in the kitchen in five minutes." Micah turned and started walking. He needed another cup of coffee this morning. After Kat's visit last night, he'd never gone back to sleep.

Ben was dressed and at the table five minutes later, fresh-faced and smiling as usual.

"Sleep well?" Micah asked, wishing he had that kind of energy.

Ben nodded, reaching for the fork on the table.

"Make sure you take—"

"Slow bites. I know, Dad," Ben said through chews. "You don't have to worry about me while you're gone. Slow bites. No getting out of my chair by myself. I'll make you proud."

Micah leaned in and kissed his forehead. "You already make me proud, son."

An hour later, they pulled into the school and Micah's gaze hung on Kat standing in the doorway, greeting the students. Sucking in a breath, he went through the usual routine: getting Ben's chair on the ground, helping Ben out, handing him his book bag and lunch. No hugs and kisses here, just a quick salute. "Aunt Clara will pick you up after school, okay?"

Ben nodded. "Yeah, Dad." He started rolling forward, stopping when he heard Micah's phone ring.

Glancing down, Micah cursed under his breath. Jessica had some timing.

"Is it Mom?" Ben asked, a hopeful tone rising in his voice. He turned and started wheeling himself back. "You only get that face with Mom. I want to talk to her!" Ben's face was as bright as it got on Christmas morning.

Jessica probably wasn't calling to talk to him, though. No doubt there was some selfish motive behind her phone call. "Hold on, buddy. Let me talk to her first." His jaw tightened as he answered, keeping an eye on his son. "Hey, Jess," he said, working hard to keep the agitation out of his voice.

"Micah," she said, sounding . . . different somehow. "I'm glad I caught you. I wasn't sure if you'd be at physical training yet or not."

"I take Ben to school in the mornings," he said flatly. Which she'd know if she was any kind of mother at all.

There was a long hesitation on the other line. "Is he with you?" she finally asked. "Can I speak to him?"

Micah's gaze moved to Ben, who was hanging on every word. "School's about to start," he said, wishing to God he didn't have to hand the phone over. But he did, he knew he did. "Make it quick."

Ben snatched the phone with his right hand as Micah offered it. "Mom! I miss you. Are you coming home?" Words rattled out of his mouth excitedly. Then he stopped for a moment and listened, making Micah squirm.

He wanted to know what Jessica was telling him—no doubt more lies that he'd have to deal with later.

"Yeah. Okay. I will," Ben finally agreed. "I can't wait! 'Bye, Mom. I love you!" He clicked off the phone and handed it back to Micah.

"You will what?" Micah asked suspiciously.

"I'll do my best at school and listen to you and Aunt Clara."

"Of course you will," Micah said, irritated. If Jessica knew her son, she'd know Ben always did those things. He was a good kid, who deserved better.

"And she said she'd be coming to visit after Christmas."

And you believe her? Micah wanted to ask. But he bit his tongue instead. Of course his son believed her. Ben was forgiving to his core and he believed people when they told him something. If only it was that easy.

"You have to walk me into the building now," Ben said. "The bell's already rung. I need you to sign me in."

Micah glanced down. Signing him in meant possibly seeing Kat, and after last night, he definitely didn't want to face her. She'd poured her heart out for him and he'd sent her away. But it was the right thing to do.

Wasn't it?

"Come on." He started walking. "After Christmas, huh?"

Ben nodded, his right arm pumping the wheel of his chair with renewed energy. "After Christmas. Mom is coming to visit me, and she said she'll bring presents from overseas," his son said happily.

Micah smiled, but inside there was a growing ache in his chest as they approached the double doors of the school. Ben was so forgiving and loving. Where he'd learned those things, Micah wasn't sure, because he certainly didn't feel that way about his ex. And despite her sincere apology last night, he'd turned Kat away. "I wish I was more like you, buddy."

Ben stopped wheeling and turned his head, looking up at Micah with those large, golden eyes that betrayed every emotion swirling in his little body. "Dad, you are. We're two of a kind. That's what Aunt Clara always tells me."

"Two of a kind, huh?" Micah repeated.

"So, are you going to see Principal Chandler again, before you leave? Maybe she'll give you ice cream, too."

Micah squatted down, giving Ben a serious look. He was about to give the speech he'd given his son a hundred times already. He didn't need anyone else in his life. He had Ben, and Ben was enough. The words didn't come this time, though. Because it wasn't enough. Not for him, and not for Ben. They both loved Kat. She was part of them now and they could forgive her anything, a thousand and one times if necessary, because that's what people who loved each other did.

Ben had just taught him that.

"You're my hero, buddy. Did you know that?" It was the truth. Ben had taught him way more about life than he could ever teach his son. And Ben made him want to be better.

"I learned watching you, Dad. You're mine."

The words made something shift inside him. His son was proud of him, even though he was leaving. The knowledge ripped him up inside. "Let's get you to class," he said, straightening and opening the door of the school.

Kat wasn't in the front office when he signed Ben in. Val was, though. She sat, alternating between smiles at Ben and disgruntled frowns at him. Hopefully, she would be as forgiving as Ben once he fixed things with Kat.

Because he was going to fix things with Kat—before this day was over.

~

T HE BUILDING WAS QUIET, EXCEPT FOR THAT occasional creak that could never be identified. Kat tapped her fingers on her desk, staring at the stack of teacher requests for time off. Then there were the office supply lists that she needed to approve. And the proposed field trips for the third quarter of the school year.

With a sigh, she shoved the stacks of paper to the side and stared at the clock. She should just go home. Julie was probably cooking, and Val might even be there. The two had gotten unbelievably tolerant of each other these days, which made Kat happy. So, she didn't have the love of a good man—the best man. She still had a sister who was loyal and sticking in Seaside indefinitely. And a best friend who made her laugh even when she wanted to cry.

A noise down the west hallway jolted Kat in her chair. She listened stiffly, hearing it a second time. No way were those vandals destroying school property again. She knew who they were now, and they'd already served their time after school.

The familiar sound of metal cans hitting the pavement brought her to her feet, though. There was no mistaking it. She started walking, getting faster as she drew closer to the side entrance. She'd really thought they'd learned their lesson, but no. She could hear the *click, click sheesh* of the spray paint writing who knows what on the wall outside.

Pushing through the side door, she was already lecturing the boys. "Just what do you think you're doing—" She stopped stone-cold as she met Micah's dark brown eyes. "You? What are you doing out here?" Her gaze searched the woods in front of her as her heart rattled her chest, and not because of the vandals. "Did you see the boys?" she asked.

Micah shook his head, but a smile was overwhelming his face. It'd been less than twenty- four hours since she'd made an absolute fool of herself, she knew, but *God,* she'd missed that face. He took a step closer to her and she stiffened, waiting for another rejection.

And she would deserve it. She'd really screwed things up with him. She knew that, but she couldn't change the past no matter how much she wished she could.

"I'm here to see you," he said, stepping even closer.

"Me? Why didn't you just come through the front door?" Her brows lowered because there was this look of mischief in his eyes. Where was the anger and the disappointment from last night?

"I decided after your whole throwing-pebbles-at-my-window-in-the-middle-of-the-night thing that I needed to do something a little more dramatic than coming through the school's front door."

"Dramatic?" She shook her head, still not following him. "For what?"

"To tell you how I feel. You poured your heart out to me last night, and now it's my turn." He held out his hands and she gasped when she saw the fresh spray paint coloring them.

Her eyes widened as she looked up. "You?" Whirling around, she gasped again at the wall of bright blue paint.

I LOVE YOU. FORGIVE ME?

Her chest pinched and her throat tightened. She couldn't turn to face him again. There was too much emotion swirling inside of her to process. Was he just clearing his conscience before leaving?

"I understand that I'll have to clean this mess up," he said in a low voice as he stood behind her. His hands rested on her shoulders, squeezing softly. "And I'll probably have to serve time after school in the Friendship Club for delinquent behavior."

She stifled a laugh.

"I may have to serve that time when I get back from deployment, though. Do you think you can wait that long?"

Facing him now, she looked up to meet his eyes through her own tear-filled ones. "I can wait," she said shakily.

"Yeah?" he asked, using his index finger to wipe away one of her tears.

"Yeah." She nodded, leaning into his chest. He didn't push her away. This was real. "But I'm the one who needs to be forgiven. I just left . . . and Ben."

Micah held a finger to her lips, gently quieting her. "I've learned that Ben and I are two very forgiving guys. So, uh, what do you say to spending more time with us? A whole lot more time. After I get home from deployment, that is."

It felt so good to be back in his arms. Like a dream she never wanted to wake from. "I will spend every second with you that you'll let me." She laughed, on the verge of tears.

He smoothed her hair behind her ear. "That's good, because according to Ben we're perfect for each other. And I have to agree. I'd be a fool to let you get away. Ben and I need you, Kat."

Her body melted into his arms. "I need you, too." And she loved them. She loved *him*. He hadn't reciprocated when she'd told him so at his house last night, though. It was written on the wall in front of her now, but no way was she saying those three words a second time. Not until he did. "You have to write me while you're gone. And call and Skype, and whatever else you're able to do while you're in the desert. Do those things with Ben first, of course, but don't leave me wondering if you're okay."

Micah locked his gaze on hers, tracing a finger down her cheek. "I'm going to be okay, Kat, but yes, I'll write and call as much as I can. And I'll think about you every second that I'm gone."

She swallowed hard. "I'm going to miss you and Ben. Tell Ben to write and call me, too." Micah frowned, looking away briefly. "Ben isn't going anywhere. He's staying in Seaside." She drew back and waited for him to look at her again. "I just assumed that Ben would go live with his mother. He told me at school today that Jessica was coming home after Christmas." He shook his head. "Just for a visit. My aunt Clara and Uncle Rick don't mind watching him for me. They've done it before."

"You know I can help, too. I love Ben." As much as she would her own son.

"And he loves you. So do I, Kat. I love you so much."

She froze. "You do?" she asked. She shouldn't have been surprised. He'd shown her in a million different ways over the past weeks.

"I love you," he said again.

She liked the sound of those words on his lips. Wanted to hear them over and over, again and again. "I love you, too, Micah." She never thought she'd love anyone else, but here she was head over heels for another man in uniform. She wasn't scared about the future anymore, though. Love was always a risk, and she was willing to take it if it meant being with this man who'd brought her heart back to life.

"I know that you'll come home to me and then we'll have our happy ending," she said, smiling up at him.

"Nuh-uh. Not an ending. We are just getting started, Principal Chandler. This is our happy beginning."

She liked the sound of that, too. And the feel of his mouth on hers as he kissed her, long and deep. Then he swept her off her feet, into his arms, and carried her home to relish every second they had together until it was time for him to leave. He wouldn't be gone forever. She believed that with all her heart. One day he'd come home to her and they'd continue what they'd started. Their happy beginning was just that, a beginning to a relationship that she hoped would be long and wonderful.

Epilogue

Ben rolled into the living room for what seemed to be the hundredth time that day and stared at the clock once again.

"Almost time." Kat offered a smile, feeling just as nervous, and excited, about Micah's return as he was.

"Do you think he'll recognize me?" Ben asked, swiping at the lock of hair that usually fell between his eyes.

She wanted to laugh, but held a serious face. "Well, you've definitely gotten taller. It'll be time for a new chair soon, I suspect. And you look older, too, with that new haircut."

At this, Ben smiled proudly.

"But I definitely think he'll recognize you. You are the spitting image of him."

Ben bounced lightly in his seat. "Can we go early? Just in case he arrives sooner?" he asked. She'd been thinking the same thing. "Sure. I'll just go tell Aunt Clara and Uncle Rick that we'll meet them back here for a family celebration afterward."

Fifteen minutes later—Kat had gotten quite efficient at loading a wheelchair in a vehicle over the last few months—she and Ben were heading through the gates of Camp Leon. They parked and Kat helped Ben back into his wheelchair.

"Here, let me." She reached out for his tightly coiled left arm and gave it a slow, gentle stretch. "Don't be nervous. It's going to be wonderful," she told him, catching the uncertainty in his eyes.

"I know. It's going to be the best," Ben said.

"That's right." She started to push his chair ahead of her, but he laid a hand on his wheel, stopping her.

"I want to show Dad just how much I've grown. I can do this all by myself."

"Of course." She followed a short distance, and then they stopped outside of a gate that sectioned off a large field.

"Your father told me he has a special surprise for you," Kat said.

"He always brings me home something when he's away. I wonder if he brought you something, too."

"Oh, honey. Your dad being home is all the present I need." Although Micah had hinted in his last letter to her that he was coming home with a question. He said he needed to ask her something that would change their lives forever.

Excitement swelled in her chest. He was probably going to ask her to move in with them, which would be pretty life-changing.

She sucked in a breath, continuing to watch the field beyond the gate. The minutes were long as she held on to the fact that the man she loved would step off that bus that was scheduled to show up in the next few minutes. She wouldn't be left waiting this time. No one had come to her door, although she'd had several nightmares about that happening. There'd been no news reports of accidents involving his squadron. And she'd spoken to Micah just last night. Everything was fine and he was coming home to her and Ben. Then they could begin the life they'd dreamt up during their many phone calls and letters to each other since his deployment.

A bus came into sight in the distance, accompanied by the cheers of the crowd gathered outside. What seemed like an eternity later, the bus stopped and its door opened. She watched each man in uniform step off. Each one that wasn't Micah felt like a pinprick to her heart.

Where is he? Where is he?

She tried not to let her fear settle in on this glorious day. Closing her eyes just for a moment, she sucked in a long breath, releasing it slowly along with a prayer that Micah would return to her, just as he'd promised. Then she opened her eyes again and relief hit her with such an overwhelming magnitude that it was all she could do not to dissolve into a puddle of tears. That, or run as fast as her feet would allow, past the gate and into his arms. She couldn't leave Ben, though.

Micah stood tall as his eyes traveled across the crowd, no doubt asking himself the same question she just had. *Where are they?*

"Dad! Over here!" Ben yelled, waving his right arm. "Dad!"

Micah's gaze connected with Ben's, and then lifted to meet hers. *No way am I ever letting this man go again.*

He walked briskly toward them, his stride eating up the pavement. Then he bent low and hugged Ben first. "Ah, buddy. I missed you so much. You're bigger. It's only been six months. What's Aunt Clara been feeding you?"

Ben grinned widely. "And I got a haircut, too."

Kat laughed, working hard to resist her tears.

A minute later, Micah straightened and leveled his gaze with hers. And if she wasn't mistaken, his eyes were glassy, too. "I've missed you so much," he said, lowering his voice.

She couldn't help it. One tear slipped down her cheek, and then another. Then she melted as Micah drew her into his arms, lifting her off her feet just slightly. "I love you," he whispered in her ear. "I love you so much, Kat."

After a long moment, he released her, glancing between her and Ben. He reached into his duffel bag and pulled out a large brown rock, handing it to Ben. "Being the scientist you are, I thought you'd like this. It's straight from the desert, buddy. I crossed the world to bring it home to you. We can put it in our garden."

Ben's face lit up. "I love it!" he cheered, hugging it to his body with his right arm.

Then Micah turned to Kat. Her breath stopped. So did her heart. "Remember my last letter?" His voice dropped and his lips curled as he looked up at her.

She swallowed, suddenly terrified in the best way. "Yes. I believe you said you had a question you needed to ask me."

He nodded. "I do. And I'm really hoping your answer is yes, Kat."

"Yes," she said, laughing. She was willing to say yes to anything he asked her right about now.

His brow pinched softly. "I haven't asked you anything yet."

"Doesn't matter. I will always say yes to you, Sergeant Peterson."

He grinned. "Oh, it matters. I want to do this right. But first I need to check in with my little man here. This affects him, too."

Ben looked at Micah as he crouched down and pretended to whisper. Kat could hear his every word, though. "What do you think about me asking Principal Chandler to be part of our family?"

Her breath hitched.

Ben's eyes widened. "That's even better than a rock from the desert. Will she live with us?" he asked.

"Only if she says yes." His gaze slid toward Kat's.

Her eyes were burning with a million tears, but she resisted saying anything. He'd told her to wait.

"And I really hope she says yes to me," Micah continued, talking to Ben, but his every word was meant for her. He was giving her time to gather her thoughts, which she appreciated. She didn't need time to think, though. She'd had enough time away from him to last a lifetime.

"You should ask her," Ben said.

Micah nodded. "I had a feeling you'd agree." Then he shifted from his crouched position in front of Ben to one knee in front of her. Even though she knew this was coming, her hands flew to her mouth. "Now don't say anything until I've had a chance to ask you properly," he teased.

She nodded.

Growing serious again, he held her gaze. "Kat, you have changed my life, just by being in it. You make each day brighter, easier. I used to wake up and just plow through the day. I grew flowers, but I

273

never stopped to smell them, to really look at them. Now I do. I see and do everything differently because of you. The last six months away from you made me realize that I never want to be away from you again. Not for a minute. I love you too much." He arched a brow. "I have a rock for you, too, Kat."

This made her laugh even as tears were streaming down her cheeks. "Oh, yeah?" She sniffed.

"Not as big as Ben's, but I don't think you'll mind." He stared up at her. "All you have to do is agree to be my wife."

"Oh, is that all?" she asked as her entire body shook uncontrollably.

"That and promise to love me and my son for the rest of our lives."

She dropped to her knees in front of him and wrapped her arms around his neck. "I think I can handle that."

"Yeah?" Micah's eyes were flooded with tears now, too. Who said a big alpha male couldn't cry? Then he glanced over his shoulder. "Hear that, son? Sounds like a yes to me."

"Yes!" Ben cheered. "Yes, yes, yes!"

The crowd that had gathered around to watch the building scene cheered also. Kat held on to Micah tighter, unwilling to ever let go again. "Yes," she whispered in his ear. "My answer is yes."

He reached into his front pocket and pulled out a box. Where he'd gotten it while on deployment, she didn't know. It didn't matter. Lifting the lid, he revealed a simple solitaire—the most beautiful rock she'd ever seen. She held out a shaky hand, allowing him to slip the ring on her finger, sealing the promise between them. A promise that wouldn't be broken.

After a long embrace, they stood.

"Shall we?" Micah started to push Ben's chair through the crowd.

"I got this, Dad," Ben said, controlling his own chair.

Micah laughed, lagging behind and holding on to Kat's hand as they followed.

Despite her tears, she couldn't help but smile, knowing that if

John could see her now, he'd be glad to know she'd found love again. That she was loved. And that she was happy—truly happy.

"Everything okay?" Micah asked, concern growing in his eyes as he studied her and the tears streaming down her cheeks.

"Yes. Everything's fine," she said, leaning in to him as they walked. "Perfect, actually."

He lifted her hand to his mouth and kissed it softly. The diamond he'd placed there reflected brilliantly in the sun. "It'll be perfect when you become my wife."

A warmness spread through her just thinking about it. She wanted nothing more than to become Mrs. Micah Peterson. "I can't wait," she said, keeping her gaze forward on the clear blue sky, and on the bright future in front of them.

Also by Annie Rains

Sweetwater Springs series

- Christmas on Mistletoe Lane
- Spring Time at Hope Cottage
- Snowfall on Cedar Trail
- Starting Over at Blueberry Creek
- Sunshine on Silver Lake
- Season of Joy
- Reunited on Dragonfly Lane

Somerset Lake series

- The Summer Cottage
- The Christmas Village
- The True Love Bookshop
- The Good Luck Café

Young Adult Fiction

- The Matchbreaker Summer

Acknowledgments

Publishing my first book was a journey I started many moons ago. There have been times when this dream of mine seemed impossible, and it would've been without the help of so many wonderful people who offered their support, time, advice, and encouragement. My heart is full of gratitude for so many.

My first thanks goes to my family, who have supported me through the years. Thank you, Sonny, for believing in me, encouraging me, and listening to me ramble about the fictional characters in my head. Thanks to my two sweet boys and little girl who know that Mommy needs "writing time," and who are willing to play nice and give it to me most days. Thanks to my parents, who encouraged me to dream big, and to my mother-in-law, Annette, who is always willing to help, whether it be watching the kids or doing research for one of my books.

I would like to thank my wonderful agent, Sarah Younger at Nancy Yost Literary Agency. Finding you was another dream come true. Thank you for giving me a literary home and welcoming me into Team Sarah. This book would not have been possible without you!

Thank you to Junessa Viloria, my editor at Loveswept/ Publishing Group. You helped me polish this manuscript into something I am truly proud to call mine. Working with you on this book has been nothing short of amazing. I also want to thank Gina Wachtel for reading my manuscript while my future editor was on maternity leave and for giving me that first yes. Many thanks to everyone at Loveswept/ Publishing Group who had a part in making this book happen, especially Erica Seyfried, Ashleigh Heaton, Lynn Andreozzi, Madeline Hopkins, and Penny Haynes.

A very special thank-you goes out to Lady Lioness. As a Pitch Wars mentor, you pulled me out of the slush pile and advanced me light-years in this writing journey. Your mentorship has meant so much to me. Thanks to the ladies of "The Pride," Marie Meyer and Sarah Blair, for all your kind words and support. I look forward to watching all of your successes in publishing.

A huge thanks goes to my critique partner, Rachel Lacey. Your input and friendship are invaluable to me. Thank you for your critique of this book, all your advice on the process, and for our many daily emails, which always make me smile. Thanks to my #girlsnightwrite crew: Rachel Lacey, Sidney Halston, Tif Marcelo, and April Hunt. You motivate and inspire me every day. Love you, ladies!

To all my friends, near and far, old and new, writers and readers, thank you!

And most important, I am ever thankful to God for giving me this passion and for putting all of these amazing people in my life to help me succeed.

About the Author

USA Today bestselling author Annie Rains lives in a small, coastal North Carolina town, full of lovable folks, scenic downtown areas, and breathtaking nature—similar to the towns she writes about in her books. Annie's love of reading and writing grabbed hold of her at a young age and never let go. Her first book was published in 2015, and she's been writing heartfelt, page-turning stories ever since. When Annie isn't writing, she's reading from her never-ending TBR stack on her bedside table, taking long walks while plotting her characters' happy endings, and living out her own happily ever after with her husband, three children, feisty rescue cat, and mischievous dog.

Sign up HERE for Annie's newsletter to stay informed about new releases and sales.

You can find Annie online at http://www.annierains.com/ or on Facebook, Twitter, and Instagram at @annierainsbooks